D1527777

# *Baby,* BABY

## Victoria H. Smith

APR 2017

HU

# BABY, BABY

Printed in the United States of America

**ISBN-10 1539314251:**
**ISBN-13: 978-1539314257**

Published by **Victoria H. Smith**
Cover Art by **Najla Qamber Designs**
Photography by **Lindee Robinson Photography**
Cover Models: **Ahmad & Reidi**
Editing by **TK's Editing Service, Judy's Proofreading**
Layout by **Something Simple Designs**

# Table of Contents

# One

## Alexander

"Complete remission? As in it's gone? Completely?"

The words felt foreign to say and way too hopeful to be able to believe in. I had been through too much; my family had been through even more.

Dr. Bradbury, an African American woman of age and experience, came around her desk. Her detailed work in this field had allowed so many leads in the advancement of medicine and more specifically, cancer. She *knew* the disease and was the most well-versed oncologist on this side of the world, which was why Chicago Community Med hired her. Even more importantly, that's why my family had hired her.

A smile touched her lips and a light glistened behind her brown eyes; she wouldn't be doing that unless she'd meant what she said. She wouldn't be telling me this if she didn't truly mean the words.

She placed her hands in her lap, taking a seat on the edge of her desk. "As in, you are officially NED, Alexander. There is no more evidence of your disease. No more signs. You are cancer free."

*Cancer free. Cancer free…*

"So this isn't a partial?"

My mom's hand came down on mine. My mother was a French woman who'd kept her accent long after she'd come to this country and married my Sicilian-American father.

I tightened my hand in hers, happy for her incessant need to come along with me to these things. Her presence kept me strong, kept me… stable, though she'd never know it. I had more of my father's—more accurately my late father's—pride than I cared to admit sometimes.

Not wanting to think about that, the reality of his absence and what ultimately took him, I looked up at Dr. Bradbury. She was smiling again, smiling still.

"Correct, Mrs. Ricci," she said, and reaching behind herself, she pulled a folder off her desk. "Let me explain better by showing you Alexander's scans."

I felt like I had seen these millions of times, but today's scans couldn't be more of an outlier to previous experiences. For starters, Dr. Bradbury's finger could no longer outline dark masses, and there had been multiple on previous scans. There used to be so many because the cancer had spread from its original site. Now, her hand waved over a general scan that was free and clear of disease. Free and clear of cancer. There was also one other difference and that had been the tears. The tears, which leaked from my mom's blue eyes, were no longer in sadness.

But rather from extreme joy.

And when she hugged me, it all felt sobering. I was no longer a ticking time bomb. I was no longer forced to wallow in the thickness of my illness. I had spent many days alone, locked up and sick as a dog in my own personal refuge, just me and my chemotherapist in an old cabin based on one of my family's countryside properties. I had all but shut myself away from the world, too much pride, too much everything, keeping me from living my life. My cancer had made me sick, but it'd been my mind that did the most damage. It damn-near crippled me most days.

My mom reached to wipe at something underneath my eye. Nothing shocked me more than when her finger came away wet. She hugged me again, and I realized something. I no longer had to worry that my mom would have to go through another heartache over a burial. She wouldn't have to bury her child like her husband. She wouldn't have to because I had something today I didn't have the day before.

I had a chance—finally.

"I'm so sorry. I had a meeting that ran late and then traffic."

My brother walked in with familiar excuses and I could only smile I got to hear them.

*I have a chance.*

"Can you believe these fuckers almost wouldn't let me in," he said, waving his hands around at the staff of the downtown office.

Bradbury's practice was associated with the city hospital, but she had her own office. Mom and I had been coming out of it when Asa had all but pushed his way in from the lobby the doctor shared with her other associates.

He pulled a shoulder bag up his arm. "Like, what the hell? I'm frickin' family. I've been here a million times."

He had been here quite a few times. Well, when I would let him visit, that is. I hated the circus-like atmosphere, and even more so the attention. How ironic as I used to be at the heart of it? Those had been different times, I supposed.

My twin's hands came down on my shoulders.

My twin... my twin, though a stranger on the street would never know. Fraternal, the two of us looked nothing alike. Asa got my mom's dirty-blond hair, while I took away with dad's dark strands and even thicker beard. I had to do constant upkeep just to maintain my small layer, having more of a ten than a five o'clock shadow. Asa had a beard, too, but it looked more like golden peach fuzz unless he grew it out for at least a month.

"Tell me it's good news," he said, and so I went into detail. I told him everything despite barely believing it myself. And on some level, I didn't think he did either.

We had all been through this thing for so long. The resections of the original tumors, prostate cancer, and then the chemotherapy that followed immediately after that. That had been the hardest. We couldn't seem to get me in remission, and each trial of chemo only took me to a deeper and darker place. Eventually, I didn't see anyone. Eventually, I gave up, but it had been Asa who told me to keep on. He told me I couldn't leave him. He told me when I had my head in a bucket and I was on the floor shaking that I couldn't *not* do this. I couldn't *not* have life. We shared thirty-one years together, and he'd said he needed me for so many more.

God, that seemed like so long ago, me in the worst of my treatment, and I guess it had been; the physical affects of the chemo on my body were long in the past. I had a full head of hair now, my weight was back up, and my body felt strong.

I placed my hands on the sides of my brother's face, feeling the best I'd been in so long.

"I guess you can't get rid of me just yet, little brother," I said, even though I was only older by minutes.

He chuckled, the sound thick and full of emotion. He wasn't one to cry, either. I guess today was full of miracles. He whipped an arm around me and I didn't fight him, holding on just as hard. Eventually, Mom couldn't take it and joined in, too.

That's when the big tears fell, especially with my mom being such an emotional woman. She cried just watching Disney movies.

Her hands went down our cheeks. "I love you both," she said, her accent rough on the words. "I know you hate that but—"

We did, but considering today's events and the journey we'd been on together, we didn't, which was why we both hugged her again. After we'd all gotten ourselves together, and Mom single-handedly drenched Asa's pocket square, we made our way into the office lobby.

That's when the fun started—and I use that term lightly.

Chaos in the form of photographers resided outside the normally docile family practice and the minute Asa, Mom, and I cracked open Dr. Bradbury's double doors, their shutters went off like popcorn over a hot stove. They knew it was the three of us easily, only glass dividing us.

"How did they—"

"That'd be me," chimed in Asa, cutting me off. He pushed his hands in his pockets, using his heels to turn his back toward the craziness. He chewed the inside of his cheek a little. "I drove the Viper over."

He drove the Viper; the *Viper* with electric blue paint and his name clear on the back in airbrush. No one in all of Chicago drove anything as obnoxious as my brother.

I pushed my hand through my hair. "Asa..."

"I'm sorry. I knew my meeting would cut things close and I wanted to get here quick."

In his haste, he made public a visit I didn't want on display. I'd been very good about not letting the photographers know when I came to see the doctor. She actually went out to see me most times unless *I had* to make a visit. I didn't want the headlines. It was bad enough when the media caught wind when I'd gotten sick.

Future heirs to our father's investment empire, all Asa or I had to do was sneeze and we'd be on the front page of a tabloid. It only got worse when we got older, cockier. At one time, I would have thrived on the attention, but today, not so much.

I framed my eyes, turning away, and Asa pushed an arm around me.

"We can sneak out the back," he said, and then raised his hand toward the doors filled with flashing lights.

Behind the paparazzi, a jet back car pulled away from the curb and I knew my driver, Esteban, would meet us around back. He'd been working for our family for many years, but my mom's car across the street didn't go anywhere. We'd gotten here at different times, which was why we drove separately.

I went to motion for hers to go around, but she stopped me.

"I'll take the front, you two. I don't mind," she said pulling on her gloves.

Mom had been well-versed on how to deal with the media since she'd come to this country on my dad's arm, and that didn't let up when her sons hit puberty. The tabloids actually dubbed us the "Princes of Chicago" at one time. They needed to call us something considering we were in the papers so much. Those people should give me a cut of the check with the many vacations they followed me on and clubs they stalked me at for a photo op or attempt to get a juicy story.

Shaking my head at the thought, I looked up when Mom's lips came to rest on my cheek.

"Mom…"

"Hush. You'll let me because I'm your mom. If I wanted to kiss your face off in front of these strangers, you'd let me."

Knowing she was right, I let my comment drop and I didn't fight the hug she gave to prove her point either.

"I love you and you will come by the house. No more hiding now that we're over the worst. You're moving back into town immediately."

*Hiding…* Interesting that was how she referred to it. Maybe in a way, I had. I didn't want people seeing when I was the worst of myself.

I came away from the hug with her hand cradling my cheek.

"I suppose your father can't have you yet, can he?" she said, the tears making their way back and putting a watery sheen on eyes as blue as the sky. She rubbed them with her gloved-finger. "I love him, but he doesn't win this one today."

My dad had been a strong man, a tough one, but even still, the battle of cancer had taken him. I thought it would take me, too.

I was glad he didn't win either.

After one more hug, she passed one to my brother, squeezing him tight, and then left us for the masses. She'd always mastered pushing her way through the flashing lights, only elegance in her stride, and her distraction allowed Asa and me to head out the back way.

He chuckled once we made it through the office, bringing his arm around my neck.

"How do you feel?"

I found this question odd. Eyeing him, I stopped just shy of the exit doors.

"Good?"

"Not sick?" he asked. "Tired?"

I took a second to evaluate all systems, and since I was very familiar with what "sick" really felt like, I had to say I felt pretty good.

Asa cracked the door after my nod and I lifted my head to the breeze blowing in.

A shiny vehicle was parked out there with Esteban standing with his back to it.

I stepped out into the brightness, the normally harsh heat of the Midwest welcomed on my skin. Today, that light felt energizing, warm and high in the sky, and with that breeze, I felt nothing but light on my feet.

Pushing my hands into my pockets, I turned around, making a full rotation, taking in the beautiful day. I found Asa after that 360 degree turn, a smile on his face for some reason.

I shrugged a little, my own smile on my lips. "Not at all. Sick, I mean. In fact, I kinda want to go for a walk. Relax a little. You game?"

I didn't know where any of that came from, and by the height my twin's blond eyebrows jumped on his forehead, I could say he agreed.

"Uh, no," he said, chuckling. He tossed his arm around me as if shaking me out of myself. "I was thinking we'd swing around the bars."

"Bars?"

"Yeah, like old times. There's this new place off the pier I've been frequenting. You'd love it. We'll have a few drinks, get into it. What do you say?"

Looking out into that day, that sun, bar hopping didn't really feel like the better alternative.

"Bro?" His hand came down on my shoulder, squeezing. "You okay? You did say you weren't tired, right?"

"Yeah. I, uh…" I pushed my hand behind my neck and then smiled when I realized where we really were. When coming to the doctor's, I usually went in and out, never enjoying the place.

I gripped Asa now. "Do you see where we are?"

Hand falling, Asa took in the back alley street. The path cleared straight down to Bernie's, an old coffeehouse the pair of us used to frequent. We'd both spent so much time there in college, the place only blocks from our alma mater, Northwestern University. We used to burn the midnight oil there, cramming for tests we'd put off studying for until the last minute. In fact, one day we came in hung the hell over, Bernie's crappy coffee the only remedy.

A grin pulled at Asa's lips. "Hell yeah."

"Right?" I said, folding my arms over my chest. I tipped my chin at him. "Remember when we convinced Bernie to pull an all-nighter with us?"

Chuckling, he tossed his blond hair back. "Oh, yeah. He normally closed by midnight, but we convinced him he'd be a part of changing history if he'd just let us finish our senior thesis."

And history was made. We'd pulled off our theses, putting them off until the night before.

Our papers had detailed the construction of a smart phone application—which totally made sense considering our majors had been finance. Dad had pushed us both into the major considering our family business with investment banking. The Ricci name had firms all over the country, and the Princes were supposed to run them when of age and experience. That had always seemed so far off. It had only been after Dad died that the reality of that hit. But in college, it definitely hadn't. Asa and I did what we wanted and technology had always been something we'd both been into, me in particular. Asa didn't do much with the courses we took, deciding to pursue law and his MBA in the end. But me, I still liked to dabble around with technology when I could. I developed quite a few applications during and after college, just something on the side really.

I looked at Bernie's, that all coming back. In fact, the place was only feet away and seemed too close just to pass up.

I slapped Asa's chest. "Let's go to Bernie's instead and get a cup of coffee. We can say hi to the old man."

The words twisted up Asa's expression, settling weirdly across his face.

He moved over to me, tilting his head.

"Old Bern doesn't own the place anymore."

I blanched at that. "No?"

His blond hair feathered in the wind with his head shake. "Sold it maybe two, three years ago? He retired early and sold it to family. I only know because I was in the area one day and asked about him."

That sat heavy on me, but it didn't remove the wind from my sails. I would have liked to say hi to Bernie, but I was sure the coffee hadn't changed. Asa said his family still ran it.

I backed away a little. "I think I'm going to go anyway. Just for old times, you know?"

If my brother asked me, pushed me on the reason behind this decision to go, I really couldn't have told him. I wanted to go so I was going to.

I did step away slowly, though, giving him a chance to join me, to which he smiled.

He lifted his hands. "I'm good on that, but how about this? You text me after you get bored and have your coffee. Because you will get bored and then you'll call me. You always do."

My brother thought he knew me so well, but I let him have that final thought. He signed off with a salute before heading around the building. I assumed to get his car and head to the bars.

I shook my head, laughing a little before treading on. I mentioned to Esteban I'd be back soon, to which he told me he'd swing around in fifteen or so to get me. I only agreed because I wouldn't have the distraction of my mom or my brother's obnoxious ride when I ultimately decided to come back to the office.

"Hello!"

The familiar greeting hit when the bell of the coffeehouse chimed moments later. Bernie always would greet his patrons.

Even if he immediately followed the salutation with a head shake after seeing me or my brother.

I smiled to myself. A girl stood behind the counter now. She read me off the specials and this all felt so familiar. Like flipping through an old book. It didn't matter if you hadn't read it in years. You still knew every page.

"I'll take a coffee," I told her while going for my wallet, but when she rang me up, I lowered it.

*The amount she said couldn't be right.*

"You said a coffee, right?" she asked after I inquired. She checked her screen. "That'll be five ninety-nine for a small."

I didn't consider myself a cheapskate by any means. I mean, my net worth easily crossed into the nine figures. That was with everything of course, like my personal assets, my inheritance on both sides, and…

I shook my head. "Just a coffee. Black."

The woman laughed as if I spoke a foreign language. She pointed behind her at a board covered in chalk writing.

"We serve only the special coffees here. Imported."

The board lined with everything from Kona to the most expensive blends from my mom's country.

*This is different… different than how I remembered.*

"I have to ring you up for one of these. That's all we got."

I paid her the amount, and then took the Kona blend—not like I had a choice. It was good, but, I couldn't help grumbling. Again, I wasn't cheap, but I didn't come here for something I could get at the places closer to the high-rise I lived in before getting sick. I just wanted the feel of something familiar.

*"Bored yet?"*

My brother's text message had me smirking when I pulled it out. I wasn't bored. In fact, I was having a great cup of coffee.

*"Hardly,"* I returned, then went for a place to sit.

That took effort.

Clearly a chill hotspot still, old Bernie's didn't have many seats to take it easy on and I pushed my way through the crowd, folks drinking coffees filled to the brim with whip cream and other fancy drinks the girl tried to offer me when I came in.

I found a seat by the window, away from the crowd of hipsters wearing knitted caps and stroking long beards. The whole feel of the place had me feeling incredibly out of place and a little old, honestly.

*I guess I did try to go down memory lane.*

I sipped the coffee, gazing out the window. Here, near the glass, I felt like I acquired my own space and I enjoyed it settling in. I was happy I'd come, but this place, the feel, was different.

Gazing around, I wondered how much did change. Asa and I didn't just study here. We'd always been surrounded by people, coming in with crowds not unlike this—trendy, I mean—and usually with girls under our arms.

The warm Kona hit my tongue and I thought about that. Up until I got sick, I was still living that life, wrapped up with it despite the years I added on.

My brother buzzed again and I picked up my phone.

*"Quit playing around, Alex. Let me pick you up already. We need to celebrate you, your life."*

*Celebrate my life.*

The smartphone warmed the palm of my hand, my gaze hovering over that last word.

"Hey."

My fingers slid away from the screen, a woman joining my side. At least, I thought she was a woman. A hoodie covered her head and dark sweatpants rested upon what I believed to be the soft curves of a feminine form. Her voice had also been light so I figured I'd been correct in my conclusion.

I shifted toward her, a light smell in the air that hinted of flowers.

"Hi, uh…"

She pulled down the hood, revealing full-on that she was impeccably female.

Strands of dark hair brushed over high cheekbones and full lips formed the shape of a heart from her side profile. She looked up at me and I stopped where I sat, my fingertips burning a bit on my hot paper cup.

I shook them out, brought back into reality. "I, um…"

Honey brown eyes popped against cinnamon brown skin, a smile placed in my direction that did nothing to help me find my words. I was usually quite eloquent, well versed in speech. This was very unlike me.

I rubbed a hand over my burnt fingertips. "Miss—"

"I'm sorry I'm late," she said, those brown eyes of hers sparkling on me.

In fact, they caught me up a bit and I had to think a moment on what she said.

*Late…? Late.*

Did I miss something? Was I supposed to meet her? This… this beautiful woman.

And she was beautiful despite how manly she dressed. Baggy clothes couldn't hide a curvy figure and her hair messy from her hoodie did even less to conceal the softest features.

I normally wouldn't complain about being thrust into a situation that would place me in the presence of such a woman, but this was… unusual. She seemed to know me, or at least believed she was supposed to meet me here today.

Stunned by the whole situation, I simply watched her. She proceeded in pushing up the sleeves of her brown hoodie, a patch on her chest that read: *The University of Chicago*, and she could have been a student I supposed, but the hoodie was worn like it'd spent some time with her.

"It's just, you know. With the CTA?" she said, and I blinked for what seemed like the millionth time in the seconds since she'd joined me.

I focused on her words, her.

"I'm sorry. I missed that. CTA?" I asked.

A wash of that flowery scent hit me like a wave when she turned her head, the soft brown coloring of her eyes like lightning in a summer storm.

She eyed me with them. "Yeah? Chicago Transit Authority? The bus gets you where you gotta go, but certainly not quick enough."

"I…"

A folder hit near my coffee with a slam and I jumped. She scooted in, erasing space between us, and whatever flowery perfume she wore layered like a wide meadow, her proximity very close.

She thumbed documents in the folder, many papers filled with this and that. All the while, I eyed the area around us.

*She really does think she's here to meet me.*

It was at this point I decided to say something. It was one thing to let her sit here and go on, but it was quite another for her to show me whatever personal information she had in this folder. It didn't matter what the folder entailed. It was hers and clearly not meant for me.

I lifted a hand. "Miss, I think there's some kind of misunderstanding."

She blinked up, frowning a little. She eyed me for a moment, her eyes shifting before slowly her frown melted into dread.

Her lips parted.

"It's because I was late, wasn't it?" she asked, the most panicked expression taking over her face, flushing her brown cheeks. She swept strands of her hair out of her face. They were strewn about from her hood, but that made her no less becoming.

She shook her head. "Because, I swear I'm not usually late. And please don't take that as a reflection of my character. I really am a serious person and take this whole process more than seriously."

"Process?" I questioned, pausing to sneak in a sip of my coffee. This was all a bit overwhelming, and I felt I needed it.

She watched me during my gulp and I had to say, I wasn't the only one confused now with the way her eyebrows drew in.

Her head tilted.

"Yeah," she said, raising and dropping her shoulders. "Carrying your baby for you and your husband."

## Two

### Johari

I was losing him.

And that had been long before he started choking on his coffee.

Jumping into action, I went to fix the problem I'd clearly created. I hit the man's back with a large *thwack* and when all he did was double over, patting at his broad chest, the terror I was making this all worse hit me full sweep.

*Jesus, Jo, don't kill him.*

But he was getting worse, hacking. His large form gasped and I gulped, trying to get it together. Such a trivial medical emergency shouldn't faze me. Hell, I *worked* in an emergency room. As a fourth year medical student, I had handled far worse conditions, but the stakes were high here, the situation more than intense. Depending on how this man took a liking to me today would directly affect my future.

As well as fix the mistakes I made in the pursuit of it.

Whatever hesitation I had, I allowed myself to let go, bringing a hand to this man's back and softly patting the coughing fit out of him this time. Sheer in size, getting close to the man was a given, and he let me, his breathing steading under my hands. I sometimes mentally had to close my nose to patients, the smells not always that great in the ER, but he made being near him easy. He smelled warm, fresh and cool, like aftershave.

"Ian?" I questioned, knowing this was his name. I read his profile online. He was Ian Reed, a flower shop owner from the north side of town.

A head of full, thick strands of the darkest tones lifted, but he didn't look at me, reaching for his coffee cup.

*Gosh, why didn't you think of that?*

Really this whole situation did fluster me.

I blamed it on the stakes, I guess.

After pushing his cup away, I rooted in my bag for a bottle of water, instead. I always had those on hand. Just came with the territory of being a medical professional, I guess. I found the water quickly and passed it to him, an arm cloaked in dark hair taking it from me.

He rose like a sleeping giant, large gulps taking my water down, a visible bob and dip in his throat with every swallow. He had the chiseled features of a man I could see gracing photographs, and he did seem familiar to me. A full beard, thin in length, covered defined cheekbones, and then there was the deep-set eyes that ticked an odd familiarity in my brain. Brown and striking, I felt like I had seen them before.

Though of course I hadn't. I couldn't have. I may have stalked the man's user profile, but it had been minus a picture.

I really felt like I'd seen him before, though, and maybe since I had found out so much about him through his profile that's where the connection came from.

I couldn't help the thorough read, as I wanted to make sure I picked the right person. Going through with this, having and basically giving up a baby for someone, was a big deal, and I wouldn't do it unless I found the right person. I needed to in order to be okay with the passing over of a child, my child.

*It's going to be all right. You have to do this. You can do this.*

The clock had started no matter how invisible. I needed this arrangement to work out and had to ignore any other factors. Especially ones of the heart.

Being professional, *staying* professional, I got this man stable then sat back. We'd gathered a nice little audience of onlookers, but once Ian's noises subsided, they seemed to move back to their coffee and conversations.

"Thank you," came from my right, and those deep-set eyes got me with their hooks. The brown color was more tawny, reminding me of a fawn's coat.

I rubbed my hands across my sweatpants, my palms damp for some reason.

"Of course," I said, and then went for another bottle of water in my bag.

What could I say? A girl always stayed prepared.

Seeing as how he finished his, I offered the second. But this one, he turned down, lifting a large hand.

"I'm good. I'm good."

"You're sure?" I said, holding it out. "It's no problem. It seemed like what happened was my fault."

Though, I wasn't sure why. Maybe he was just tense, nervous like me.

A wide smile coming from his direction showed me even more reasons why.

This man was hot. Like seriously smokin'. His cheekbones, slightly hollow, only added in the pouty look he inadvertently created with his full, pink lips, and I think my heart died a slow death for my entire gender that he wasn't batting for my team. What, since he was gay and all that.

*Jo, he could be your employer in minutes.*

And that.

I pushed my hair back. Really, I had to get my head back here.

Placing the water bottle down, I let my shoulders relax. He'd seemed to come out of the worst of the coughing fit, rubbing at his chest. A casual t-shirt and jeans covered his brawny frame and my thoughts triggered that he'd be better suited in something more like a three-pieced suit and shined shoes.

*Had I seen him before?*

I was unsure where the thoughts were coming from. Perhaps, the proper way in which he sat, his hands folder on his crossed legs and hair so perfect and parted slightly to the side. A piece of it curled over one of his eyes, catching on his lashes.

"You okay?"

He asked because I was staring at him.

My gaze averted.

Laughing my way out of being caught, I swept a hand over my face.

"I feel like I should be asking you that," I said, making my gaze far less invasive this time. I simply let it fall on him casually.

I got the same back, but that did no less in making my face hot across the short distance of our coffee counter.

"Um, yeah," he said, scratching a little into his hair. "I'm good. Great."

"You're sure? That definitely went down the wrong pipe."

My words gifted me with cool laugher, nice and low from the confines of his broad chest.

"Yeah, I'm fine. I can breath now. So..."

His tone had lowered on the end there, fading away while he stared at me. He reached for his coffee cup, but didn't drink, his finger tapping at the paper.

"Um, so you were saying um..." He swept his hair back, the dark strands popping up when his hand left. "I'm sorry you said something about a um... carrying a um, for me and my um.... carrying a..."

"Baby," I finished for him, confused a little by his lack of articulation, but then again not really considering all that just happened.

He had nearly choked to death.

Sobered by the fact, I decided to apologize again for something I was sure didn't help the overall situation.

"And again, I'm so sorry for being late," I said. "It's usually not like me and if you'd let me show myself to you and explain who I am, you'll see I'm the right person for this job."

I really hated putting this all in those terms, that carrying his and his partner's child was a job. But for all intents and purposes, this arrangement was exactly that. He had a need for a service, a service that paid someone for a completed task on the other end and well... I needed that person to be me.

It had to be me.

Fact of the matter was, I needed money quickly, a *large* amount quickly, and this unfortunately had to be a job to me. I literally couldn't afford for it to be any other way and knowing that, I had to treat the arrangement as such. Every day on the job, I had to separate myself from emotional connections. Life in the emergency room was full of opportunities to get one invested during my clinicals. I learned quite fast to keep that wall up. That's just what one had to do as a medical professional.

I'd do that now, separate myself now.

I had no other choice.

Going into it, I thumbed through the docket I rustled up for this meeting. I filled it full of documents, jam-packed with things about myself. Everything from my medical history to how I lived my life from day-to-day filled its pages and it was all for this man. I really wanted him to know me, to show him I was the perfect candidate to do this for him and his spouse.

I pushed the folder toward him. "So here, you'll see I've taken the liberty—"

"Wait a second. Miss, I—"

"Johari," I said, feeling kind of silly that in all rushing to show him about myself I left out the simplest thing—my name.

I had answered an ad, my identity anonymous to him. The surrogacy matching website certainly had a lot of information about him and his family, but as I'd answered the listing, nothing about me.

"My name. It's Johari Russell," I finished. I supposed I should have started with that.

His shoulders relaxed.

"Johari," he said, almost as if testing my name in the way he said it.

A smile slightly on the end of it, he opened his mouth again.

But it snapped shut when that folder once again got closer.

His hands came up, almost in protest.

"Johari. Just hold on a moment. Let me explain—"

"First off, I'm a very responsible person, reliable. I'm actually a medical student and near the top of my class."

I started with this information, as I believed this to be one of my strongest attributes. It was and I had worked hard for it. "I'm in my final year and money is hard so…"

"Hence, the job. This job. You carrying the um…?"

Why couldn't he say baby?

I sat back. "Baby, yes. Hence me carrying the baby for you and your husband."

I wanted to be open with my purpose. I believed honesty was the best policy here. I did need the money and he, well, he needed a child. Even still, this shouldn't be just about that. Not when it came to something so sensitive.

"But this wouldn't be just a job," I went on. "This entire process I take as an honor and my background in medicine makes me an excellent candidate."

"I, um…" he said, pushing a hand behind his neck. He swallowed. "I wouldn't disagree with that sentiment."

Him saying this meant more than he knew; it meant that he was seeing me more than just a potential candidate here.

Feeling hopeful, I once again slid the folder in his direction. "Here you'll find everything about me. Well, everything that can be put on paper."

That surprise once again touched those brown eyes and one would have believed my folder had the plague with the way he refused to touch it.

"Johari, I, uh… Wow," he said, his gaze sneaking away. It fell on the folder and he placed his hands down, slowly toward the table.

"You're, uh, you're very prepared," he stated matter-of-factly as his sight lifted from the pages. "You've got a lot here."

"Yes," I said, grinning a little. I seemed to have snagged him for at least a little while.

And I didn't waste a moment.

I pointed to the page he was on.

"As you can see, I have no major illnesses. No broken bones or even any allergies."

"Yeah, yes," he said, reaching back to push a few fingers into his hair. "Tip-top shape I see, and very thorough."

"Completely. And thank you for noticing my attention to detail with all this. I feel I need to be in this situation. I really will take this whole arrangement seriously. Yes, the money brought me here, but I truly do want to do this."

And I did. I got into medicine for a reason, to help people and I… I wanted to help him. We'd all be getting something out of this. He'd be helping me just as much as I'd be helping him.

Thinking about that, I watched as he finally began to slowly thumb through the folder. I didn't want to break his focus now that I had it.

Especially as he seemed to really be getting into it.

His gaze traveled the pages with an intense intrigue and every new one seemed to draw him in more and more. He got through half the folder before I allowed myself to say anything.

A smile touched my lips.

"I can think of no greater thing than to help someone bring a child into the world," I went on, fully believing that. Like I said, that's why I got into medicine.

I watched him continue to read. "I love children. I don't have any kids of my own, but I do have a younger brother myself."

And he was my light and joy, the pair of us two peas in a pod. Mama worked a lot, so I got that little tyke a lot of the time. I loved him.

"So you've never done this before, Johari?" he asked, then shook his head. "I mean, you've never have children before?"

There came that reminder again. Like I'd seen him before someplace or somewhere…

His face, his voice… especially when he said my name with a hum of properness over the word.

A sudden wish I would've presented myself in a better way fell upon me—maybe I should've chosen a dress for today and heels instead of my old undergrad hoodie and sneakers.

I gripped my hoodie sleeves, playing at the hem with my fingertips.

"Technically, no," I said, allowing myself to make eye contact. He made it hard since his were so intense.

"But don't think that means I'm infertile or anything," I went on. "I've been through all the tests. My body is completely ripe and ready for this."

His bottom lip parted from his upper and I bit mine.

Was this too much information for him? It couldn't be considering the situation.

"I can do this," I said placing my hand on the table. "You probably have a lot of people to choose from, but no one who will take this task as seriously or with as much care as I will. I know what to do. I know the body quite literally inside and out."

"You're confident," he said, and it wasn't a question as he closed the folder. He smiled a little at me and I nodded underneath that steady gaze.

"I am," I agreed. "And I believe I should be on your short list. In fact, at the very top considering my qualifications."

Had I been perhaps… too confident? Cocky even? I couldn't help thinking that as his gaze averted. It was just… When he smiled at me it seemed like that was a desired trait for him, and maybe I'd gotten a bit carried away because of it.

That smile wasn't there now, though. With his expression turning grave, his fingers moved up to rub his trimmed beard.

"Johari," he started, turning my way. My name sounded different this time. Proper still, but not in the same way. There was no warm hum.

He placed his hand on the table, too. "I've misled you. I'm not who you—"

"Is it because I'm older?" I questioned, suddenly feeling like this was all going south. I had to push, panicking.

*I can't let him get away. I need this opportunity.*

I couldn't risk the potential blowback.

He blinked at my sharp cut in. "I'm sorry? Older?"

"Yeah, I'm twenty-six. Well, twenty-seven soon. I'm sure you've got younger candidates, but just because they're young doesn't mean they know what to do. I do, Ian."

"Ian?"

Now, I blinked. Maybe he wanted to be called by his last name, Reed. I just assumed.

*God, I'm really messing this up at all angles.*

"Mr. Reed, I feel you're about to let me down easy here, and you shouldn't. I want to do this for you, for you and your husband. Robert's cancer story was so—"

"Cancer?"

The word had been soft coming off his lips, rough and patchy.

And I nodded, watching that gaze hone in on me again.

"You both had been through so much," and as I said this, I thought back to their story. There'd been so many listings for surrogates, but theirs… theirs stuck with me.

I smiled at him. "Your husband's prognosis was so grim, but you stayed positive. You didn't let go. You fought just as much as he did, and that was so inspirational."

How much people like me could truly gain from that kind of strength. Those people in those situations traveled their own wavelengths, and never, I repeat never, let anyone else drag them down. Thoughts of my own battles came to mind, both the trials of being a woman of color climbing the ladder of professional medicine and then some battles even closer to home.

He went silent after my words, and I got closer to him. Thick and woodsy, his smell lingered on the precipice of my senses.

I turned away from him a little. "Please give me a chance. I won't disappoint you."

Dark hair feathered when he looked up at me, his gaze gripping, racking. He closed his eyes and when he opened them, he faced the casual traffic passing by our seat on the other side of the coffeehouse window.

A sedan pulled up, black and directly in front of where we sat, and from out of it, a man came, one with a billed hat and a nice smile behind a white beard. He stood in front of the car, patiently waiting with gloved hands.

And he looked to be staring directly in my direction.

"Use this to call my office."

A card was in front of me now, white and with bubbled lettering. I couldn't read it because I followed it up to the eyes of the owner, which were brown and forever warm.

Mr. Reed stepped down from the ledge that our table and chairs were on, but the step did nothing to sever his height or the amount of space he took up in the room.

He smiled at me again, and I forgot that I missed seeing that expression. It took being away from it for a little while to remember.

"Do that and we'll arrange a meeting," he said, stepping away. "Discuss further what we talked about today. The um… the surrogacy and possibly moving forward."

I nodded, standing from my chair. Almost as if to follow him, but I didn't. I just watched him go to the door, a chime sounding when he opened the coffeehouse doors.

"It was good meeting you, Johari," he said, and then dipped his head when he went out into the sun.

His long strides took him to the driver outside and the car he stood in front of. The driver opened the door for him and he got in.

*Alexander Ricci,* the card read, then followed two words: *Ricci Financial.*

*Alexander Ricci... as in...?*

His car pulled away as he lowered the window, giving me a slight wave from behind it. I followed the few feet the car traveled with my steps, but soon I was cut off, the car too far and out of sight.

I gazed at the card again, my mind running with so many thoughts and emotions.

He was Alexander Ricci, *the* Alexander Ricci, of what I knew to be a billion dollar investment empire, and I wasn't the only one who knew that. The entire city had. He and his brother, Asa, the sole heirs.

They'd also both built a rapport in the city, the pair a motley crew and considered well-known playboys by the media. But Alexander was also something else. He had something else.

Cancer.

I popped my hands over my face.

*Holy crap.*

# Three

## Alexander

Calling my office wouldn't have made sense for Johari. I had given her my card. I'd let her know the truth about my identity.

So why did she make contact just a few short days later?

I hadn't spoken to her directly. The number on my business card went to my assistant, Penny. She'd been the one to tell me Johari called, wanting to meet with me. Penny had scheduled her for an appointment with me in the near future, two weeks from the day she called, and I used that time to reflect. I needed that time to think about what all this meant and what I meant by giving her my card.

Truth be told, I questioned my sanity many times while going through treatment. I asked myself if my mind could handle the physical trials I put my body through. I asked myself if I was strong enough and even if all the fight would be worth it in the end when it came to me and the current life I led.

My brother and I had left a solid mark in this city, but for me, I didn't feel it'd been a particularly good one. I wasted a lot of time over the years, slaved for a life and job I'd been seasoned to fulfill. It had always been destined for me and Asa to work for my father. We were essentially supposed to take over and carry on our late father's legacy eventually, when we were ready. Currently, one of my father's business associates was the company's head, but it was all there for one of us when we decided to take the reigns.

My father's legacy allowed for a comfortable life, which I had more than my fair share of indulgence in.

I got into things. I took things I felt I deserved just because of the simple fact I was born into a family that'd given me a means to have them. I actually thought those things made me happy at the time. Money, toys… women. But when I thought it'd all be taken away by my disease, those weren't the things I grieved for. I ached for all the highs I wouldn't get to do and those weren't trivial things like skydiving, traveling to the handful of countries I *hadn't* seen in the world, or anything else my bank card could get me in a single flash.

I wanted the things I couldn't think of yet, the stuff my mind couldn't even compute they were so wonderful. That's when I knew all the important things I *thought* I'd done hadn't meant much to me. All my corporate triumphs and financial gains didn't mean much if I wasn't happy. It was then that I'd finally realized that I wasn't.

It was funny how it took almost dying to realize that.

It was shocking. It was insane, but I…

I wanted Johari's offer. I wanted to be able to have what she was so graciously offering me and the funny thing was, I didn't find the notion crazy. I didn't think the desire to want to have children at this stage of my life was unusual. I found I actually *wanted* to have children and not only that, but that I should. I questioned my sanity many times recently.

But this decision was the first time I hadn't in a while.

The only piece of the puzzle I needed now was Asa. A lawyer as well as a financial businessman such as myself, he had all the tools I needed to move forward with this potential arrangement with Johari. He'd gotten both his MBA and law degree at the same time and was knowledgeable in both the legal and financial side of our family's company. Asa knew business. Asa also knew contracts, so he had exactly what I needed to make this surrogacy plan happen.

Now, if only I could convince him to give me back the paperwork.

"What the hell is this?" he charged, tossing the documents on my desk.

I had a carrier run it over to him this morning, documents I had drawn up and wanted him to go over. I took the initial steps to get a basic surrogacy contract drafted up, but I wanted him beside me in all this as far as legal representation.

I was beginning to regret that decision upon seeing his initial reaction to all this.

He put his hands on my desk. "Why would you need this? Are you sick? Because if you are, tell me that now."

I wasn't ill. In fact, I couldn't be more clear-headed.

I stood, pressing down my tie. I came into the downtown office today for a formal meeting space. I wanted this all to be done right and for Johari to feel comfortable. I was sure she'd have a lot of questions for me.

Especially considering how I left her.

I had Penny inform her the meeting would be about a potential surrogacy arrangement, but really, not much else besides being open to a background check and sending over some necessary identification documents. She sent over her own paperwork detailing her personal history in response, so at least, we'd both be on the same page about what today would be about.

I guess that was a start.

"I'm completely healthy. I assure you," I said coming around to my brother. "And think about it, Asa. Why would I be trying to bring a child into this world unless I was? If you'd just let me explain—"

"You damn well better," he said pushing off the desk. Hair so blond, his reddened face made him look like a cherry. He forced a hand through blades of hair made sharp with product. "You ignore me for over two weeks, Alex. Wiped from the planet like you don't exist, which made me not even know what to think."

He was right. I had. Like I said, I needed the time to think. I did that thoroughly in the time away, so I would give him one there. The last time I went away like that, I actually *had* been sick, going away for treatment. Though, at the time, he did know about the reason, my entire family did.

"And then you come back with this," he went on, his hand toward the documents to emphasize the point. "A contract for a baby agreement to have a child with a complete stranger with no more details but an, 'I need this, Asa. I need you to do this with me and I'll explain later.'"

"Later is now. Later is why I asked you here to explain."

"Oh, no you didn't. You needed someone close with a legal background. I mean, you're going to meet this girl in…" He paused, checking his Rolex, and his eyes only bugged out at what he saw. He dropped his wrist. "Minutes? Jesus, Alex. Where did you even find this woman?"

"A café. And if you'd just let me talk for a goddamn minute I could make you see that this whole thing isn't as crazy as you think."

His finger went down to the page, to the contract. "Why do you need this? *Why?* Like you said, you're healthy. You're fine, so why would you make such a rash decision after quite literally getting a second chance at life."

"Because I do have a chance," I shot, nostrils flaring. I jabbed my fingers to my chest. "I have been given another chance to live my life."

"And living your life means having a baby?"

"Part of it, yes. We're thirty-one, Asa, and it's not unreasonable to want to have a child at this stage of my life. I'm young, *healthy,* and we're both fortunate enough to have been born into a family where we've never had to worry about anything. I'm stable. I'm established and I want to have a kid."

"That's all fine and dandy, Alex. It's completely fine, but you're clearly forgetting something so let me check you with reality. Up until this moment, you've never in your life desired to spread your seed in any other way than to bust a nut. I know because I know you. Hell, I am you. We operate completely the same way and that's always been okay for us."

And see there was the problem. The two of us fed off each other, never allowing the other to move forward. We enabled each other's sophomoric decision-making, and used our money, power, and status as an excuse to get away with it.

I gripped my hair. "You're not listening to me. I don't want to be that way anymore. I was nothing that way before."

"You were nothing, huh?" he asked taking a step back from me. "So what does that make me, as I was there alongside you?"

The ridiculousness of his statement only had me crossing my arms. I shook my head. "Don't do that. Don't make this about you. How you live your life is fine, but don't ask me to continue doing the same if I have no desire to."

A stream of air expanded from his nostrils and reaching forward, he took the documents off my desk before I could stop him. He took the contract.

He tapped it on the chair meant for clients and colleagues in front of my desk.

"What if I don't want to help you?" he asked, completely serious. He tucked the document under his arm. "What if I say fuck all of this? What if I say fuck you?"

"Then I find another lawyer." I took a seat on the edge of my desk, putting my hands together. "And my perception will change of you."

At the end of the day, my brother could threaten all he wanted. He could ream me with everything from jabs at my intelligence to questions about my current mental state, but that wouldn't matter. I was going to do this with or without him.

He passed a glance outside. I was sure seeing so much. On the seventy-fifth floor, the entire downtown area of Chicago could be seen from my corner office of polished glass and steel beams. The area in which I conducted my business was quite literally an executive fortress and the biggest amongst the offices in the *Ricci Financial* Chicago office. I won the tossup. I won my father's office.

The document sliding from underneath his arm, he handed it to me.

"Don't make me lie to Mom about this. I don't want to keep this from her," he said, and I wouldn't.

At least not forever.

# Johari

The place was like Emerald City. And that was just the first floor.

*Ricci Financial* glistened with sparkling floors and crystal chandeliers, the clientele just as polished.

Straightening my pencil skirt, I attempted to blend in, my heels short but my strides sure as I made my way through the bank's exuberant halls. I'd already been caught once looking out of place in front of someone clearly *on the level.*

And I wouldn't do that again.

My mind blew that I was here, seeing... Alexander, Alexander Ricci of a massive fortune, this fortune.

*Keep your wits about you, girl, and stay optimistic, open.*

Sheer curiosity brought me through these halls today, the man I was scheduled to meet one of mystery. He clearly hadn't been at that coffeehouse to meet me, *discuss* having a baby with me. I was supposed to sit down and have coffee with someone else— that very person canceling the meet-up only minutes after Alexander had left me. It seemed the couple found someone else and forgot to tell me, and well...

That almost felt like fate to me, fate that I had met Alexander instead. And fate that he wanted to discuss the arrangement further. I was on a time crunch for this arrangement. I... I really couldn't afford for this *not* to work out, the stakes too high.

The reasons for needing this money quickly came to mind. I had made many sacrifices to get myself through medical school, my life consumed by the decision to make something of myself and *do* something for myself. I came from a low-income household on the west side of the city, raised by a mama who broke her back every day for me and my brother to have something of anything. My drive to do even better, better for myself and represent my family well pushed me in to the direction of medicine. I worked long hours both physically and mentally to do it. But even still, I came up short. Medical school was hard. Medical school was *expensive* and I needed to find some way to fill in the gaps.

Even if it meant taking the funds from somewhere I shouldn't have.

I was about to correct that choice now, though, make amends now.

Standing tall, I made steps forward, my thoughts awhirl at all this around me, the opulence of the building and the man somewhere inside it.

*He really wanted to have a baby? Truly?*

I mean, he asked for all the documentation needed on my part and did have me submit for a background check.

*I suppose we'll see, shall we?*

I approached a woman standing inside of a circular desk before a four-set of golden elevators. I bypassed the bank area completely and just went ahead and met with her to get directions. Upon quickly giving her my inquiry, her eyes had just about fallen from her head upon hearing who I wanted to see. As it turned out, that floor was actually restricted to the general public. She had to make a "call" and didn't seem too happy about being bothered.

"Thanks," I said, my tone more polite than it should have been, and if I hadn't been used to folks treating me any way they felt I might have sported an annoyed look myself. In the ER, people unfortunately treated you how they felt when they came in—and that was pretty dang crappy. I was currently serving out my clinicals in the emergency room of Chicago Community Med.

I received a chin tip in response but ignored the chill and took my travels where she directed me.

Behind the elevator doors moments later, I pressed a button to the seventy-fifth floor, the top floor, and for all intents and purposes, the penthouse of *Ricci Financial*.

He was somewhere up there on that top floor, no doubt walking the halls in those shiny shoes and that fine suit I envisioned that day in the coffeehouse.

I really *had* seen him before. In fact, he quite literally consumed my television and magazine articles daily. And let's not even touch Alexander Ricci's well-known presence on the Internet. That kinda happened when one came from a family of a billion-dollar empire.

And I'd worn a hoodie and sweats in front of him.

My massive failure in that regard had me on my game now. I had on a pair of heels, making me a little taller, and the fit of my skirt and smart blouse was slimmer compared to the sweatshirt I'd wore last time we met. Alexander Ricci wouldn't see me so unkempt and fresh off a shift at work. He'd see me polished, proper like himself. It might affect his decision if he really wanted to do this.

*Breathe, just breathe.*

The elevator doors cracked open and a wide berth of granite tiles met my eyes. They stretched on for what seemed like forever and surrounded me the moment I stepped out of the elevator.

I expected desks lining the interior walls, hustle and bustle not unlike what had been downstairs, but up here, there was only one desk. A girl stood behind it, petite and pleasant in her gaze. Of Asian descent, her cloak of silky dark hair flowed behind her when she came around a marble desk, to me.

"Ms. Russell?" she questioned and I nodded, a bit on autopilot.

I smoothed my hands down my skirt.

*Hold it together, girl.*

"Um, yeah. That's me," I said, slightly mumbling. I could stutter now. I had to get it out of my system before seeing Alexander Ricci.

My nerves only seemed to make the girl smile. She held out her hands, gesturing to the right.

"Mr. Ricci and Mr. Ricci are ready to see you," she said and that had me blinking.

She said two—as in more than one.

Before I had the chance to load my questions on her, she took me on a journey. We went behind the wall where her desk resided and on the other side, were two wide, glass doors the shape of an arch. They were located at the end of a road, which glistened in beige, fancy flooring up here on the penthouse floor.

*Emerald City indeed.*

My secondhand shoes took me down the hall, behind the girl, and I knew I only had moments. I still had time to turn away, head back into the land of the familiar and leave behind that of the unknown.

I had no idea *why* Alexander actually entertained my ramblings that day, or where his interest in having a baby now and in this way, came from. Alexander Ricci was a powerful man in this city, his entire family was, and up until the day I actually met him, he didn't seem like the type to really *want* to settle down let alone jump the hurdle of a spouse clear onto fatherhood. My sources had only been that of the media of course, but I was hard-pressed not to see anything but truth in what they fed the general public about Mr. Ricci himself. Was he truly serious about this? About me and wanting to go through with what I told him that day at the café?

I caught sight of the man with all the answers the moment my escort opened the doors to her boss' office.

And he was just as handsome as that day he met me at the coffeehouse.

Standing upon my entry, he wore that fine suit, though minus the jacket. A baby blue button-down synched in at his waist, a black skinny tie going long down his broad chest.

He had his hands in his pockets; I couldn't help but notice coarse, dark hair running thickly over his chiseled forearms. He had his shirtsleeves rolled up part way and I saw them well, his skin far from fair with its honey-glowed complexion. I supposed that made sense considering his last name. He almost looked European in his darkness.

Hand extended, he came toward me, thighs hitting the seems of his pressed pants like his shirt did over his frame, and thoughts of how I even believed for a second this man was gay astounded me. He was polished for sure, *clean,* but no way gay.

No. Freakin'. Way.

"Johari."

His hand cradled mine when he took my hand, one on top and the other underneath, and for a moment, I forgot the simplicity of breathing.

"Thank you for coming," he said, a smile tugging at his full lips. He stepped back and when he did, he took me in.

"You look very nice," he said, shaking my hand.

He called me nice looking, the subtlest compliment but more than sweet.

My face saturated in heat, I meant to say something of a similar fashion, about him and how he looked, but the moment passed. He lowered my hand and when he did, his returned to his pockets.

"I appreciate you meeting me today and your willingness to go over everything. I'm sure my interest in pursuing this was a surprise."

And just like that, he confirmed what I believed.

*He's serious about this.*

So many questions raised, his reasons and thoughts behind them. But I guess, really that wasn't my business. He just needed a surrogate, a means to have a child, and that's all the information I no doubt was entitled to.

I couldn't help wondering, though.

"Um, yes," I said. "It was. It is, Mr. Ricci."

His smile widened. "Please. Call me Alexander."

That heat surged my face once more.

"All right. Okay, Alexander."

His bright white teeth revealed even more with his grin, a sharp contrast to his full dark beard. He put out a hand and I realized we weren't alone, a man with his back to us standing on the other side of the room.

Alexander's hand went behind my own back, as he released his assistant of her escort duties.

"I'd like you to meet someone," he said to me, and soon enough, we were headed toward the man fully dressed in a tailored suit, his hands behind his back.

"This is my brother, Asa," Alexander introduced him as and right away, the contrast between the pair was evident.

Asa had blond hair, gleaming and flaxen in the strong light in the office. He also carried himself differently, a stiffness to his shoulders when he lowered his hands from behind his back.

Alexander gripped his brother's shoulders.

"Asa Ricci," he finished. "He's my lawyer and will oversee everything today."

*Lawyer...*

This really was official.

This really was happening.

Blinking, I extended my hand toward the man I now knew to be Alexander's twin brother. The pair really couldn't be more different. Though, their heights did match, as well as the general size of their frames. He had a trimmed beard, too, but his was of course blond instead of Alexander's thick raven color.

"It's good to meet you, Asa," I said, genuinely feeling that way. Alexander put off an overall warmness to him that I assumed Asa would as well since they were twins.

I guess that was why I'd been so thrown when his posture changed.

"Mr. Ricci," he corrected me, his shoulders stiffening with the words.

His handshake also went firm and I didn't miss the look Alexander passed in his direction, his body shifting that way to give it.

That's when I knew I wasn't supposed to see it.

Feeling a sudden tension, I tried to ignore the fact, smiling a little before dropping Asa's hand.

"Mr. Ricci," I returned, not at all bothered by the preference. If that's what he wanted to be called I would. I stepped back. "But feel free to call me Johari. Or even Jo. My friends all do."

Head lowering, a smile touched Alexander's lips I found hard to miss. It only made him that much more handsome. I got no smile from Asa, though, his look deadpan.

He cleared his throat.

"Very well," he said, straightening his tie before gesturing to an open door on the right side of the room. "Shall we take this in the conference room then?"

We could do whatever he liked. I had no problem adjusting.

I followed the men to that open door, a wide room of mahogany-colored walls and polished wood flooring. Vast, the table in the center could quite easily hold a couple dozen executives. Today, I got two and I tried not to let that intimidate me. Alexander made that quite easy. He could have sat on the other side of the table, next to Asa, but he sat near to me, a few feet away with his legs crossed.

And Asa didn't miss that, eyeing him before digging right in. And dig in, he did. He had a ton of paperwork in front of himself and from what I could see, some of that had been the documents Alexander had me send over to his secretary. Most of it was my medical history like I'd brought the day to the café, then other things needed for a background check, my driver's license and stuff.

Asa read a little before he spoke.

"You're very thorough, Ms. Russell."

I noticed he still refused to call me by my first name, but decided to let it go.

I nodded. "Thank you."

"Clean bill of health," Asa went on, reading. "This is very important as I'm sure you know. We can't have any issues if you're going to carry my brother's child."

Alexander dampened his lips after he said that. Like he wanted to say something but decided against it. He passed me a smile before glaring a little at Asa, but he of course missed it as he was well into eyeing my paperwork.

I wanted to show Alexander none of what his brother said bothered me. What he said was true and as Asa was acting as his lawyer, I supposed it was technically his job to be straightforward like this.

I placed my hands on the table.

"I agree, Mr. Ricci," I said, having a *very* high tolerance for stuff like this. I worked in the ER and had to stay on my feet when it came to folks and their sometimes heavy attitudes. I'd simply handle this like I did there.

Professionally.

"That's why I provided it," I went on. "I'm glad you find it thorough, sufficient."

His gaze lifted from the page, his eyes green unlike the sweetened brown of his brother.

Closing the folder, he shifted in his chair. "I suppose that only leaves one issue then before we go over the paperwork."

In the back of my mind, I wondered what he had for me. But never would I let that show.

I gave him the floor.

"Go for it."

"Why do you want to do this?"

"I'm sorry?"

Asa finally passed his gaze over to my left, staring at his brother.

"I know my brother's reasons," he said, moving to face me. "But I want to know yours now, your true intentions for wanting to go through with this. Is it just the obvious—money, or is it something deeper? Fifteen minutes of fame perhaps? Because I'm going to shut down that glimmer of light for you right now. You'll definitely be signing a nondisclosure agreement, Ms. Russell. No one will know you're carrying my brother's baby. So if you think for one second you'll be—"

"Asa!"

Alexander's hand came down with a crack to the conference room table, but his word had been stronger, more forceful.

"Enough," he pushed through his lips, burned through them with the intensity of the sound.

Asa's jaw worked. "These are honest questions. They need to be asked and are in your best interest. That's my job as your lawyer, and hell, your brother."

Alexander's lips tightened. I hadn't seen him angry before and it made me kind of sad. It didn't really sit well on him; look good at all.

Rubbing my hands, I waited it out, Alexander choosing to respond to his brother.

"They are honest questions," his said agreeing when he lowered his head. "But they're invasive, as well as inappropriate."

Asa stood, putting his hands on the table. "We need to know her intentions. You need to know. These things need to be asked, Alex—"

"I think we're done here."

Asa blinked, standing tall. "What?"

"We're *done*," he said again. "At least with this part of the meeting. We'll bring you back in when it's time to go over the details. I need a moment. I'd like to speak with Johari without you here."

"Well, as your lawyer I don't advise that."

Dark eyebrows descended like storm clouds. "Duly noted."

Things couldn't have been more intense, a stare off between two brothers. Alexander won, though, clearly, and without another word, the blond pushed my folder away. He left the conference table in a fury and Alexander didn't even look at him as he made his way toward the door.

Nor did he watch when his brother slammed it.

Alexander's fingers went to the bridge of his nose.

"I'm sorry about that," he said, facing me with the kindest eyes. He did seem kind, at least sympathetic.

He lowered his hand toward the table. "He shouldn't have acted that way toward you and I apologize."

Today hadn't gone exactly like imagined. But I suppose I had no real expectations.

I didn't want anyone fighting, though.

I chewed my lip. "It's not a big deal, really. He was just doing his job, right? As your attorney?"

"I wish it had been only that. He was being protective, ridiculous."

Again, proving my earlier statement.

"Like I said, his job. He is your brother."

I'd do the same for mine and would do so every day and any day.

And I think Alexander understood that about his own, the realization in his eyes.

I was sure he'd do the same.

"Yes, he is," he said, then surprised me when he wheeled his way closer to me.

Space erased and then, he was there, that cool aftershave suddenly in my direction.

I dampened my lips at his unexpected proximity, my heart leaping a little.

"I really did want to talk to you," he said, lifting curly lashes to me. "Without him here."

I swallowed.

"Okay," I said, trying not to shift in my seat. He wasn't disrespectfully close or anything, but unlike at the café, he wasn't gay this time. And because he wasn't, I couldn't reason not being attracted to him, and Alexander Ricci was quite attractive.

Almost devastatingly so.

*The tabloids didn't do him justice.*

His body wide and features masculine, he had an intense presence about him that fastened attention and I found myself susceptible to his draw.

"I wanted to get your thoughts on everything," he finally said, tapping the marble table.

He shrugged. "Just see where your head is, I guess. Today isn't a commitment to anything. And actually, I do advise you to take a moment and think things over. Meet with your own lawyer and look at everything before you decide."

The reality of what he was saying settled, his want for this, *to do* this, have this baby with me.

Have this baby for himself.

*"I know my brother's reasons,"* his brother had said only moments ago.

But what were they? I guess he had his own. Just like me and my… my debt.

Breathing, I crossed my legs in my pencil skirt. "I wasn't lying at the café. I want to do this. I've been thinking about surrogacy for a while and…"

Chewing the inside of my cheek, I wanted to reiterate my reasons. I said them before but I wanted no secrets.

"Money is a big reason. Your brother was right on that. I do have a lot of school debt, but that's where this stops. I had no idea who you were when I met you that day, and now that I do, who you are doesn't change that."

His expression warmed.

"I know and I do appreciate your honesty. You did that before you even knew who I was and that means a lot. As far as money, you won't have to worry about anything on that front. I've put together a list of figures well-above the standard. I did some research and found what I believed to be a fair figure. I feel a higher amount is necessary for you considering your valued secrecy in all this. We really can't tell anyone about the arrangement. I enjoy my privacy."

I was sure he had, his life, his world a fish bowl for any casual onlooker.

"And it's all negotiable," he went on. "The figures. I wanted to give you something to start with but we can go anywhere you want with it. You'll also be covered for everything from healthcare to everyday essentials during the pregnancy and I've taken the liberty of opening a checking account in your name, as well. I wanted it there, ready just in case. You can draw off it immediately. I made sure the balance was more than sufficient for you."

He was saying so much, *doing* so much, and with each word, he had no idea how much of a burden he was lifting from me.

Ian and Robert were offering a hefty some for a surrogate, but they definitely hadn't been billionaires. Truth was, I didn't need billionaire money. I just needed a break, a little bit of hope to undo myself and pay someone back who'd been there for me.

I could return the favor now and soon.

And what a relief that was.

The relief washing me, I smiled at Alexander, laughing a little as I thought back at how truly thorough he was about all this. He sounded like me and all the neurotic steps I took to have my bases covered in all this, basically throwing my entire life at him in a single folder.

My shoulders shook with the laughter. "And your brother said I was thorough."

"Well, I have to be," he said, opening and closing his hands with a smile. "I'm a businessman."

And I guess this was business as sensitive of an issue as it was.

Alexander watched me in my silence, a man I never believed I'd be having this conversation with. As I thought before at the coffeehouse, he had a history, and after meeting his brother, Asa, I felt my preconceived notions had been spot on—at least about Asa Ricci. Alexander himself on the other hand was an outlier. He truly wished to have this baby. I guess I just didn't understand why.

He watched me. "I feel like you want to ask me something. I'll be honest. You were with me."

Okay, so we were being honest then, him giving me the floor.

I put my hands together, deciding to take the opportunity.

"Your brother said something. About… About your reasons," I said. "For having this baby and in this way? I mean, a guy like you doesn't need a surrogate. You could just get any old girl to—"

And now, I was crossing a line.

Clamping down on my lip, I felt the heat flush my face, embarrassed about using his invitation to take the floor as a means to make assumptions about his personal life.

His smile allowed for some of the embarrassment to fade away, though.

"You're right I could," he said, being honest about that. "But I'm choosing not to. Going this route is an agreement, an understanding between two people with one objective."

And no complications, though, he left that out. He wanted nothing confusing here. He wanted this child and that's where it ended. I got that, I supposed.

"As far as why," he went on. "I guess that has to do with the new state of my health. I'm able to do something like this and I'd like to. I'm ready to."

"So it's true? You're no longer sick? I mean…" I bit my lip. "The media said as much."

The Internet had been a small explosion about him since we'd run into each other, much like it had during the time of his original diagnosis. The heir to the Ricci Empire had been dying, cancer…

The same disease that took his wealthy father.

Alexander's gaze shifted then, moving outside, and he smiled at the day behind his glass fortress.

"I used to measure my life in days," he said, his chair swirling in my direction. "But, yes. Now, I get to measure them in years like everyone else. I almost feel like it was fate. Not just getting better, but when I did. I met you right after I was told."

*Fate… Fate.* How interesting I'd thought that right before coming up here.

I guess it had been in the clouds, the stars.

He placed those big, brown eyes on me and my chest caught, my arm rising in goose bumps when he placed his hand on the table near mine.

"I never really thought about having children before. But then, well, you came to me; you with all your medical and extreme tardiness."

I laughed lightly. "That really never happens. I see patients every day. I have to be efficient with my time."

"I know. I believe you. I really do. And this won't affect that, right? Your pregnancy affecting your education? I know you said you were in your final year."

I guess I forgot to mention that, my plan for the logistics.

I shook my head. "It shouldn't. I'm actually graduating this winter early and I'm taking a year off before starting my residency."

Something I had already decided even before thinking about surrogacy to cover some of my debts. I had big plans for my future, big moves, and needed time to prepare for them. I wanted to help my mama out in the year before I left. I guess give her time to prepare for my absence. She'd never ask me to do that of course, but I wanted to. I'd always been here for her and now I wouldn't be.

That year would ease us all into the separation, myself included.

What I said must have pleased Alexander, his handsome smile once again on me.

"I want this," he said. "I want to move forward with this if you do. With my condition, I took the initiative of freezing some samples before my treatment."

That's right. With his particular cancer, having children would already be difficult. I read he had prostate cancer and though it's not impossible to have children after that, with as bad as I heard he got, I highly doubted he'd be able to have children without medical assistance.

My heart hurt for him, him being so young. He wasn't much older than me from what I understood.

"It's all ready," he went on. "And I've already looked into getting a donor."

"I was going to offer Robert and Ian an egg. I don't have any immediate plans to have children."

"That wouldn't be too hard for you?" he asked completely serious.

And I understood. This would be… this *was* an emotionally charged experience we were both about to dive into. Especially myself.

*I'd be okay. I will be okay.*

"To carry, essentially, your own child," he went on, unknowingly tugging at my heart a little. He swallowed. "Our child?"

It was the way he said it, *our child* as if he could already imagine it.

Getting out of my head, I reminded myself that this was his child. *His.* Not mine.

*You're doing this. You will do this.*

*It won't be like before.*

I nodded to the thoughts, breathing. I was going to be professional about this.

That was my job to be.

I moved in. "It would be an honor, truly, Alexander. I'd love to help you and as I said, I was going to with Robert and Ian. This is no different."

I made myself believe in that. This wasn't different. Just because it was him, someone of his status, that made no difference. He was still a man who had a genuine need, a want he should and had the right to have.

"Robert and Ian," he said, laughing a little with it. "They wouldn't mind you doing this for me? Giving you up?"

And so, I told him of the cancellation text I got from the married couple shortly after meeting with him.

This really must have been meant to be.

# Four

**Johari** The door slammed behind me and I paused, waiting a moment before continuing.

Upon not hearing anything, I let my breath escape, hiking the bag of groceries I brought in up on my hip.

I ended up taking my travels through the basement. I'd come through the back door of the house, but that route was the only way to get upstairs and to the kitchen to place them.

"I heard you slam my door," came before I could even get barely in and I sighed.

Stiffening up, I took the few feet to make my way into my mama's basement sitting area. She was there. They were all there, she and her customers. Mama had her hand braced around a hot comb, steam coming off aged, gray locks as she transformed her customer's hair from curly to straight.

She gazed up at me. "I don't pay rent for you to break my stuff."

"I know, Mama," I said coming in.

Adjusting the groceries on my side, I ignored the smile she exchanged with the woman she worked on. I knew the woman well. In fact, all three of the women in the room. The other two were under hairdryers, long-time customers of my mama's basement hair salon.

"I didn't mean it," I said coming over to give her a kiss on the cheek. "Door just slipped and I couldn't get it in time."

She put her face out to receive the peck, the soft heat of the room and her constant labor leaving a shiny glow to her dark skin.

"Mmhmm," she responded, going back to her customer's head. She sent a pass over a curly strand near the woman's ear, glancing up after she did. "What you got there?"

I showed her, pulling out a loaf of bread and some non-perishables I picked up on the way over. I shrugged. "I noticed you had a list started the other day on the fridge. I wanted to bring it over before I headed in to work."

I tried to bring stuff over when I could. It'd never been much in the past, and only what I could afford on a student income.

*I guess that was about to change, wasn't it?*

I hadn't signed with Alexander yet, but fully intended to. I planned to go over everything I got from him today the moment I cleared from work tonight.

What I brought Mama today was on my own little earnings, but I stretched them to relieve things for her when I could. Especially once I moved out and decided to pursue school. I'd been living on my own since I left for undergrad; the place I was in now was small but functional. I basically only went there to study and sleep, and knew it would only be a means to an end. I'd be getting out of the city entirely eventually, though, starting my residency.

Mama analyzed the stuff with a quick once-over before stepping back behind her client, Mrs. Anderson.

"I think I got most of that when I took Javan out yesterday, but thank you," she said, looking at me over the hot comb. "I appreciate it."

And I knew she meant that, but that didn't mean she had to start the way she had, that she didn't need the food or the gesture.

Knowing that was her way, though, I stepped around and out of her way, greeting the other ladies in the room.

"You've been scarce, Jo," one of them said, and I smiled, bending down to give Ms. Sherry a hug. She'd been my mama's neighbor for literally my entire life.

I stood, shifting my grocery bag a little. "Been busy."

"She gon' be a doctor, you know," Mama said, lifting her head a little as she said it. "I'm sure you won't see her much at all after that. She's always trying to get away from me and my nagging."

My heart racing, I turned, tiling my head. "It's not that, Mama, and you know that. I just want something different. I've been in the city my whole life."

An "mmm…" left her lips, and I didn't know why I bothered. My mama was notorious for only hearing what she wanted to hear and I could kick myself for even trying.

Ms. Sherry squeezed my arm. "Don't pay your mama no mind. You get out of here. You should. There's so much to see and California sounds nice."

The whole neighborhood pretty much knew my plans; our community was big but tight. Especially when one of us chose to get out. Following school, I wanted to be matched for work on the West Coast, intrigued after I spent some time there recently with a friend. I actually met Roya when I started medical school; she was a nurse at the hospital I was doing my clinicals at. She had family back in California and asked for me to come with her on a mini vacation, and I guess I fell in love, the sun and the beauty of it all. I'd get a change there. I would get something new.

I smiled at Ms. Sherry, not surprised she got it, me wanting to go. I stayed at her house almost as much as at home growing up. Though we were apart by many years we felt kindred, staying up to watch old movies and play card games. This woman got me. She knew me.

"Javan around?" I asked generally of the room. They all knew my brother, just as much as me. I reached into my paper bag, pulling out some cookies. "I got his favorites."

It'd been Ms. Sherry who answered me, smiling wide. "You always spoiling that boy, Jo."

"Don't she, though?" Mama came around Mrs. Anderson. Putting the hot comb down, she exchanged it for a curling iron. She took it to Mrs. Anderson's head. "He's rippin' and runnin'. You know him."

I did, my brother was super popular. At twelve years old he was just starting to really get into that pre-teen freedom and I was happy he got to do that. At one time, we all thought he might not be able to.

I said goodbye to everyone, heading upstairs to put the things I brought away. I wanted to do so quickly as I had a shift tonight.

Mama got me before I went too far.

"That riffraff came around looking for you," she said behind me. "That boy?"

I tried to play off what she'd said, turning around casually. "What did he want?"

A dumb question I knew. If Jared was looking for me there could only be one reason. He only had one reason now, as we hadn't dated since I left home.

It had ultimately been the reason that sent me into surrogacy.

This had been the wrong question to ask Mama, though, impatience in her eyes as they lifted toward her ceiling.

"What do I know, Johari? Nobody's got time to deal with your—"

"Okay, I'll find him," I said wanting to cut her off before she hit the ground running. "I'll see you all later."

I went back through the basement the way I came in, hearing, "Did you hear that? What she said to me?" come from my mama's lips before I was well out of earshot. But it had been what I heard when I pushed open the door that had me shaking my head.

"That girl always thinks she's so much better."

The words pinched at my chest, didn't matter how many times I heard them before.

I made sure the door didn't slam this time and didn't have to go far to find who I was looking for. Jared was walking down the sidewalk where my mama's driveway met street.

And he was walking with my brother.

I could see Javan's smile from here. There weren't many like his. It was very unique and that made him only more special because for it. Down syndrome wasn't a rare disorder but still wasn't without its obstacles when it came to raising a child with the disorder.

My mama had it rough when she raised us. She had to do it alone with a child that needed extra care. Because of that, I overcompensated. I needed to in order to make things easier for her, not that I minded it. I loved my brother and respected my mama for her fight as a single mom. I lost my dad to the system—he'd been incarcerated all my life—but Javan's still lived around here.

That's why he didn't show his face, his clear abandonment of the child he felt was damaged. He'd actually said that once. He'd said Javan was damaged, flawed.

*Motherfucker.*

My mama ran him out of here after that and we rarely saw him. It was better that way. She didn't need him, and neither did Javan. They had me.

Smiling, I shielded the sun from my eyes, raising my hand. I waved and Jared noticed, coming up the driveway. Beside him, Javan played with a plastic plane, zipping it and zooming it through the air. He got to me and I hugged him, rubbing on that knot head of his.

"What you doing?" I asked him, and so busy, he just continued to play. I smiled. Reaching in my purse, I managed to get his attention back.

He beamed, trying to get at the cookies I bought for him today.

"Come on, Jo!" he said, reaching for it. He was starting to get so tall, reaching my height.

But still I had him on some inches.

I lifted the cookies. "Boy, you better say thank you."

"Thank you!" he said, grinning, and I gave them to him, shaking him a bit before making him hug me again. I had to work tonight and didn't know when I would see him next.

After he got his cookies, he cruised inside, fighter plane and cookies in hand and I shook my head.

"Thanks for walking him home," I said to Jared, and he nodded, pushing his hands into sagging jeans.

"No problem. He was playing with Erick."

Erick was his own little brother, the pair of ours pretty much blood brothers. We kind of got together through them. As my brother got popular in school, made more friends, he brought them around and that's how Jared came to be; him picking Erick up from time to time when he came to my house. Javan actually spent a fair amount of time in general classes and was quite the socialite. He did things even doctors didn't think he was capable of, considering how sick he was growing up. He beat the odds and made us all see.

I shrugged my purse up. "I wouldn't hang around here too much longer, though."

"Why?"

Mama's laughter could be heard from the basement. She had the window to the basement open. She had to considering how hot it got down there from the curling irons and hair dryers.

That answered Jared's question.

"Right," he said, shaking his head in the general direction. "Never did like me, did she?"

He really shouldn't beat himself up about that because my mama didn't tend to like many people. Sometimes I even questioned her like when it came to me, though, as I got older, I understood that was silly. Of course she liked me. She loved me.

But my mama always had been a hard one to crack, even from the time when I'd been a little girl. She'd just been through so much; the life of a single mother was hard, and that could put a toll on anyone and their attitude.

I started to walk away. I needed to get to the bus stop to go downtown to work, but Jared asked me to wait, and I'd be lying if I said I had no idea what the confrontation would be about.

I hadn't been ready to talk to him yet—about the money I owed him. I was still in talks with Alexander about everything regarding the surrogacy, the paperwork unsigned.

"You'll have it soon," I told him, at least knowing that. Once I'd gone over the contract, squared everything away, I'd pull Jared aside myself. He'd get what was owed in full no problem.

He looked around in response to what I'd said, up and down the street actually. Upon facing me, he lowered his voice.

"When, Jo?"

"Soon. I'm going to be getting some extra money coming in the near future."

That was putting it lightly. I hadn't read through everything involving Alexander's paperwork, but I was sure his offer was more than fair. He'd even said it would be negotiable on top of that.

"And when I do, you'll get it in bigger installments."

"That's the thing, Jo. We can't keep doing installments," Jared said, pushing his hands into his pockets. "I'm going to need cash quick, which was why I'd been asking you about it. You know I borrowed it from 'Keem."

Like he knew, the local drug dealer gazed our way. He'd been across the street, staring at us from a neighbor's porch. I normally wouldn't have taken a dime from Jared, knowing exactly where he'd get it, but when he offered, knowing I needed the money for school, I foolishly said yes. I didn't have a full ride through med school like I had my undergrad and wasn't trying to start life in debt up to my eyeballs in student loans. Jared's own personal loan helped fill in the gaps scholarships didn't fill.

I just didn't realize Hakeem would be coming back for it so soon.

"I caught him looking at Erick today," Jared said, breaking my gaze of Hakeem.

I faced him. "Looking at him for what?"

"What do you think?" he said, his voice tense through his teeth. "He got me young. He was looking at Erick and hell, Javan too because he was with him."

He'd said the wrong thing. The wrong damn thing.

I put a finger to his chest. "He wouldn't touch him. Javan couldn't even push for him. You know that, his condition."

"That wouldn't stop him. I'd been able to protect Erick. Keep him off his radar. But then, I asked for a loan."

He did ask for a loan...

He did so for me.

I folded my arms across my chest, suddenly feeling cold. "How long do I have?"

"You know there's no deadline. But then again there is. I would just take care of it sooner rather than later. Please."

He started to walk away, but I grabbed him. I had a habit of doing foolish things, this I knew to be one of them. But Hakeem couldn't look at Javan or Erick. Those boys wouldn't be selling drugs. They couldn't.

Especially because of my selfish decision to leave.

Reaching into my bag, I pulled out a checkbook. It'd been for a new account, one that had been opened specifically for me. Alexander told me he arranged for it just in case I said yes to the surrogacy arrangement and wanted to move forward with everything.

I did want to move forward. I had every intention to especially after meeting him. He'd been so welcoming, genuine, and how much I really did want to give him his wish for a child.

But at the heart of it all, I did need the money, too. This, Jared and the loan, had been why, and though I hoped to sign with Alexander more formally, professionally, Hakeem wasn't giving me much of a choice.

*I'll cut the check now, but then send the papers to Alexander's office first thing. He'll probably get them before the money's even taken.*

Knowing I didn't have much of a choice, I filled out that check from the account in my name, the *Ricci Financial* seal underneath my fingers. It was beautiful, official and made this whole thing real.

Jared's eyes bugged out while I did. "Is that for real?"

He didn't even know the half.

I ripped the check off then gave it to him.

"The full amount," I told him, the reality of that crippling by the many zeros on the check. My education had been so much.

I breathed. "And only *you* cash this. I'm trusting you. All you have to do is go to the bank the check is drawn on. They'll cash it for you no problem."

He simply stared at it, and then slowly raised his fingers toward the pretty paper.

Taking it, he studied the writing with a thorough gaze. I gave him what he needed and then some. Just in case Hakeem tried to pull one with interest or something.

"It's good?" Jared questioned, lowering it.

I nodded, shrugging my bag up. "More than. And remember, just you cash it."

"Just me," he repeated, folding the check.

He slipped it in his pocket and how much anxiety flooded from me there on my mama's driveway. I hadn't realized how much of a toll the burden of the debt had taken on me, a weighted blanket that affected me both physically and emotionally.

*I can... I can move on now. I can go toward that next step, California. Medicine.*

Kind of emotional with those thoughts on my mind, I hugged someone who used to be my everything. I really did love this boy. We just... we went different ways, our lives and destinies taking us in varied directions.

"Thank you," I told him, squeezing him. "For everything."

Jared had given me the greatest gift, a wonderful gift.

"Just thank me by getting out of here," he said.

And when he pulled away, I watched him. His gaze had traveled behind me, over my shoulder, but it hadn't been toward Hakeem or even the other drug dealers across the street.

He stared through a basement window, a woman laughing while she worked on an older woman's hair.

# Five

**Alexander** "What exactly am I looking at?" I asked, forcing the blurriness out of my eyes with rapid blinks. Asa had called at…

5:32 a.m.

*Christ.*

I pushed my hand through my hair, the hour just as ungodly early as I'd believed. Pressing a button on my cellphone, I went back to my email, where my brother had sent me to go the minute I answered his call. I didn't even get a hello, just a, "I sent you an email. Wake your ass up and look at it."

"You're looking at a big freaking mess of 'I told you so.' Do you see that shit? Tell me you see it."

I couldn't see it, my vision still blurry. Pushing the sleep out of my eyes, I finally did and my eyes widened at what I saw.

"Why am I looking at my bank account?" I asked, kind of pissed about it. I redirected. "Why do *you* have a screen shot of my bank account?"

"Because I kinda sorta own the bank with my brother."

He overinflated the hell out of that statement. Asa and I didn't own *Ricci Financial* and all of its entities. We held shares, a fifty-

fifty spilt of half the company divided between us. Upon our thirty-fifth birthdays we got the majority via my father's will, but until then, we were definitely checked by the shareholders.

But that was beside the point.

"Tell me right now why I shouldn't reach through the phone and strangle you for calling me so early?" I snipped, turning over in my bed. It was barely daybreak, my room the orange color of too-early-in-the-morning. I frowned at the ceiling. "Because if it's seriously not the end of the world, Asa, I swear all that is—"

"She drew off your account."

"Who?" I had to take a second to think, which wasn't made any easier by how tired I was. I pulled my hand down my face. "Stop being cryptic. Who are you talking about?"

"That *woman*. The one you just hired? The one who's supposed to have your damn baby."

"Johari?"

"Give my brother a prize, everyone. He's just come back to reality."

He really needed to stop with all the sarcasm. It didn't bode well on him and I wasn't ever one to have the patience for such things. In my life, I needed the real. Real answers, real statements. I was a guy about facts not this BS.

Calming down, I held my face, trying to figure out what to say to my idiot twin without completely coming off as an ass to him.

"Just relax, okay?"

"Relax? Relax! What the hell are you talking about? Relax? You knew about this?"

I tilted my head back, knowing he wasn't going to be happy about what I was about to tell him.

"I did know," I said, rising up. "I gave her checks to draw off the account during our meeting."

Though I didn't know she'd be so quick to use them. But actually, that made me very happy. I wanted her to think about everything and bring her own representatives in if she desired, so if Johari cashed a check that meant something. It meant she decided.

A hard smile spread across my lips.

*She said yes. She's doing this.*

The reality I tried to wrap my head around. Maybe I should call her. Maybe we should talk or… or celebrate or something? I didn't know the next moves for something like this.

I think I just wanted to see her.

"Have you completely lost your mind?"

I unfortunately had to deal with Asa first.

"No, and I'm about over you calling me crazy."

"Well, Alex, I'm gonna call you crazy, you know why? Because crazy people give complete strangers checks when they haven't even fully committed to a process yet."

"But she is committing," I said. "That's why she drew off the account. She wouldn't unless she had. She probably just got a little overzealous."

"Overzealous? Right. Alex, overzealous is fifty dollars. Maybe even a thousand if she was truly a creep."

"Watch it. You won't be saying things like that about her. And if you say one more goddamn word about Johari that isn't the utmost of fucking sweet, I swear to God, Asa."

"*Ten thousand*, Alexander. She wrote a check to someone for ten thousand dollars. People don't do that, and they definitely don't unless they signed a contract to legally be able to do so. It was so goddamn unusual the bank put a twenty-four hour hold on it and since it's from one of *our* personal accounts, they called me."

They should have called me. But I guess I understood why they hadn't. He'd been handling all the financials for me once I really hit the rough patch in my illness.

*And ten thousand…*

That was unusual, but then again, not really. Johari had said she was in a lot of debt and maybe she just wanted to take care of it right away. I would have.

I touched my beard. "She confessed to me she's in a lot of debt. I bet she was just taking care of it. I wouldn't get alarmed just yet."

Getting out my bed, I decided to go ahead and get myself together. I wasn't going to head into the office today. I officially was not ready to go back to work, but being in that space I might think better. I could call Johari in or maybe we go somewhere a little less formal. We could get coffee or something and talk.

But then I dropped my pants at what Asa said.

"Well, considering her debt is most likely drugs I think you should be pretty alarmed."

I wouldn't lie. I did a double catch of the phone.

"Excuse me?" I questioned, pressing it to my ear.

"You heard right, Alex. *Drugs.* I did a background check on the guy she wrote a check for. He submitted his license to get the money."

Him running a background check on someone was definitely very illegal considering the reasoning behind it, but I let that go, listening.

"He's got a rap sheet a mile long and has served time in and out since he was fifteen."

A sad case, but I'd heard of it. The city of Chicago lost a lot of youth very early in life unfortunately. This guy probably got handed a crappy life, which left him vulnerable to be on the wrong side of the tracks just as I had been fortunate enough to be handed my opulent one. Our lives both were a roll of the dice, nothing but DNA and chance.

"Maybe she was just giving him money." Because I couldn't jump there. Not yet. "She told me her debt was medical school."

"Had she really? Do you know that for a fact? I mean, she said so, but do you know for certain?"

"Technically, no. But—"

"Because you don't know. You know nothing about her but what her own background check said and her medical history. This woman gave a known criminal a large sum of money on your dime and the fact that you don't know whether its drugs or something else is very alarming. This woman is supposed to be carrying your child, Alexander. What if she's an addict? What if she comes from a family of addicts and you don't know? We're talking about your child. And if this woman has any shred of anything even remotely close to a drug history you need to stay away from her. Think of your kid. She could pass all the drug tests you want her to take before conception but what's stopping her from doing drugs after you've both committed? After she's *conceived*."

I hated what he was saying. I hated every word. Because… he was right.

Swallowing, I attempted to temper my thoughts, my anger. I'd gotten so involved, my hopes, my faith in her…

A perfect stranger.

"I know this is hard and I take that by your silence," Asa went on. "But we'll get you another surrogate. Someone suitable, someone you should be having a baby with."

I had no idea what he meant by that, but I had nothing for him, spent. He told me he'd talk to me later and I dropped the phone, the screen crashing down and then cracking when it hit the hardwood. I went to pick it up, but I found something else instead, something tucked away under my bed frame.

*The cleaners must have missed it, since I'd been away.*

I had only spent a short time back in my high-rise apartment, not even fully moved in post my free and clear diagnosis. Like I said, I had spent my days going through treatment away and figured by the time I got back, I'd be in a new headspace.

I picked up the photo of my dad and me. We were both in business suits, his arm around me while we smiled into the camera. Asa had missed this photo, off being himself somewhere in some foreign country. I had always been the worker, fighting the hardest, wanting to please our dad more.

I ran my fingers over the broken glass, not caring if cut. I threw the frame at a wall the day I'd been diagnosed, the wall ahead still chipped from the dent. I worked so hard to be in his photo, smiling with him, pleasing him.

Only to die from the same thing that took him.

Slowly, I tossed the photo on the bed, and then reaching down, I picked up my broken phone. I dialed, waiting to hear my assistant's voice. Penny would be in now, always was by five to get everything started even without me.

"Good morning, Mr. Ricci," she said. "How can I help you?"

I eyed the photo, dropping my arm across my knees.

"I need you to stop a check," I told her. "And cancel an account."

# Six

**Johari** "Wait a second. Slow down," I said into the receiver. "What happened?"

"Jo."

My gaze collided with the nurse ahead.

Bent over the nurse's station, my stretched body covered a stack of papers as well as someone's chart.

I jumped back, letting the cord of the phone placed to my ear extend. I cringed at the nurse who called me on my flub.

"Sorry," I told her, and she raised her hand, allowing me to rest easy I didn't hold anything up too much. She grabbed the chart and went on, but I waited. I shouldn't be on the phone and definitely not in the middle of the emergency room. I couldn't help it as I'd gotten a call right in the middle of my shift.

I turned, the phone cord wrapping around my body. People used this phone to talk all the time when they shouldn't, but that never had been me.

"I said your check is no good," Jared said into my ear, and I shook my head.

"What are you talking about? What do you mean it's no good?"

"I mean, it's *no good*. I went to cash it, but the bank put a hold on it. I'm assuming because it was so big. That's pretty fucking shitty but I got over it. But then I got a call that the check was bad. A stop was put on it."

I held up my hands. "Wait. Back up. The bank stopped it, or it was bad?"

"What difference does that make?"

"A big one."

A deep groan went into the phone. "They told me the check was stopped and I couldn't cash it. Don't matter either way to me, since I ain't got the money."

My lids fell over my eyes and my heart hammered at what this meant.

The check was good, the account good, as the man behind it had a net worth beyond what thoughts could even imagine. So if the check didn't work, the checks meant *for me* in connection to a prospective agreement, I could only formulate one conclusion for the interruption.

Alexander. He stopped it purposely, or his people did. Either way they did and...

The reality of what was happening right now blasted through my awareness at full speed, and I felt like a frickin' idiot for even giving Jared the check in the first place. It didn't matter the intentions behind it. I had no right to considering Alexander and I hadn't finalized our agreement.

*Oh my God, what must he think? Of me...*

I checked the clock above the ER entryway as a few EMTs guided in a body, the linens around the patient saturated in blood while he held his arm. One attendant pushed the gurney while another held an IV for the injured man.

This was my life. This was what I worked so hard for, to help people.

"Give me the afternoon," I shot into the phone. "I'll figure this out."

"Jo—"

I slammed the phone down, and then handed the chart under my arm to an available nurse behind the counter.

"Hey, I'm going to take my lunch a little early, okay?"

She nodded, letting me know she'd inform the appropriate people. I unfortunately had to get downtown.

I needed to explain myself.

Since I was on my lunch and needed to get somewhere quickly, I decided to sacrifice the money for a cab. Money always tight, I never did that. I couldn't afford the leisure.

But this was an emergency.

Upon arrival, *Ricci Financial* seemed, if at all possible, even busier than the morning I'd come in, people coming in on their lunch hours to bank. I went to the familiar desk and asked to speak to Alexander. The lady from before was there once again— the snooty one who shot her nose up at me the first time.

And my heart sunk at what she told me, what she said after she made a call upstairs.

"You're not on the list, Ms. Russell. Nor do you have an appointment."

I knew I didn't have an appointment, but horror chilled me that there was a list outside of that, a list that may have restricted me.

A list that blacklisted me by the man himself.

I shrugged my bag up my shoulder. "I'll only be a minute. I know the way."

"I'm sorry, ma'am. But unfortunately, I've already told you that— Miss? Wait!"

I didn't wait. I went around that damn desk of hers and went onto the elevator. Alexander had to see me.

I had to explain myself.

The doors closed, cutting the panicking receptionist from my view, and I dropped my bag to the floor, pulling out documents. I had already signed them last night and would have taken them in already if I didn't have to work this morning. I planned to cruise in after my shift.

Dropping my head, I felt so foolish. I should have faxed them first thing, so he'd have them right away.

So he'd understand.

I let a mess form around me that shouldn't have. How much shit had this man already been through, his illness, and I added to the pile. He seemed so happy when I told him I would commit to him, relieved.

*And you put the notion of having a child into his head in the first place...*

I had to fix this.

This seemed to be a day of familiarity because that same petite girl faced me the moment the doors open. Her expression deadpan, she didn't have the same welcoming smile she had before and I assumed she'd been warned, warned I'd be up here.

That proved when she put a phone down, the receiver previously on her ear.

"Ms. Russell," she said, folding her hands in front of herself. "I know your purpose for being here, and meeting with Mr. Ricci cannot happen today. He's not in. I'm sorry."

I called her on her bluff there. Because if he hadn't been in I wouldn't have gotten as much resistance as I had downstairs.

I could only tell the girl, "Sorry," as I went around her desk, and as my legs were longer, she couldn't catch up to me while I charged that sparkling tile road. I needed to see the Wizard himself, the man locked up in his ivory tower. It wasn't unknown to me that Alexander Ricci had become a recluse. After he was diagnosed, he pretty much fell off the globe. The media went crazy for weeks, months after his disappearance. They wanted to know what happened post diagnosis, where he went and why, but for me, I seemed to be the only one not in the dark.

The man had just gotten diagnosed. He was told his life was about to change and he might not get one. I saw that not every day, but often at the hospital. Alexander shut down. He locked himself away to deal because despite his money and power, he was like the rest of us.

He was human.

And that mere mortal sat behind glass doors. I pushed them open and got a clear view of his executive chair, a light setting it aglow from the surrounding sun. I couldn't see the man himself, though. He kept the chair's back toward the door, but he occupied it.

I knew because he rocked back just once in it.

"Alexander?"

"Mr. Ricci?"

We'd said the words at the same time, his assistant and I.

But he didn't respond to mine.

"It's okay, Penny. I'll see Ms. Russell."

The vacuum sucked away in my chest, and if not for his voice, the depth of it, I would have thought his brother sat there in that leather throne.

"Very well, sir."

His assistant, Penny, backed away, leaving us alone.

I hoped once she'd gone, once she left the pair of us, the tone in the room would be like when Alexander's brother Asa first exited the office. I felt relaxed last time I'd been here, calm.

What wishful thinking I had.

The nerves boiled in full, my hands gripping the folder with nothing but harsh silence filling the room.

I decided to break it.

"Alexander?"

His chair moved slightly, but no turning.

And then came even more silence.

Swallowing, I approached his desk, my footfalls audible in the back of my head. I pulled the folder out with the documents, the contract.

I placed it on his large desk. "I signed these. I'm sorry I didn't get them to you sooner."

I had half a mind to believe those documents would sit right there, untouched until I left the room. But somehow, I got the Prince of Chicago to turn around.

I wished he hadn't.

A sharp contrast hit me now, a different man in front of me than the previous one before. For starters, he wore a full suit today, perfect and pristine not unlike his brother, and it brought out a difference in him, a seriousness.

It matched his eyes.

That amber-filled gaze wouldn't move in my direction, and when he reached forward, I thought he'd pick up the folder.

More wishful thinking.

Instead, he opted to push the papers toward me, placing his hands on his desk.

"I think you should take these yourself."

A chill backed the words, a harshness to the tone.

His lips went tight and that firmness, that seriousness continued.

"That way you can make sure they're properly disposed of and not tampered with."

I felt hallowed out, carved and cut internally.

The swallow traveled hard down my throat. "What do you mean? Why would I do that, Alexander? I've agreed to the process. In the document? If you'd just…"

He had a look that said he wanted nothing more to do with this, his head turning away.

But I couldn't let this go.

"This is about the check," I said, a statement and not a question. "Because I wrote one out to someone."

What I wouldn't give to get those eyes on me, his attention for just a second.

His Adam's apple bobbed in his throat.

He put his fingers to his lips. "I think you should go now, Johari."

I should have gone, left without another word. I had been in the wrong, completely and fully.

So why did I stay?

"You gave me your trust," I said, stepping forward. "You did and I overstepped, but I wouldn't have unless I knew this was happening. Our agreement? I wanted to deliver the contract to you this morning but I had an early shift. I should have faxed them over once I got in and really, I have no excuse for that, but time got away. And I guess I really wanted to give you them myself anyway, personally."

I guess… I wanted to see him again, see the look on his face when we made this thing happen.

Made it real.

But that was no excuse, no reasoning for my quick actions to relieve a debt that had nothing to do with him.

There was no excuse.

Reaching forward, I went to grab the folder.

"What did you need the money for?"

I lifted my head. "What?"

His lids fell over his eyes, his jaw working, moving slowly.

He looked up at me. "It was a lot of money to take out very quickly. What did you need it for?"

Shock rattled me still, not knowing what to say.

My hands came together. "I… I don't believe I'm required to tell you that, that I'm obligated, I mean."

I read the contract since our meeting, front and back and nowhere did it detail I needed to provide what I planned to do with the money he was compensating me for.

*Compensating…*

God. This really was business, wasn't it? Having his child.

I breathed.

"You're not but…" His jaw ticked, tight. Pushing out a breath, he slid the folder toward me. "Please take the papers. I'm sorry we wasted each other's time."

He stepped out of his chair and long strides took him to the glass windows of his office. They surrounded him, caged him.

I did take the papers, but I didn't let this go… either.

I slid my bag to a chair and then headed in that same direction toward the same windows he was standing at.

"Why do you need to know?" I said, shaking my head. "Is that how this was going to be? You monitoring the funds? Me?"

His head shifted my way. "Of course not."

"No?"

"No."

And turning around, his gaze collided with mine. His face had flushed, charged with color.

I just didn't know why.

"Why did you give money to a drug dealer, Johari?"

I had to have misheard him, blinking.

"What are you talking about? Drug dealer? Who told you that?"

"So it's true?"

"No. What? Where is this even—"

"I know where the money went, Johari," he said, nostrils flaring. "It was my bank account. You gave ten thousand dollars to a criminal, and believe me, I've thought about it. I went long and hard with it, but I can't come up with a single reason as to why you would ever do such of thing that didn't end in trouble. There can't be a reason. There isn't."

Each word shocked me to no end, but despite what he was saying, whatever he was accusing, I didn't miss the judgment. He was judging Jared and me.

I folded my arms over my chest. "I told you I was in debt."

"Yeah?" he asked and had the nerve to sound sarcastic about it. "Drug debt? Are you even in medical school like you said you were? Or was that a lie, a way to get yourself in so I'd agree with this?"

"You know I didn't know who you were before all this. You know that and said so yourself. I came to you not knowing a damn thing about you in that café, and actually, I do know more than I thought I had. You're a rich man, Alexander Ricci. You're rich and you are entitled, and everything the media says about you is true. And how do I know that? Because of this."

I tossed the folder at him and he caught it.

"Your judgment," I snipped. "You stopped that check, this arrangement, before you even got the full story. Did it ever occur to you that maybe that 'drug dealer,' as you referred to him as, might be a good person? In fact, he is. He's a great person. He just wasn't blessed to live such a privileged life as you. But you know what? Your life isn't a privilege. It's a curse. It curses you in your elitist attitude and drowns you in judgment."

I moved away before I said anything else.

And before my eyes foolishly leaked.

Picking up my bag, I turned to him. He was still by the window, holding that folder with wide eyes.

My lips trembled despite myself, my eyes hot. "How about you get the hell over yourself? And when you do, maybe then you'll be ready to hear it. The truth."

I waited until I left the building, escaped those ivory walls, but I did have to take a tissue to my eyes. I couldn't pinpoint the emotion, frustration... loss, I didn't know. Either way the tears did fall, but I wouldn't succumb to them. After tossing the tissue away, I hailed a cab.

I had to go back to work.

# Seven

## Alexander

"Alexander?"

My pen pulled away from the sign-in sheet, then left completely when I recognized someone familiar. Naomi, my ex-girlfriend, came toward me in a set of blue scrubs and lengthy white jacket and actually looked… happy to see me.

At least someone was.

I tried to push Johari out of my mind as I lowered my arm to the side, turning toward Naomi, but truth be told, Johari had consumed so much of my head space lately that I didn't know which way was up these days. *That* in itself said something to me, something big.

Something that got to me.

I was a businessman. I did nothing but multitask and handle complicated situations daily. But the thing was, Johari wasn't a situation. She was a person.

And I very much had disrespected her, jumping to conclusions. I basically called her a drug pusher, her and that guy she gave money to.

How many times had I asked Penny to dial Johari's number this week, only to change my mind no more than a moment later?

And in any case, what kind of person had his assistant call to connect him with someone on such a personal issue? I knew the type of person, my father. Having my people "call" would be something he would do. It was professional, but it was also disconnected, cold.

And hadn't I already been harsh enough to her with my accusations about herself and the people in her life? She'd been right. I had overstepped in my assumptions about her, who she was and the people she surrounded herself with. This was also something my dad would do. He'd disconnect from others; his obsession with business and making money allowed him to do that.

But it hadn't been my father who made assumptions about Johari, judged her. That I did all on my own. Asa may have planted the seed, but I ran with it. Almost like I was looking for a reason to.

I tried to smile when Naomi came over, but only mostly because she herself was smiling, which I definitely didn't get…

Considering how we ended things.

Despite the fact, I didn't argue. I had no desire to stare a gift horse in the mouth. Especially, not of late.

"Alexander," she repeated, and really did smile genuinely. She reached up, pushing a blond curl out of her face. "My eyes, are they working properly? Seeing you out and about?"

Her questions to herself came as no surprise. My scarcity was of no surprise to anyone in my life, her especially as she'd been so close.

I rubbed the back of my neck. "Yeah, I'm here. And no, you're not seeing things."

"Yeah, I suppose I'm not, am I?"

Her gaze analyzed me in almost wonder, then flew behind me and stayed. Since the only thing there was the sign-in sheet I just filled out, I gathered that's what she looked at.

"Everything okay?" she asked, redirecting her attention to me. "I heard you were doing better, past the worst."

I was sure she had, as well as anyone else with access to the Internet or television. My recovery was breaking news for solid weeks. I couldn't have gotten away from the circus if I tried.

I took my coat off the counter, putting it over my arm.

"Fine, fine," I told her, stepping away to let someone else sign in.

The lab department of Chicago Community Med was always bustling, people having their blood tested for many different reasons than I was.

I shrugged. "Maintenance mostly. I'll probably have to be pricked with a needle the rest of my life."

A small sacrifice to pay for reassurance, certainty, and I'd wager Naomi got that. She herself was in the medical field, an obstetrician specifically.

"Of course," she said, and I knew she did get that. Moving to the right, out of the fray of the rest of the patients in the waiting room, she gestured me over.

"How have you, um… How have you been otherwise? Healthy? Clear?" she asked. "Your mom kept me up to date during treatment."

While we'd been dating, my mother had been my and Naomi's biggest cheerleader. I supposed that was why it'd been so difficult when things turned out the way they had between us. I ultimately ended it, feeling it was best for both myself and her. We were two very different people and I think I understood that the most, which was why I bore the responsibility.

"I've been well," I told her. "Just taking things one day at a time. It's nice not having to worry." I laughed a little. "I guess I'm kind of scared not to."

"Don't be. You can't live like you're going to die. That will only make you anxious, paranoid."

Chuckling, I lifted my head. "Yes, Dr. Randolf."

She cringed, shoving her hands down into the pockets of her white coat. "I'm doing it again, aren't I?"

"Just a little."

Naomi was far from a psychiatrist, but I'd be lying if she didn't feel the need to play armchair doctor whenever I had any type of hiccup in my life, whether that be stress or a chest cold. It didn't matter that she only worked with babies and new mothers.

Her sentiment, though, did ease the tension a little. I laughed again, and that made her happy, her smile widening again.

"I don't know if your mom told you, but I kept up with your place a little. While you were gone? I had a key and it was no problem. I had a few things to get out myself."

She had, hadn't she? We broke up right around the time I had been diagnosed, though, I hadn't been sick then. At least, I didn't know I had been.

I nodded. "She hadn't, but thank you. Actually, more than thank you. Anything off my mom's mind during that time is appreciated."

And I meant that genuinely.

The busy lab hustled and bustled around us, the people. Doctors, nurses, and their patients came and went and I figured that's how Naomi spotted me, on her way herself to continue working.

Someone bumped into her and we both said excuse me, the two of us clearly in the way of a path.

I pushed a thumb behind me. "I better take a seat. They'll be calling me."

"Oh, right. Right." But she didn't look any closer to walking away. Pulling her hands out of her pockets, she crossed her arms. "Let's catch up sometime. Get a drink? You know I jump at the chance to read a juicy lab write-up."

I chortled. "Sure."

"Yeah? How about tonight? I get off pretty soon."

I honestly had agreed as quickly as I had because the prospect of an actual drink I believed would be far in the future. I really wasn't in the mindset for that tonight.

"Maybe some other time. It's not that I don't want to, though."

It was actually because I didn't understand why *she* did. I very much had broken up with her; a decision I was well aware of hadn't gone without hurt on her side. The two of us had been through a lot and I more than gave her reasons for ending things herself. Despite the fact, she stayed. She hung in there.

Even when she shouldn't have.

"No?" she asked, but then stopped herself. She rubbed her arms. "I guess I just thought…"

"What?"

She dropped her arms. "With you being sick? Us ending, I thought…" She shook her head. "I suppose I believed that's the reason why, the reason why you ended it."

I had been afraid of that. In the back of my mind, I had.

I pushed my hands into my jeans pockets. "Naomi, we had problems well before that."

Too many to count, and that had been on both our parts. Naomi had her fair share in the trials and tribulations of our relationship.

I had just made the final blow.

"I know, but I just thought…" Lifting her hands, she waved me off. "You know, what? Forget what I said. We'll still do drinks, but just as friends. And tonight does stand. That is if you're game."

Drinks before sounded like just friends, but drinks now, after what she said… didn't.

Sighing, I decided to let her down lightly. But I found I couldn't.

I saw her.

*Johari.*

Her and in her element, hair brushing across cheeks that flushed and lips that vocalized commands. She was in her scrubs, pushing a gurney with a patient on it, and if she hadn't told me, I wouldn't have believed *she* was the medical student, the EMTs listening to her.

In the wings, she did have assistance, a burly man in a white coat flanking her. His hands in his pockets, he had a wide smile on his face, saying nothing and letting Johari do her thing.

"Some other time," I said to Naomi. Johari and party had pushed the man on the gurney toward the ER rooms, my current location of the lab adjacent. I turned to Naomi. "We'll catch up later."

Hands in pockets, Naomi shifted in the direction I stared. But so much was going on out there, she quickly lost interest and turned to face me.

"Of course," she said, but something in her voice told of her disagreement of my decision, her disappointment. "You'll have your assistant call?"

She got my attention again, with that.

A "Right" left my lips, so much familiarity in that. I really was my father's son, and Naomi, well, she knew that.

She squeezed my arm just once, nodding before leaving to do her job. And once gone, I found Johari again. It seemed everything with her patient had gone all right.

She stood back from the fray now, letting the nurses handle the rest as she'd already stabilized the patient.

Her doctor friend patted her shoulder and brought light into eyes I recalled being so bright in the café. They'd gone wide when they stared at me that day, and then creased softly in the corners with her smile.

The doctor left her, heading away and down the hall. After he had, Johari came out of the patient's room, pulling a curtain for privacy.

I took a step toward her.

"Alexander Ricci?"

My name had me turning back toward the lab.

The nurse behind the desk looked at me.

"We're ready for you now," she said. "To draw blood?"

I turned back toward the ER. Johari had long gone, heading toward the hall and approaching a set of glass doors.

*I'll lose her.*

And I couldn't help thinking in more ways than one if I didn't follow her.

After telling the nurse to move on with the rest of the list, that I'd be back, I picked up the pace, hoping those doors didn't lead to somewhere restricted.

"Jo—"

Getting on an elevator, she missed my voice down the hall behind those glass doors. I caught up to the lift in a few strides, but even I wasn't quick enough to catch her before the elevator doors closed.

On my heels, I thought to make a sprint toward the stairs, but took a moment, looking up at lit numbers.

*One...*

*Two...*

*Three—*

*Two.*

She stopped on the second floor.

I had no idea how pointless my laboring would be. By the time I scaled the two flights, I still might miss her. I was currently on the basement level of the hospital.

I had to try.

Urgency in my step, I made that ascent, grateful for every step I made. Not so long ago, I might not have been able to do such things. So many things were out of reach in the past for me and because they were, I refused to let that happen again.

I found her behind a door at the top, one right near the stairwell.

Catching my breath, I watched through the glass window, the most interesting scene before me. Johari was in a room, but she wasn't alone.

In fact, far from it.

She hovered over a bassinet, one of clear plastic with holes on the walls.

And the child inside was so tiny. Actually, all of them were, the babies surrounding her.

*Neonatal Intensive Care Unit.*

I dropped my gaze from the word above the door, shifting to Johari while she stared over the tiniest infant. Beside her was a woman, one wearing scrubs, but also, a colorful scarf over her head.

But one would have thought Johari was alone the way she interacted with the child.

It was as if no plastic barrier were between them, between any of them, as Johari made rounds. She gave the babies the most intimate attention, cooing at them with a smile that radiated light, radiated sunshine.

The woman in scrubs followed her, speaking to her, and even she couldn't keep the warmth off her expression watching Johari and the tiny babies. Johari would speak to her, and then the woman would nod as if getting advice.

The pair came upon a young couple, one viewing another child and they spoke to Johari, a welcoming expression telling they'd definitely seen her before.

In the back of my mind, I wondered if this was it for her, where she'd be once done with her studies. If not, it should be. She seemed so at home here.

She and the woman in scrubs suddenly left the couple, rerouting.

And that's where they spotted me.

It had been her friend who saw me first, and then she placed her hand on Johari's shoulder.

I got those eyes then, that light in the brown. They revealed themselves between strands of her hair, which fell from the way she gathered them above, her lips parted below. She had such a slight pink of them, a soft contrast to her mahogany-colored skin. Seeing her, I really did wish a potential child would take on more features of hers than myself.

I really would be lucky to have a child with her, fortunate.

A space taken up by a door and vast air seem so short between us now, the space so small. Our gazes intermingled and they stayed together, her head tilting at me.

Moments later, I found myself backing away from the door, and when she came out, I'd been put on the spot, caught watching her.

Her arms moved over her chest, her eyes narrowing slightly. "What are you doing here, Alexander?"

A simple question, but one that gave me pause initially.

I thought to tell the truth.

"I saw you downstairs. I was uh, getting blood work. Maintenance you know, something that has to be done occasionally."

Her chin lifted and dropped. "So you followed me?"

Quite unusual, I supposed. But was it really?

I pushed my hands into my pockets. So many words I wanted to say, but finding none of them. I had my assistant phone her with those words on my lips, and even I had dialed her with intent to voice them.

But they were lost now, my thoughts a mass.

"I suppose I wanted to talk to you," I said. "Could we go somewhere?"

*Johari*　We took our talk upstairs, out of the fray and from prying ears. There's this space up there, on the roof with a patio deck and tables. Hospital staff tended to take breaks there and since I was still technically on mine, that's where we went.

"You wanted to talk," I said, moving my arms over a guardrail.

Before us, the city went vast, the hospital a looking glass into a concrete skyline ahead. One could even see *Ricci Financial* from here, Alexander's building. The shiny beacon stretched high in the sky, a crystal tower amongst the ordinary buildings it shone so bright.

The prince of that building pushed his hands over the hospital guardrails, muscular arms extended that pierced through his casual shirt. It seemed he walked amongst the peasants today. He said getting blood work.

He turned on the railing, hands together.

"You said a lot of things at my office," he said. "Interesting things."

I thought, "Which ones?" and going back, I hated I'd allowed him to make me come out of myself, lose my cool. I usually handled situations with a very level head, as I had to in the intense environment I would dedicate my life to. I wouldn't be stone, but I did have to be rational.

I guess Alexander made that a little harder, difficult.

Choosing to nod, I remained silent, irises of a toasted almond-colored tone pinning me in place. Framed lashes rose above them, not breaking his focus of me with even their blink.

He got closer and pushed the air, pushed me even if he didn't know.

He stared at my hands on the bar. "I suppose I'm ready to listen to you, Johari." When he lifted his head, he was smiling. "Get the hell over myself?"

I didn't miss the shock in his eyes that came with those original words, but this time, they made him different.

They made him smile today, hadn't they?

I dampened my lips, fighting my own grin. "Yeah?"

"Yes. You know, I uh... I never let people usually talk to me that way. At least, no one's ever had the audacity to try it."

"Maybe they should," I said, pushing the envelope and that chance I took faired in my favor.

The smile only widened.

Teeth went over his bottom lip, his eyes sparkling ever so bright. The evening was starting to settle in the city, those buildings in the sky blinking on lights like fireflies.

Pushing his hand over his beard, Alexander nudged the expression away, a seriousness to his lips that wasn't bad this time.

It only made him more handsome.

"Tell me," he said nodding once at me. "Tell me about before with your friend. I want to know."

And so I did, not the dirty details, Hakeem and all that mess. But I told him about Jared, that boy and his big 'ole heart. He did me a favor and I didn't care who knew. I just wanted him to be seen as he should, a man, and a good one, who just happened to find himself in the hood, and yeah, with a history of selling drugs.

"And you used to date?" Alexander said.

I did mention that, too, and wasn't ashamed of it. I still did have love for my ex. I just wasn't in love with him anymore. We had chosen different lives, different journeys.

Broad shoulders rose and dropped with my nod and turning around, Alexander took his gaze toward the city.

He stared down at his open hands. "I guess I would have known about all this had I just asked. You were in a scrape and just repaying a friend who helped you out."

"You know now," I told him, removing that final bit of space we had. There was no more anger now and hadn't been for a while.

Alexander sighed, his lips turned down.

"Yes, but not without complications," he said, closing his hands. "Unnecessary ones."

He took a step away and our gazes collided, this man so large before me in so many ways. Alexander Ricci was such a presence, which in turn, made him kind of intimidating.

He dampened his lips. "When I first found out about the

check, I questioned trust. I had no trust for you. I couldn't, so moving forward wasn't possible for me."

"That's understandable," I said, nodding. And it was. "I probably would be the same way. I was out of line."

"But how the tables have turned now. I managed to shift things, take away any trust you may have had for me by what I did. That's not a good place considering what we're about to do and the contract we're about to make."

I could see what he meant. I didn't know Alexander Ricci, but up until he single handedly severed any agreement we had, I had no reason to fear going into any type of business with him. We had a clean slate before. But now, things were complicated. We'd both managed to do that.

But…

"You said *about to* make," I said, smiling a little with it. "That means you want to do this? You want to have this baby?"

His dark hair feathered in the wind when his gaze shifted upon me, that dimple pressing into his right cheek.

"I want to have a baby with you."

Perhaps, it had been the way he said it, words so light and dare I say vulnerable. His heart was fully open and on display for apparently me and my decision. We had a lot riding on this, the pair of us, and that went far beyond any monetary value.

It couldn't be helped when it came to matters of the heart.

"I think I want to have your baby," I told him, and that made us both laugh, a deep chuckle humming from Alexander's throat. What a weird situation, a different one.

He pushed off the bar, taking space, and I felt the loss of it, the air clouding around me like a wool blanket.

"I should probably get those papers back from you," he said, and I had to fight, to watch his eyes over his lips.

I smiled, feeling shy. I guess it's good I never tossed the contract then.

That I waited in the end.

# Eight

**Johari** The mirror could tell time. In fact, it did tell time… eventually. But for now, all its reflection did was unnerve me.

*Of course you won't show. It's too early. Too soon.*

But that didn't stop me from staring in the mirror.

Slamming my locker door, I grabbed my scrubs top off the bench in the hospital's locker room. I finished getting ready for my shift by pulling it over my tank top, but my mind was no less clouded and the only thing that could relieve it a little was the one thing I wasn't allowed to do.

Pregnancy tests were explicitly prohibited after a round of in vitro fertilization. They were inaccurate. They could give both false positives and negatives and as an almost-doctor myself you'd think I would know that. I did know that, but the logic made keeping myself from taking one no less difficult. It seemed like the only thing that would relieve this… anxiety, this craziness I found my headspace in.

We were at two weeks now, Alexander and I. We were two weeks post the day we both walked into a shiny, *expensive* clinic where they got me set up, got me going on the first steps of creating a child the non-traditional way. It had been a surprisingly easy process; at least for me since I didn't have to do anything but lie there. Alexander and I had already decided we'd be using my eggs to have this baby. I just needed him. He came with me of course and that had been... interesting.

"I'll just wait outside," he'd said, stepping away and rather awkwardly at that. I found the whole thing cute since he always seemed so sure of himself and I was sure he was. Generally, I could imagine he was the boss-man in his life, but when it came to babies... when it came to this, he had to sacrifice a lot of control. The tables turned to me and the specialists at the clinic. All he could do was sit back and let that happen.

And so began the two-week sweat fest. Well, I guess they called it the "two-week wait," the period in which Alexander and I had to wait out to see if the pregnancy stuck, but my definition seemed like a far better one in regards to what was going on in my head right now, my body.

I felt very *aware* of myself if that made sense. I felt aware of every sensation and ounce of movement going on from a tummy ache to indigestion.

*"Is that the baby?"* I would ask myself like I could physically feel it growing at two-weeks young. It seemed all logic went out the window when one was *possibly* pregnant and even being a medical professional myself I couldn't talk myself off the ledge of paranoia.

I spun my fingers across the dial of my locker's lock, more than ready for my evening shift. Working these days seemed to be the only thing to keep me out of my mind so I welcomed it. I headed in the direction of the emergency room, but upon catching my work bestie, I only made it halfway.

Roya slowed down from a group of other nurses she walked with, her purple scrubs blending seamlessly with the colorful material of her hijab. This girl didn't *not* coordinate. Everything went together, everything was a statement of fashion and she taught me a thing or two on how to dress up the old hospital scrubs. I didn't try every day, but when I did, I was the best-dressed medical student in the entire hospital and only thanks to my friend.

She waved her friends off, and then came over to me, a "You. Over here. *Now,*" on her lips when her hand slid around my arm.

She pulled me off to the side, just a few shades lighter than me due to her ancestry. Her family hailed from the Middle East, herself second generation.

"So do we know anything yet?" she asked, a light in her brown eyes.

She'd been the one person I told that I *might* be currently pregnant right now. Quite frankly, she'd been the only person I could trust with that information. One of my first friends here, we had history and her working in the Neonatal Intensive Care Unit, she constantly dealt with situations such as mine when it came to ways in which people conceived children.

She also happened to be the only person who didn't violate Alexander's nondisclosure agreement—which of course I signed before doing this whole thing. She spotted Alexander that day outside of the NICU, nothing but questions on her lips when I got back. I held out for as long as I could, but in the end, Roya had her way. I broke down and asked Alexander's permission to tell Roya. I wouldn't tell her without it, legal or otherwise, and surprisingly, he'd been reasonable about it. I trusted Roya, so she got that trust by extension from him.

I boiled it down to our own trust we were attempting to establish.

I was glad he had allowed me. Roya would be the only one who'd be in on this besides Alexander and his family. At least— until I started to show. This was a complicated situation. This baby wouldn't technically be mine and not a lot of people could know. Especially my family, my mama.

I'd figure out that hurdle when I got there, got close there. My mama definitely couldn't know about this pregnancy. For so many reasons besides the obvious.

I shook my head in response to Roya's question, eyeing the area while I did. I felt *walls* had ears these days and hospital gossip could truly be worse than an office.

I dragged her out of the fray of the busy halls, taking a vacant wall to have a chat.

"Just left the two-week sweat fest," I told her and she fully knew what I was talking about. Anytime I had a cramp I ran up to her to relieve my nerves. I swear to God you'd think with what I do I would be better at handling all this.

No one told me a woman went crazy once preggers.

Roya nodded like I knew she would, understanding. "When will you both know?"

"We go back to the clinic at the end of the week." I silenced waiting for a few doctors in white jackets to pass by. After giving them a nod in acknowledgement, I shrugged.

"And it couldn't come faster, girl," I said, sighing. "I'm dying here. I can't even pee these days without thinking it's pregnancy related. I'm seriously losing my mind."

Again, my neuroticism was full blown. But it would be relieved very soon. Like I told her, we'd be going back to the ritzy clinic later this week and it would be all too soon to alleviate my stress.

Roya's laughter bubbled in the hallway.

She pushed an arm around my shoulders, rubbing. "It probably is my friend. It probably is."

"Oh, dear God, don't tell me that. I'm already paranoid about every little thing."

Her shoulders lifted and dropped. "I'm just saying everything your body does from now on can't be ruled out in regards to pregnancy. You opened yourself up to that I'm afraid."

"Don't remind me. I'm sweating bullets here."

Chuckling, she dropped her arm from my shoulders. "I'm still shocked to hell you're even doing this."

"Why?"

Her dark eyebrows lifted. "Why? You, Ms. Not-Having-A-Kid until I'm at *least* thirty and definitely not until I finish my residency?" she singsonged, sounding only a little like my own raspy voice. "You were always that gal with the plan, and this wasn't in the plan."

I thought about what she said, so chilly in the fact. I was that way and I decided that a long time ago. I made too many mistakes in that past and promised myself, moving forward I would no longer go off course. I couldn't afford to, not if I wanted the future I desired. I couldn't slow down. I wouldn't let myself.

Not again anyway.

"Well, neither was accruing medical school debt," I told her, shaking my head.

Her hand came down on my shoulder again. "I get it. That's why my butt went into nursing. Only a fraction of the time and not even a smidgen of the debt."

Smart lady she was, but being a doctor for me seemed to always be in the stars. I'd wanted to be one for as long as I could remember. I even remembered pretending my melted down ice cream was medicine, taking it to relieve make-believe illness. My friends and I always loved playing that game, pretending to be doctors at sleepovers and such. The thing was, they all grew out of that, but I never stopped. I couldn't stop playing pretend until I made it happen.

"I can see all of that resistance change though when you start to feel it, start to show." Roya's brown eyes shifted in the direction of my tummy, her pink lips smiling. "Especially, with his fine self. You'll be fighting him for his half child. Just you wait. His genes can't *not* be beautiful."

Chuckling, I couldn't disagree with that. But I played it off.

"Feeling it?" I questioned, tapping on something else she said.

A warmth spread across her expression. "Yeah, being a mom. I did when I had my two. That connection runs deep and I know it will with you."

My heart squeezed. "How so?"

"Because of how you are upstairs. At the NICU. You say you come to see me, but I see how you are with the kids. I see."

I wondered how much she did see, how much I truly did enjoy being up there, and I also wondered how right she was, about feeling it.

Would I... this time?

I let that thought go, the past go. My friend and I finished up chatting, but before we did, we made dinner plans. We usually broke for it at the same time if we worked same hours, heading to a place down the street. Safety went in numbers when night fell over downtown and that was the only time I'd venture away from the hospital if I had her.

"See you at six?" she said. "There's a new place I want to

check out across the street."

"Oh yeah?" I asked, pausing. I had started to step away, standing in the middle of the hallway. "What place—?"

"Excuse you. This is a hospital. Pay attention please."

The force came at my right side, smarting my shoulder.

Turning, I faced a blonde I had seen before. She frequented a lot upstairs in the area Roya worked.

And always looked at me funny.

I assumed the "looks" had to do with the fact that I didn't work up there, but was constantly in the area. But with some people that didn't matter. There were doctors around here you couldn't get to crack a smile even if you presented them with a giant piece of chocolate cake. And who didn't love cake, right? Just some people were like that and this woman seemed no different underneath her crisp white coat and perfectly managed hair. She always had it pinned and perfect, a seriousness about her face.

"Sorry," I said, letting her pass by. Roya put her hand behind me, allowing the doctor to pass as well.

The doctor lifted her hands. "Just pay attention. And Roya, please don't stay down here too long. I know Doctor Grant was just looking for you about a patient."

Roya's expression was the utmost of professionalism, only a calm demeanor beneath her gaze, but behind those nut brown eyes I knew the truth. Like I said, we had history.

She was giving this doctor a big old bird to the ceiling... as well as a subtle, "Bitch, please."

"Of course, Doctor," she opted instead, smiling a little. "On my way."

Doctor-Takes-Herself-Way-Too-Seriously nodded, going about her way, and Roya and I followed her with our stares.

"Doctor Randolf has been here three months and is *still* a pain to work with," Roya said, shaking her head. "I thought I needed to just learn her style. She came from Rushvill Med."

Rushvill Med was a good hospital. In fact, great. If I wasn't trying to go to California I might have thought of practicing there actually.

"But I don't see her getting any better," Roya continued,

sighing. She faced me. "Promise me now you won't turn into that, the clear power trip."

She didn't have to worry about that. I hadn't been doing this whole doctor-thing long, but I did know there were various ways to deal with the trials of working so close with people, different ways of coping with the emotion that came with it. One could be cold, disconnected so as not to feel. Or could be something else, something less intense.

This woman obviously chose the former.

My shift started later that evening the way most of them did—chaotic. A bus accident downtown brought in over a dozen people and I found myself on the front lines as per usual.

"Russell?" came at me from across a rolling gurney, Dr. Orval McCarthy the caller. "I want you to get the IVs set up. This woman suffered heat exhaustion along with her injuries."

The second one this evening. From what I'd heard, these folks had been trapped for a while before the fire department could get to them. Most of the people on the bus had been fine, but the multiple car pile-up around them made getting rescued a challenge. It seemed some idiot ran a red light. Crazy how one person's foolish decision could affect so many. I worked on at least three cases like this in the last hour alone.

I nodded at the doctor, other things I had in my wheelhouse far more intricate than that of a simple IV. I reached for the appropriate materials, getting the patient set up and secured with the IV in little more time than a snap.

"You people get the *fuck* off me!"

My adrenaline already pumping heightened at the sound of a struggle, a man thrashing and throwing his fists toward several staff.

Set up on a gurney just outside my own patient's room, they couldn't even get this man to his assigned area, attempting to hold down erratic arms. Face red and sweating, this man had the classic signs of coming down off something. Clear track marks railroaded down his arms and the vomit on his shirt only added to my theory.

He jabbed. "Get off me!"

There were several people, both men and women, trying to

hold him steady and when I saw a white jacket, I knew what was going to happen next. The doctor wearing the coat, who I knew to be Dr. Reed, readied a syringe.

The patient's eyes widened at the sight. "Hell no. Hell no! Don't you crazy fucks stick me with nothing!"

The man struggled, nearly leaping from the bed, and the attendants wrestled with him. Dr. Reed tried to stick him, but wasn't getting anywhere. The man was simply thrashing too much.

The doctor held her ground. "Anyone who can offer a hand, please assist. We have to get this man down now!"

My patient stable, I answered the call for help.

I went into action without thought, and any other time, I think that would have been okay. I think it would have been all right for me to go in, act because it was something I did every day, and though every shift was different, every patient different, more often than not I would have been okay. There were those few times, though. There were those rare occurrences of chance encounters that staff and doctors dreaded. They were the ones in which a patient lost control.

The ones in which a doctor herself was caught in the crossfire.

The man kicked his ankle out of my hand the moment I touched his skin and the automatic jerk caused the rest of the staff holding him down to jump back. It was a snap reaction. They just couldn't help themselves. Dr. Reed flew back as well, her full syringe still in hand, but she cleared. She got away.

I was the one who hadn't been quick enough.

I didn't miss that second kick, the man going for whoever was in the way of his escape, and the hit sent me clear to the floor.

A sharp burn shot through my palms the moment I attempted to catch myself on the hospital tiles, but that was nothing. It *felt* like nothing compared to what the man did when he finally wrestled his way off the gurney to the floor.

He found me there on those hospital tiles. He *wailed* on me there since I was the only one in his path of escape.

That first kick that slammed into my back ran deep. Like a baseball bat to my skin and the second I felt myself disconnect. I fell outside of myself, watching in horror as this man reared back, his foot charging through the air with the force of an angry tornado. I knew exactly where he was headed, where he was going. He'd get my abdomen.

My stomach.

So many thoughts traveled through my head in that moment, the world, time as if in slow motion. I thought about Alexander. I thought about him and his want for his child. And then my thoughts traveled there, to that very small life. It was a life I hadn't gotten to see or even feel yet.

*No, please. Not again.*

My body balled, I waited for the impact, my arms cradling so hard around myself. I didn't want Roya to be wrong. I wanted to feel it.

I had to.

# Nine

**Alexander** "Where is she?" I asked Johari's friend, Roya. It'd been she who was the one to call me and deliver what I didn't know to be my greatest fear until notified.

I attempted to work recently, God help me. I took on a few of my old clients, ones who had always been easy to work with. I thought being active, working, would help to alleviate my recent stress surrounding the surrogacy situation.

How foolish I'd been.

Johari and the pregnancy had been a constant on my mind. The "two-week sweat fest," she called it, and how right she'd been when she joked about the process the day of conception. When I wasn't thinking about her, the baby, I was finding ways of thinking about her or the baby. Hence, my recent work schedule, which had been more than a disaster. I caught myself slipping in mentions of babies and the like into meetings, which did nothing but confuse the hell out of my colleagues. I was constantly backtracking, *apologizing* for the slips but nothing could save me from the flurry of the racing thoughts in my head.

All thoughts of mergers faded into the ether, and the topic of pregnancy cycles somehow phased themselves into the forefront of my mind. I was becoming a madman and in all my forced distractions, business dealings, I'd been completely tied up when the news about Johari finally did get to me.

It took me nearly an hour to get to the hospital. I had been in a meeting, one I had to first drop, and then explain why I had no time to reschedule. Between that and the Chicago traffic, getting here felt like it took me a short millennium when if I'd just stayed put... been at the ready for her...

I could kick myself.

Roya I'd remembered well when she called me. She'd been the nurse that day when I found Johari in the NICU, the one wearing the scarf.

"She's in here," she said, pulling back a curtain. She'd said, "She's in here," and that's the last thing I remembered before my heart beat its way from my chest into my throat.

And my vision turned red.

All alone, they had Johari on a gurney, turned on her side and in a white hospital gown.

*Where's her damn doctor?*

"Johari?"

She turned and my temper did nothing to ebb. A small maneuver had her cringing and any movement at all had her cowering into herself, her arms shaking as she attempted to raise herself up.

"Alexander," she said, and I didn't know what it was about that word, my name that had some of that anxiety inside relieving a little. She still looked to be in so much pain, but it had been her voice and the way she said my name. Dare I say, there had been some relief there. It seemed my presence helped a little.

I went over to here, pulling my driving gloves off. My driver, Esteban, had been at the ready to assist me to the hospital. But as much as I loved my old friend of the family, I didn't trust him to have the speed required to get me here in the time needed. I drove my Jaguar today.

"I'll leave you both alone," her friend Roya said, leaving us, but her voice faded to the wind. It couldn't be helped.

I put my hand on the railing of Johari's bed, wanting to touch her but....

She looked so fragile.

Fighting the urge, my hand folded close and she cringed, watching me.

"I'm so sorry," she said, dark lashes coming down over her eyes. She rubbed her nose a little. "I didn't mean to put myself at risk, the baby."

She thought I was worried about the position the baby had been put in. I mean, I was but…

"Are you okay?" I asked her, hunkering down. She had a chair beside her bed so I took it.

A shrug hit her shoulders, but she nodded.

"Bumps and bruises," she said. "Lots of bruises, but I'll bounce back. My arms took the brunt of it."

Solid purple masses on the outside of her forearms told me that, her deep-toned skin swollen and tender. Roya told me on the phone Johari had fallen to the floor and had been kicked on her sides. I could imagine her front had been in the line of fire, too, but with her arms in the condition they were…

Had her arms taken such a thrashing to protect herself, the baby?

"Johari, where is your doctor?" I needed to know answers, the status of her condition yes, but I needed to know she was okay.

I had to know.

She adjusted herself and another cringe had me tightening my hold on the damn bed.

"He did some tests, then stepped out. Said he'd be back soon," she said, and I helped by adjusting her pillow for her. She smiled at me. "Thank you."

"Of course." While sitting next to her, getting a real read on all she'd injured was hard. She had a sheet covering everything but her arms, and seeing as how the condition of those had been less than favorable…

Then there was how she lay, curled up on her side with her back not even touching the bed.

*Had that bastard gotten her back, too?*

A crack slicked the air when I braced my hand over my fist and unable to remain restless, helpless, I stood, heading out the way I came.

"Where are you going?"

"To find your doctor," I said, pausing just long enough to face her. "There's no excuse why you should be in here alone without any answers in regards to the status of your condition."

"Yes, but Alexander—"

"And after that, I'm going to speak with whoever runs this place. My family has been a benefactor of this hospital for decades and how they run things here is unacceptable. Their staff is basically sitting ducks for trash to come in here and do this. There's no reason why this should have happened to you."

"But what happened was my fault." She tried to get up, using those shaking, bruised arms, but just as quickly her strength sent her back down for the count.

"Johari!"

I wasn't back to her fast enough, holding her up a little as she tried to find a proper position to sit.

"Please don't get the director of the hospital," she said, wincing as she braced the bed. Giving up, she lay back where she'd been. She grabbed my hand on the way down, squeezing while she gathered herself from, I assumed, the pain the movement caused. She looked up at me. "And the doctor said he'd be back. I work with Dr. McCarthy all the time. He's a good doctor and what happened isn't the hospital's fault, Alexander. The accident, the oversight, was on me. Those occurrences unfortunately sometimes happen when working the hospital floor. And definitely comes with the territory of working in the ER."

"You have the right to a safe working environment regardless of that. You work in a hospital, sweetheart. Not some damn war zone."

Laughter touched the air from beside me and she leaned over, touching her cheek to her pillow.

"Sweetheart?" she questioned, eyeing me and I smiled.

"Is that okay?" I wouldn't say that if it bothered her, call her that.

She nodded and I couldn't help noticing my hand still firmly placed in hers. I didn't even think she realized how hard she held it, how long. Turning, she used it to lie on her side and I assisted her, bringing her a sheet from behind to go over her waist.

"I'm glad you're here," she said, and finally, she, too, noticed our hands. The hold softened then, but remained ever steadfast. She looked up at me. "And I'm so sorry again. I'll never forgive myself if—"

"Let's worry about you, okay? Just you. Let's... let's worry about you."

Her head lowered, as I retook the chair I sat in before.

I watched here there, lying on that pillow so bruised and broken. Her hair had fallen from her bun, long and fine against one of her shoulders. Dark skin peeked from underneath the strands, her shoulder escaping the material of her gown.

I covered it, the blanket smoothing over the perfect mahogany color.

"I'd never forgive myself," I told her, finding her eyes. "If you got hurt."

Because even though she'd been here at the hospital, I couldn't help feeling some responsibility. It didn't matter how unreasonable. I felt a sense of protection for her now. She was mine to protect, she and our... our baby. That was, if the conception took of course.

Our hands remained together, my other still in attempts to wrap her up.

She let me, watching my eyes while I messed with her blankets. A warmth lingered in her gaze, and all too soon, I felt the tone in the room change. My anger, so heightened before seemed to decimate, and I had a feeling, that had something to do with those deep, dark eyes. They were so close, so warm on me.

"Johari Russ— Alexander?"

My gaze with Johari broke at the sound of our names and the caller couldn't have confused me more.

I started to get up by Naomi's presence, but a reminder in my hand caused me to sit back down. I didn't let go of Johari, but I did watch as my ex entered the room.

She pushed blonde curls out of her face, clearly surprised by my own presence here. She looked to say something, but then stopped. She stopped when she took inventory of the room, Johari and me of course.

Our hands.

It'd been a voice beside me that chimed in first.

"Can I help you, Doctor?" Johari asked and I had to say, she looked more stunned than the both of us, bewildered.

Blinking away from me, Naomi faced her, raising a clipboard.

"I have your chart," she said, but then stopped herself, dropping the paperwork to her side. Her curls flew in my direction when she turned her head. "But I don't understand. Alexander, what are you doing here? *In* here and..."

Her blue eyes didn't let up on Johari's bed, her head shaking over what I knew to be a clear handhold before her.

"You know each other?" Johari asked.

I had no idea who or what question to answer first. Like I said, this was a surprise.

I ended up with Johari, my own questions on my lips. "Naomi's your doctor—"

"No," she said, then her eyes scanned over to Naomi. "At least she wasn't. Where's Dr. McCarthy?"

"He called me." Naomi came into the room, Johari's chart still in hand. "He called me after finding out the situation. Alexander, what are you doing in here? Are you two together? I mean..."

She raised the chart now, her lips parting a little. "Is this baby she's having yours?"

*Baby...*

She said baby as in present, as in now.

As in no longer just a possibility.

I think Johari realized the same information as I had. In fact, I would wager at the exact moment in time. I'd bet money on it, a sure thing.

Dark eyes found mine and the shock between us was surely apparent across both our faces. I could only see hers, but mine had to be the same, my heart racing like I'd ran a marathon. Like I ran forever with her.

Johari's lips parted. "She said baby."

"Yeah," I said, awed.

*Is this real?*

Shaking my head, I faced Naomi.

"You said baby, right?" I asked, needing to confirm. I had to.

Naomi blinked in response, but then lifted her chart again. "Um, yeah. By my count, about three weeks?"

"Two."

We'd both said it at the same time, and then fell into laughter.

"Uh huh. Give or take a couple of hours." I said the words to Naomi, but I stared at Johari. Jo. "Did you hear that, Jo? What she said? Did you hear it? I'm not… I'm not imaging it?"

Her smile started slow and she found our hands, squeezing the handhold we still had together. "If you are, then so am I."

I could only compare the feeling to one other moment in my adult life, but even then, my clear diagnosis didn't compare, which blew my mind. Is this what people talked about? When they said your child rose above everything else? I didn't even have one yet and I was feeling this way. Just the possibility changed any and everything.

I wished I could say I remembered everything that happened next. And though I didn't remember *how* it happened, I definitely recalled the final result, the feeling.

Johari in my arms felt like home, my hand in her hair, and her soft cheek against my scraggly beard. I think I tickled her, because she laughed.

I pulled away a little.

"Sorry," I said, but I didn't let go. I just stared at her.

She touched me, too, covering my hand.

Her cheek was pressed into it.

"And two weeks, you hear that?" she said. Her breathing had picked up, a quick rise from her chest. "Our baby is so big they think it's three weeks."

"Yeah," I said, laughing a little. I could count how many times I had cried in my entire adult life on one hand. One of the most memorable had been after I'd been told about my cancer, and even then, it had been months after the diagnosis. I had held it in, steeling myself to the reality, and I allowed absolutely no one to see. Tears were vulnerability.

*Weakness...* my dad would always say, but today if those tears happened I didn't think I would care.

Least of all who saw.

A surprising sheen in Johari's eyes took me back and I think she noticed because she looked away, trying to stare at anything but me.

I brushed her cheek with my thumb, bringing her back. "We did it."

Smiling, she covered my hand. "I'm glad I could for you."

Staring at her, I couldn't help hoping, wishing the baby would take more traits of hers than my own. What I couldn't give for him or her to have her eyes, the light in them.

I guess we had to wait and see, didn't we?

A throat clearing had us pulling apart a little, Naomi. I supposed I had forgotten we weren't alone.

Her swallowing told of her discomfort and her eyes told of something more. She looked away. "So, um, I guess a congratulations is in order then."

At that moment, I allowed Johari's hand to leave mine as I stood up. I felt Naomi deserved an explanation. Both ladies did. Johari especially as she'd been caught in the middle, and Naomi…

She needed to know something because we had a history—a long one. We dated for such a long time even the tabloids believed we'd been headed down the aisle. Hell, and not just them. Naomi herself, her family, and mine all had a similar belief about a possible matrimony. It had been me who'd been the outlier and only for reasons my brother had already presented right in front of me.

Asa had been right when he mentioned what he had about me, Johari, and this whole surrogacy situation in my office. Once upon a time, the concept of children had been so far out of the ballpark for me. The thoughts were in a different stratosphere completely, so in regards to today, Naomi had to be confused about what she was seeing before her now.

I would if I was her knowing our history.

I opened my hands. "Naomi…"

But she stopped me, raising hers. "I supposed the other day made sense then, didn't it? God…" She shook her head, gripping the chart a little. "Of course it did because the drink didn't make sense. You're with someone else."

"Alexander?"

Poor Johari. Lying there, bruised and banged up, she had nothing but questions in her eyes. Inadvertently, she'd been thrust into a multitude of situations that weren't required of her. Both of these women had, in a way.

Releasing a breath, I faced Johari first. "Johari, I want you to meet, Naomi Radcliff."

She laughed a little. "Oh, I know Dr. Radcliff, Alexander. Well, I don't *know* her. But know of her. We work together."

"And she's your girlfriend. Your fiancée?" Naomi threw out there, a hand raised in Johari's direction. "Your wife, it doesn't really matter. I just wish you would have said something, Alexander. I'm an adult woman. I'm not going to—"

"Johari is my surrogate, Naomi," I said, but not because I wanted to explain myself or talk my way out of a situation. Johari being my surrogate was a fact and I wanted her to know. I wasn't ashamed of it.

Her jaw dropped like I knew it would. I mean, I could imagine that was the last thing she believed would fall from my lips. Especially since me *not* wanting to have children in the past was definitely understood between us. In fact, chillingly so.

"Your surrogate," she spattered. Like really spattered, her hand coming over her mouth. "You arranged for this woman to have your baby?"

"Yes, Naomi. And, Johari, Naomi, who's apparently your treating doctor now, is my ex-girlfriend."

Her lips parted, a slow, "Oh," falling from her lips. She turned, moving around in her bed. "Let me just give you both some space…"

The rapid movements of course had her cringing, her injuries ever present between all of us.

I sighed. "Sweetheart, you don't have to do anything. Just stay put, okay? You didn't do anything wrong."

My acknowledgement of Johari, the term, right away I could tell had someone else cringing in the room.

And it wasn't Johari.

Naomi took a step back, the floor taking her attention, and I pushed air through my lips again. I believed she'd been the last person I called that. Though, obviously it meant something else.

I was screwing this up, royally, and needed to get myself together. There was a lot that presented itself in this room today, so many feelings considering the situation, and because of that emotions were high. They were delicate and I needed to tread lightly.

How had things taken such a bad turn so quickly? We'd been on such a high before, Johari and I.

"Naomi, can we talk in the hall?"

She nodded, dropping her clipboard to her hip, as well as the situation when she escaped the room with active steps.

"I'm so sorry."

Would this woman stop apologizing? But that just seemed to be in her nature I supposed.

I put my hand on Jo's pillow, hunkering down to the level she lay on the bed.

"One more apology and you're going to make me lose my mind," I said to her. "All of this happened well before you, and none of it you should concern yourself with. Besides, I think we both have other things on our minds these days. Other worries."

My glance to her stomach had her own gaze heading that way, a smile spreading across her full lips.

She nodded, and then let me arrange her covers again. After telling her I'd be back, I went into the hall, closing the door. Naomi stood there of course and arms crossed, she was just as out of sorts as when she left.

She raised and dropped her arms. "What is going on, Alexander? A surrogate? This is madness. Insanity."

And yet more people questioning my mental state. I could imagine I would get this a lot as more people found out, but unlike Naomi, I hoped to do this on my own terms.

Asa had only been silenced recently because I stopped answering his phone calls. They'd flooded in after I told him I was moving forward with Johari and not surprisingly, he'd been resistant. The choice wasn't his, though.

It was mine.

I came over to Naomi, pushing my hands into my pockets. "The notion isn't as wild as you think."

"No." She started to say something else, but then resisted,

biting her lip.

She lifted a finger toward me. "Children weren't on the table *at all* for us. That's why we broke up. What it all boiled down to, right?"

She was right, but she put it so simply, hadn't she? I was a man of many faults and that's something I had no shame in admitting. But Naomi Radcliff wasn't without her own. It had been the actions of the pair of us that broke us up. It didn't matter that I had been the one who called it.

I blew out a breath. "Things changed. I've changed, my thoughts on the subject."

"You're changed?" She nodded with the words, shaking her head a little. "And with all your changes now you want children?"

"I do. And I'm not going to ask you or expect you to understand. Asa already let me hear it."

"And your mom?"

"She doesn't know. I'm not sharing anything with anyone else until Johari is at least past her first trimester."

Something I had already decided. Many couples chose that route anyway to share news when it came to the arrival of a new life, so this wasn't uncommon and with the already emotionally charged process, this decision seemed best.

"I only told Asa because I needed the legal stuff taken care of," I told Naomi, then silenced for a second when a few hospital staff came down the hall.

Naomi crossed her arms. "So this is legitimate? You didn't just knock this girl up and you're feeding me this to get me out of your hair?"

Though I didn't like how she said that, I got her frustrations. She really did want to have children, but in the end, I didn't.

"This is an arrangement between two people," I explained. "A legitimate one."

"And what about me?" she asked, shaking her head. "What about us and why we broke up?"

I had no words for her, so I gave her nothing but silence.

She faced away and I again got that. I just knew at the time, when we were together, I had no desire to have children. And now that I had… they wouldn't… well, they wouldn't be with her.

I drew a hand down my beard. "I'm sorry, but my thoughts are singularly on the child."

"And that woman," she said. "Johari?"

"Yes. My thoughts are on her and baby. Especially after today. Can you tell me anything good? You know with the accident I—"

"She's fine," she said, and though, it didn't look like she wanted to, she lifted her clipboard, turning a sheet. "And everything looks good with the baby, too. Her assailant managed to miss the fetus. There's no issues on that front. Mom and baby will be fine, no major injuries."

*Mom and baby will be fine.*

Rubbing my hand down my face, I wanted to tell Johari directly, but resisted, giving Naomi back the floor.

"I'd like to do a full work-up on Johari just to be sure. But yes, for now. She's fine."

She managed to calm so many emotions for me in that moment she couldn't possible understand. The baby was fine and Johari was fine, too.

"Thank you. You don't even understand."

She nodded, dropping the clipboard at her hip. "You're really serious about this? Having a baby?"

"Yes, very. And I do need your confidentially here. I really don't want anyone knowing until she's farther along."

Her arms moved over her chest. "I couldn't tell anyone if I wanted to. Doctor-patient confidentially."

"Yes, but do I have yours?" I understood what she meant, but I wanted her to tell me that *she* herself wouldn't say anything regardless of her position in all this.

That thickness moved down her throat again, and she swallowed hard. This had to be difficult for her.

I made this difficult for her.

"I will not say anything," she said, and then followed up with, "you have my word."

# Ten

**Johari** When Alexander said he'd like to make a short stop before dropping me off at home from the hospital I never, even in my wildest, would place us at the Wrightwood. The posh hotel I stifled all thoughts about due to the hefty price tag, but here we ended up, curbside.

"They have the best ice cream in town," Alexander said, grinning as he turned off the Jaguar.

His Jaguar, yes his Jaguar, and I sat in it, tender flesh and all on the heated leather seats.

I unbuckled daintily—mostly because I hurt. But, putting my own posh on sure was tempting in such a nice ride.

"Ice cream?" I asked, and sure enough my question was answered in the form of a waiter skipping down the many steps of the ritzy hotel. He had a platter on his hand, a single item balanced while he took steps two by two. He ended up directly on Alexander's side and Alexander pushed his window down with a single gloved finger.

"Yes," he said, pulling the clear container off the platter. He tipped the waiter with a folded bill to the man's pocket, and though, I couldn't see the amount, the inventor's face on the bill allowed me to see the gratuity was quite handsome indeed.

He handed the cup to me. "I know it isn't much, but ice cream never hurts in these situations. I devoured a carton or two whenever I injured myself as a kid."

He stopped here to get me ice cream.

He stopped here because I was hurt.

Schooling my features, I attempted to keep how sweet the gesture was from reflecting across my face. But I wasn't stone, and well, what he did was pretty sweet.

I accepted the gift graciously, tipping the container to him. "Thank you. You're right. It definitely doesn't hurt."

Perhaps the only thing that hadn't in my fragile state and he'd done that. He managed to. I'd been grateful just to get the rest of my shift off, so all this was a wonderful bonus.

He simply bowed his head in return, restarting his car, and my gaze couldn't help wandering to a tapered waist and sizable arms. He had his shirtsleeves rolled up to his forearms again and a singular vest minus the jacket fit snug around his muscular frame. He braced the steering wheel, the leather of his driving gloves stretching over the thickest fingers.

He panned over to me. "Ready to go home?"

Breaking my gaze, I nodded. The car went into gear underneath me, but he didn't take off yet. I assumed waiting for me. I hadn't buckled up yet.

Popping my ice cream spoon into my mouth, I held my cup in one hand while I tried to get my seatbelt back on with the other. The maneuver was more than awkward and in my movements, I managed to jostle already tender flesh. I hit one of the many bruises on my waist with my arm and the white-hot pain caused tears to sting my eyes.

I clamped down hard on my spoon.

"Hey. Wait a minute, Jo. I'll help."

The car clicked into park and I saw his hand. It stopped, though. It stopped, I assumed, at the sudden raise of my shirt hem.

I just wanted to check the damage, instinctual at the sudden spike of pain. My skin would show me nothing different of course as I'd seen all my injuries before. But Alexander hadn't. This was the first time.

His eyes narrowed at the purple skin, the bruise large enough to cover my entire right side.

I covered it quickly, but the damage was done. His entire body language changed, that almost jubilant expression completely gone.

"I will be speaking with the director," he said, and then reached over, taking my ice cream. The container procured new space in the cup holder next to my thigh, and then Alexander took my seatbelt, pulling it over my chest.

I sat back, letting him. He stayed close, his beard near my cheek, his hands all around me. He clicked the seatbelt, making sure the device fit snuggly but not too tight. He faced me then, again so close with his smell, him.

He started to draw back, but I touched his arm. His shoulders stiffened, his lips parting as he looked up at me.

I brought my hand down his arm. "And if I asked you not to again? Speak to the director?"

Because doing so wouldn't do anything. He was fighting a losing battle and would just make waves. He'd create unnecessary drama. Especially for me as I was on my way out.

His breath warm, the current brushed softly across my lips.

"Don't ask me not to," he said, the words coming from somewhere low, deep.

I swallowed. "I have to. I think you saying something will just get me into trouble. I don't want to make waves."

His lids fell over his eyes.

Pulling back, he found his own space again on the other side of the car.

"Very well," he said, putting the car into gear. He checked his surroundings and then we were off. As stated before, he sat so differently. On the way over to the hotel, Alexander had been very much at ease, but now he remained stiff, tense.

"I'm sorry," I said.

But that only made things worse.

He shook his head. "One more apology, Johari."

"I can't help it. I'm a public servant. All day it's my job to take care of people, to serve."

"But you don't serve me, Johari."

In a way, I did. But that's what I signed up for I supposed.

In all my silence, I got his brown eyes.

"And I know what we are to each other," he said, staring at me. "You being my surrogate and everything, but I don't want you to feel like you serve me. So please, no more saying sorry. You try that and I'll try not to be so…"

"Stiff?"

He laughed a little. "I was going to say overbearing. That's what I do all day, too."

We were both victims to our occupations, our lifestyles.

"But yes, I'll try that if you stay firm in your decisions and even your screw-ups as you can learn from them."

Look at him being my life couch all of a sudden.

I sat back, smiling. "Okay."

"Okay?"

I nodded. I could try it I supposed, the no apology thing if he could try to do the same with his control. I had a feeling abrasiveness really was a thing for him and his willingness to try to let go might be an indicator to his disagreement of that part of himself, his dislike of it.

"Good." He turned away, a subtle grin to his full lips. "We don't want people walking all over you. So you do that and I'll do mine. You have my word."

*Walking all over me…*

My thoughts surrounded what he said and I almost missed when he asked me a question.

"Can I show you something before I drop you off?" he asked, turning the wheel and rerouting us away from the busy downtown area. "I want your opinion on something. Won't take long."

My door cracked open to a back alley moments later and if not for who escorted me there, I might have been a little put off. Something told me when it came to brutal murders of pregnant women, Alexander Ricci wouldn't be the one getting his hands dirty. He had too much money and would hire out for such a thing.

I eyed him, deciding to jab him a little despite the fact. "You haven't brought me here to rough me up, then hide the body, right? Because I have to say, there are better places than the neighborhood where I grew up to do it. I know a few people here that might not let you get away with it."

I'd been surprised to find myself only blocks away from my apartment complex and only houses away from my mama and brother's house. We were in a local commercial area, restaurants and hair stores just on the other side of the alley.

Alexander grinned, holding my door. He'd come around to retrieve me.

"I like to think you'd find me more intelligent than that," he said, resting a bicep on his open car door. He leaned in. "And I'd hire someone, Jo. I wouldn't do it myself."

How did I know this man so well already? I laughed inside at the thought.

Licking my spoon, I placed my empty ice cream cup in his drink holder, finishing the vanilla bean ice cream off well before we got here. He was right. It was the best I had ever had and I had a lot in this city. I unstrapped, but like getting in, didn't do the task without Alexander's assistance.

He reached down, aiding me, and I only resisted arguing, poking him about his control, because of his hands. They felt too good, too warm when they touched me.

*Don't get too close.*

*Don't get hurt.*

But all the internal arguments in the world couldn't change the way my body naturally reacted to him. But this was natural, though. I was holding his child now and *naturally* felt connected to him. This was normal.

*Right?*

"Can you manage?" he asked me, falling back a little. "To get out, I mean? If not, that's okay. I can point everything out from where you sit."

Seeing as where we were, my curiosity wouldn't allow me to sit back. I needed to see his reasons for taking me here, the location so unusual. I had no idea he even knew about this neighborhood let alone knew exactly where to go. But driving here, he knew these streets. He knew them well.

I braced his Jag's chair. "I'm too curious. I gotta know what this is about."

His deep chuckling drew pinpricks down my arm, as well as his hands when he went to aid me. I attempted to keep any tell of pain off my face when I moved because I knew exactly how he'd react to it. I had seen it. I could imagine he felt guilty about what happened to me. But even though he had partial responsibility for my pregnant state he had nothing to do with my physical pain. That was on me.

*No more apologies.*

I promised him that.

I rose on my cross trainers, allowing him to take my arm.

"Are we moving too quickly? You cringed."

*Damn. I hadn't been as careful as I believed.*

I slid my arm from his hands, putting my big girl panties on. "We're good. So what is this you want my opinion on?"

He didn't look too sure, but he did step back, allowing me space. "I feel like I've pumped a lot of hype. Like I've given myself some pressure here and you'll be underwhelmed."

I started to walk. "Oh, you have. But I've been here before, so it's nothing I haven't seen. I just want to know your reasons for bringing me here."

And I did. Deep in the heart of my neighborhood, the back alley behind the local shops was nothing but dumpsters and the occasional dealings, neither of which would mean anything to a wealthy man who lived far from this area.

*And there you go judging him again.*

I was trying not to do that. I got him for doing that, so it wouldn't be fair for me to do the same.

He just had me wondering so much still, who he was…

He followed me, crisped trousers extending with the length of his legs. He got ahead, and then turned, walking backwards in his shiny leather shoes. "I guess I just wanted to know what you thought about the place? The feel of it."

My feet slowed, arms covering myself. "What do you mean? The alley?"

Now, I felt I missed something.

He chuckled. "Not the alley per se, but…"

He panned the area, then reached over.

Taking my hand, he led me toward a wall, my heart in my throat.

Focusing, I noticed the wall belonged to *Pop's*, a black owned business that served the best flapjacks this side of the city. I could smell those flapjacks. In fact, the soft notes of butter and fluffy cake radiated through my senses.

I moved my tongue over my lips almost tasting it, then laughed at myself. "I'd like to say this was the baby, but…"

"What?"

Alexander came over, nearly alarmed and I felt kind of bad— at his alarm. He no doubt assumed the worst, seeing as how I lead in about the baby.

Cringing, I pointed toward the building. "*Pop's* is on the other side of this wall, a diner. I want the flapjacks and the smell has me seriously *on* right now. I doubt it's the baby, though. It's too soon."

His gaze went warm, his hands sliding into his pockets. "Wouldn't that be something?"

Yeah, it would.

Breaking away from this silliness, my foolishness, I gestured to the area. "So what did you want to show me?"

My words had him recalling something, dark lashes blinking away from the moment, too. He took a step back, staring up at the brown brick wall of *Pop's*.

"This," he said, framing it when he lifted his hands. "This piece. The feel of it. The feel of the whole area."

I took a step back as well and it made sense why I didn't understand what he was getting at before. Graffiti art was so common to me that my gaze passed over the work without a second glance most of the time. But this man, Alexander, the imaging had him awed.

He moved his arms over his chest. "I jog back here from time to time."

"You do?"

His cheek dimpled with his smile. "You sound surprised."

"Well, yeah. I am. There are so many other places you could

jog. Gyms. Country clubs?"

My words had him turning. "You really have made up your mind about me, haven't you? Summed me up?"

Because he was right, I fell silent. I really tried not to force him into this conversation, but that couldn't be helped. Alexander was such an anomaly sometimes, a complete contradiction of the tabloids that had been my only peek into the wonders of his opulent life. But when things like this occurred, him bringing me here, as well as his desire to have a child...

Then there was me. The fact that he picked me at all. I was kinda plain, and well, very *normal*. I was not like him or the company I was sure he kept.

He didn't let me answer, only stared up at the wall with a small smile. "Well, you're right. I would never have known about this place if not for a business deal. I had an opportunity to tear the place down not that long ago. Put up a strip mall."

God, the people around here would be pissed.

"You're not still going to, are you?" I asked kind of nervous. "So many people live here and so many local businesses are in the area."

He passed a look over his shoulder. "Oh no, I couldn't. I argued against it." He looked away from it. "We ended up putting the development in another part of the city. But even after the deal, I still came back here."

"Why?"

"I guess the reason I fought for it. I love the work. The art."

His gaze circulated the area, so many pieces around us both. The brick walls were a mashup of colors and thoughts which were given life by the taggers who placed them there.

He pushed his hands into his pockets. "It all just tells a story. I see it all over the city, but this location is where I felt it. I really like it and I would love to do something similar for the baby's room."

The very thought had my eyes widening, so surprised. "You want to tag the baby's room?"

He chuckled, pushing a firm hand behind his neck. "Not tag, per se. But I want the same feel. I want the story. I'd love to find some of the artists who contributed. They could teach my contractors a thing or two."

"You know I'm from here. I could ask around. People around here don't mind helping each other. Especially if they found out you kept this place from being a strip mall. And if they were paid too I guess that would..."

"Oh, money wouldn't be an issue. And you're serious? You could put out some feelers? I'd really love their input. The baby's room is coming along but the artists could be very helpful still to the process."

"You've already started?" My heart warmed at the thought. I mean, we just found out today the pregnancy stuck and here he was already nesting.

His face spilled in color a little, his cheeks turning a bright shade of red. "I know it's a little soon but..."

He came over to me, heightening my senses and overwhelming my heat. He placed his gaze on my stomach, then me when he found my eyes.

"I wanted to be ready," he said. "And I want you to see it sometime. That is, if that's in the cards. I know the technical logistics of our arrangement. You have the baby and then that's it for our contract. But things like this were kind of open. I don't know how emotionally invested you wanted to get, how involved with things like this, but I'm open to them. I'll take your input wherever you'd like to give it."

His words had me lost for many reasons. Mostly because they felt attached to other things and those other things did nothing to disconnect me, sever me from this man who already had me latched so strongly to him. I held his child and because of that, I had a natural connection. I had a tether and even though this was all new, all foreign...

I broke the eye contact with his stunning eyes immediately.

"I'd like that," I simply said, then turned in the direction of the car.

"Jo, this way," hummed deep from my side, and Alexander pulled me back, taking me in indeed the direction of his vehicle. I had gotten backwards somehow, confused.

I'd like to say he thought about it. I'd like to say *I* thought about it, but when he brought me to him, his hard chest to my breast no resistance came from my direction.

His lips came to crash on mine and he unleashed a fervor of any and everything that shouldn't happen. This *shouldn't be* happening, but it was. It was and I let him, his fingers traveling up my arm, then across my shoulder blade.

His mouth opened and he had my cheek, guiding me in the most delicate ways to his lips. Arms held me carefully, hands touching me intimately. He pressed into me and his hard length against my stomach trickled heat through my veins.

He touched the wall, that very art he found so inspiring behind us and used it to pin me, hitching me up with a hand to my bottom.

Why couldn't I stop kissing him? Touching him?

His beard, I pushed my fingers through, his hair so perfect and rough beneath my fingertips. I shouldn't want this. I shouldn't want him.

*We're complicating things.*

I braced his cheeks, aching inside and his hands went to my hips. He was so gentle, cautious with every kiss and every touch. I had no idea if that was because he knew I was injured, pregnant with *his* child, or how much that was just him, and that last thought was what scared me most.

It terrified me.

It almost hurt to kiss this man, hurt because it felt so good, so deep, and I wasn't ready for the gamut of emotions that came with it. Damn, my hormones, pregnancy or otherwise. Damn them to hell.

Using my bruised arms, I attempted to get closer to him, almost claim him in a way, but weakness sent me back, and that's what sent him back. But he didn't stop. He simply tapered me off, smiling before bracing my cheeks again.

He got me in a soft kiss, tender bursts of pressure across the surface of my lips. He guided my gaze toward him when he lifted my head, vision darkening when he studied my face. His lips went to return when some commotion came from my right, chatter. A group of people cut through the alley from the side of *Pop's* and he stepped back, but not before the people saw us. I knew they did, because their talking stopped flat. It stopped and…

A slow dread filled me at familiar faces, shocked expressions I never anticipated seeing, but I should have anticipated this. I should have because what I did, what Alexander and I were just doing was so wrong.

Mama stared at me, a hand in hers. It was my brother's, but she had him turned. Almost like she was protecting him and beside her was Ms. Sherry, her shoulders falling a little.

"Ma—?"

But she pulled Javan away, tucking him under her arm and away. It was Ms. Sherry who stayed, albeit only briefly. A sympathetic look on her face, she followed Mama and Javan. They took this way often. They always cut through the alley to get to Pop's always.

*What was I thinking?*

I moved my hand to cover my mouth, knowing it was pointless, foolish even to try to go after them and explain myself. My mama had made up her mind and came to her own conclusions of what I'd been doing in a back alleyway.

Kissing a man who looked well out of my league, my scrubs dirty from work, my hair messy and fallen. That very man's hand came down on my arm, his fingers touching me tenderly, gently like before.

"Johari, what's wrong? You know those people?"

Bracing my mouth, I choked down tears he couldn't possibly understand. No one did unless they knew. Unless they knew her and how she was. I once told Alexander he was judgmental. But my mama made him look so apathetic in comparison.

"She'll never let me forget this," I nearly cried. I cried for myself. I couldn't help it. I was so careful to do things a certain way when it came to my mama, live my life a certain way, and not do anything that would put me negatively on her radar. She always had something to say, about everything I did no matter how small. It was because of that I refused to give her fuel. But this would do exactly that. She saw her daughter tonight, her daughter messy from work and kissing a man in a grungy alley like a streetwalker. Like whore.

It only made things worse that Alexander was white.

Biting my lip, I pushed away from him and my chest hurt. "Johari. Jo!"

His steps brought him to me quickly. He reached for me, but I pushed my way out of his hands.

He blanched, looking so hurt and my stomach tightened.

I raised my hands, trying not to shake and even more not to cry. "I need to go home."

"Well, let me take you—"

"No. Don't take me. Don't touch me."

"Don't touch you?" He stepped back now and that hurt really did drill a hole through me.

"I'm sorry," he said. Stepping back, he pushed his hands into his pockets. "I'm sorry if you didn't want me to kiss you. I…"

I started to walk away again. I couldn't bear it, that expression on his face, and though he caught up to me again, he didn't reach for me. Not this time.

He had a phone in his hand, lifting it. "I'll call my driver. He'll take you wherever you want to go if you don't want me to take you. But I'm sorry, you're not going anywhere by yourself. Not like this with it getting dark. Just let me call him, and then I'll wait with you until he gets here. I won't touch you. I promise."

The way he said it… Like he did something wrong before…

I nodded, turning away, and then heard his voice in the distance. I would let him call, and then let him wait.

But that's all I could do.

# Eleven

**Alexander** I stared at the photo in my hands, paper-thin, but the image more than clear. A baby lay. Though at this stage of development, the child took on more of an oval shape cocooned in a mother's womb. Despite being so tiny, I could definitely make the tiny image out in the photograph I had.

I sat back, awed in my office chair. My fingers brushed across the surface of the photo and I tried to feel the underlining layer, capture it all if possible. It was the closest I could get.

"Did you get the sonogram, Mr. Ricci?"

My assistant's voice traveled through the air via my interoffice intercom.

I pressed the button to give her my voice.

"I did and thank you," I said. "Thank her."

*Her.*

She who had phased me out, the woman who was doing this all with me, but no longer beside me.

"Of course, Mr. Ricci. I'll tell Johari you got the package."

Penny meant no harm, but her simplifying the delivery of the image of my only child did unnerve me if not a little. The photo had come in a box, wrapped in brown paper and pristine. Care had gone into the delivery, but the cargo inside was more than a simple parcel delivery.

I drew my hand down my beard, stroking it when I placed the image on the center of my granite desk. It lay there, tiny in a sea of black and luster, and I attempted to ignore the feelings that went with that. I felt I started to get good at that, disengaging myself from any attachment that went outside of the child in this photo.

I had to after so many weeks.

*Were we at just under two months? Already?*

I wouldn't know if not for the calendar, the time that had past. I had no word, no reports but that of the physical exams. Johari sent the results, never a day late outside of the contractual agreement she signed when this whole thing began, and though I knew she signed such a thing, I never imaged that's how all this would be. It was professional yes, but so disjointed.

I thought I would get to *see* her during these visits to the doctor, wait outside if anything. And on top of that, the photos wouldn't be my only indicator to see how my baby was doing. I would get to see the mom, see her grow along with the child.

I had no idea if Johari was showing. I had no clue how she was feeling or what being pregnant was doing to her, for her. I knew she was healthy of course. I knew the baby was healthy.

I got the reports.

*Why had I kissed her?*

A thought that plagued me since that day, since I realized our contact would turn into this. She'd established that very clearly. Any calls could only be about things related to the baby and nothing to do with us, her, or what happened that day.

And what *had* happened? I felt I would never know. I just knew she knew those people who came into the alley, and because she had, what we'd done wasn't okay. I gathered that much and didn't need my Ivy League education to tell me that. But even with the fallout, I couldn't find myself regretting what I'd done. I wanted to kiss Johari. I needed to.

I just wish she'd felt the same.

Tapering my thoughts, my emotions once again, I attempted to go on with the monotonous work of the day. I was fully back into work now, fully back into the life I lived before I'd taken ill minus the social. I had too much on my mind to be around people and still had to come up with a way to tell the rest of my family, my mom.

I sighed, knowing D-day was definitely coming. I owed my family that, my mom that, to be truthful. I didn't tell her I was sick at first and if I kept something like this from her, something so important, so big, I might not get her forgiveness so easily this time.

An afternoon meeting at least took me off my stresses for the present, but a call to the office brewed them once more.

"Ms. Radcliff has called for you, Mr. Ricci," Penny chimed into my office at just after two o' clock and I waved the call off. Penny knew how to handle it. Naomi had called my assistant more than once in these past few weeks.

She had to as I'd been ignoring her calls to my cell.

I would like to chalk that up to the anti-social thing, but I didn't need any complications now. She knew about Johari, our situation, and me not interested in anything outside of that right now, but even still, my ex may believe something was possible between us. I had promised her a drink and right now, I couldn't take the risk of any misunderstood feelings.

I had enough of that on my part these days.

My next meeting, I managed to get out of as I decided to leave early for the day. I usually did that on sonogram days, taking the time to relax and just think. The baby's room had been done for a bit now structurally and I'd been putting the finishing touches on it with photos.

*I wish I had been able to get her input.*

The room was missing something and that wasn't just the graffiti mural I wanted to put in. It missed a feminine touch and I wanted… well, I wanted hers.

My phone buzzed just as Esteban pulled up outside of my office building. I waited at the corner for him like most days.

I didn't have the mental energy to even drive.

I greeted my old friend, and then slid into the back seat of the Bentley. That's when I had been able to get the phone and I only felt like a heel by what I read. The text was from Asa.

And he was more than pissed.

*"You going to actually make it to dinner tonight with Mom?"*

he buzzed in, and then, *"If not, I suppose the two of us will both have a reason for our perception changing of the other."*

My own words coming back to bite me, he was right. I had been inadvertently cold toward my mom and him, too.

After texting him I'd be there, I explained the change in route to Esteban. The Bentley went out of the heart of the city then and well away from downtown. The concrete jungle of Lincoln Park took over the landscape, the Chicago skyline in the distance.

My mom's property took over a five-acre lot, my childhood home nestled between that of the rich and even richer. I used to find how boxed in my family's estate was with its gated restrictions normal. That was until I went out of the city, lived in the freedom of the open air and breathed natural life around me. My family's cabin resided well out of the thicket of city progress, and though, I had been sick as a dog there, I had to admit I had never felt so free.

Esteban was buzzed in through the driveway gates and he drove me up to the side entrance of the house, parking outside wide wooden doors.

He got my door for me, passing on his good wishes to my mom and I smiled at him. He worked for me even before I knew who he was; as a small child going to and from the park with my mom or whatever other errands she had to do with twin newborns in tow, I'd never paid much attention.

I hadn't decided yet how all this, a life like mine, would affect my own child yet. My mom was active in my life, present in it, but there'd been more than a few times I saw nannies more than anyone else.

I saw my busy father even less.

Esteban passed me the bouquet of flowers we'd picked up along the way from a local street vendor on our way out of the city. I guess I felt I needed a peace offering after being away so long, but upon traveling through my mom's pristine floral gardens on the east side of the home, what I brought seemed pretty minuscule in comparison.

I let the bouquet fall to my hip and a columned stairwell led me inside.

The door was open for me as if I'd been expected. The

gatekeeper who let Esteban and me into the property I was sure was responsible for that.

Getting inside, I greeted Maybelle, one of my mom's housekeepers, then found my way into the entryway of the grand estate.

Hardwood floors and expansive white walls surrounded me at every turn. So much space for just three people growing up, but my dad always desired the best, opulence. In all of his exuberance, I wished he would have thought about the rest of us. Mom in particular. With Asa and me out of the house now, this place resembled more of an enchanted mansion than a home, my mom all by herself.

Maybelle let me know one of my family members was in the kitchen so I headed there, waving at my mom's butler, Gerald, on my way. He mixed drinks in the butler's bar located under the stairwell, which led to the second floor.

He offered me a drink as he always did, but I passed, the Tuscan-style kitchen only just to my right. This place was well older than I was, but with its fine refurbishing one would think I outdated it. The kitchen had a full breakfast bar and everything, and sitting singularly at the kitchen's rustic island was my brother.

Still in his suit from the day, he sat atop a bar stool, full rotisserie chicken on a plate in front of him.

Pulling off a leg, he devoured the thing like an animal and I laughed, announcing my presence.

He sat up, passing a glance at me over his shoulder, but just as quickly I lost his attention. He went back to his abundant meal in front of himself and I shook my head.

*I guess I deserved that, being away as I was.*

And I had been away, so very much so.

I brought myself into the kitchen, the flowers, but there was clearly no Mom.

I tossed them on the table, gripping the chair across from my twin. "Hey."

He lifted and dropped his head once in acknowledgement. Taking another bite of chicken, he simply went on with his food as if I wasn't here.

Something felt weird about that.

I tipped my chin at his plate. "I thought we were eating dinner with Mom."

A mere shrug met me, then another bite from him. The whole thing really did seem rather odd. I saw chicken, but nothing else. My mom had many cooks, but not one of them worked over a stove. I figured for a second maybe the two of them ate without me, but there was no smell. In fact, no aftermath at all.

I eyed my brother. "Where's Mom?"

And finally, I got his attention, his blond eyebrows rising to the air. He used his drumstick, pointing behind himself.

"For what it's worth, it wasn't me who said anything," he announced taking another bite of chicken. He swallowed it. "It was just my job to get you here."

A red flag went off like an alarm bell, the reality of it buzzing from ear-to-ear and I left Asa, nearly pushing the chair I handled away from underneath my hands.

"She's in the library, Alex," came from behind me and I picked up my feet, my heels squeaking on the polished for. What had he meant by what he said?

What did my mom know?

She was in the library like my brother said and I recalled finding her here so many times when growing up. My mom had the capability to run many businesses and she had once upon a time. But that had been before she met my father, though, the two actually coming together over a business arrangement. He swept her away after that, away from her home and everything she knew. If she hadn't told me, if I hadn't seen her in here so many times schooling my own tutors, I never would have known all sides of my mom. She was that of an extremely intelligent and educated woman.

So how had she become a trophy wife?

She sat on a chaise lounge, staring out the window and into the day. We had lots of scenery out there; my mom's gardens seemed to go on for miles before the gates started.

I held onto the door. "Hey, Mom."

She turned and I only remembered the last time I saw her, the expression she gave when she left me, so happy, all of us happy.

But that seemed long gone now.

Her aged eyes had none of that light from before and her tight lips soured. She didn't anger easily, my mom usually laidback.

She waved at me, gesturing to come in, and I felt as if I was walking some sort of plank, finality to something important, something big.

*D-day.*

Papers rested on an old, oak table and I stood in front of them, the stack high.

I pushed a hand in my pocket. "It seems Asa started without us in the kitchen."

"Do you take me for a fool, Alexander?"

The vacuum sucked away, a depth inside my chest.

I rose up, facing her full on. "Of course not, Mom."

"So what is this? This foolishness?" Her hand gestured toward the papers, but she didn't pick them up. Her fingers went to her lips. "I'm apparently going to be a grandmother and didn't know."

A steady current passed through my lips and I dampened them. "Who told you?"

"What does it matter? It's true, correct?"

"Yes. Yes, it is."

She faced away, as if she couldn't keep the contact. Like she couldn't bear it.

"And am I to find out on my own?" she questioned, her accent so strong. She never lost the crisp tones of her French roots even many years after becoming an American citizen.

"I wanted to wait until the pregnancy was further along," I started, explaining. "Until the surrogate had reached her first trimester. We're barely at eight weeks."

*Surrogate…*

Is that all she was now?

Trying not to accept the reality of that, the finality of it, I studied my mother, but like before, none of this seemed to be boding well with her. She was shut off. She cut me off.

Her head shook above her fingers. "And she's black? African American?"

The statement sent a heat firing through veins and cruel words pulling at my lips.

I eyed her, my respect for my mom the only thing keeping me from saying them. But she wouldn't be exempt from what she said, though. I may not be able to speak the harshness of what I truly wanted to say, but that sure as hell wouldn't keep me from calling her on the carpet.

"Is that right, Mom? I have to say," I paused, laughing only too cynically. "I didn't take you for a racist."

"Racist," she said, rolling the word sharply across her tongue. She sounded, of all things, disgusted by the very notion. But didn't she realize how she sounded? What her statement of before implied?

Sitting up, she finally faced me, her arms crossing. "I live in the real world, Alexander. And I thought you had too. How will you look carrying around a black child?"

"Watch it, Mom."

She was testing me, *trying* me far too hard. I didn't let anyone speak to me this way and if she continued to do this, disrespect me…

My nostrils flared. "I want to be fair here. I didn't tell you about all this, so I'm giving you that. But if the conversation keeps moving this way, if *you* keep moving this way, I can't be held accountable for what I say to you."

Her eyes narrowed, harsh at me. "Are you ready for the implications that comes with this? The questions? The whispers? You can love this baby, this family and I can love this baby as much as we want, but society will always have an opinion otherwise."

"And what have I ever cared about other people's opinions of me?" I asked, unable to hold back now with my tone. "When I was plastered across the cover of magazines? The bad boy billionaire off getting ass in Cabo or Bali? Well, where were you when I was out doing that for over a decade, huh? You, society, and their opinions? I could get shitfaced in the middle of damn Millennium Park with nothing but a pat on the shoulder and an, 'It's okay. That's just how he is.'"

"Now, you watch it," she said rising up on the couch.

"Why should I? It's true. I fooled around, jacked off for

*years*, and you never once cared. But the minute I actually want to do something that means something, and heaven forbid, have a mixed-race child, I meet so much resistance from you, from Asa."

"It's not about you wanting to have a child, Alexander. Or even the color of the child's skin. I want you to have a baby. I've always wanted that, to be a grandmother."

"So what's the issue then?"

"The issue is you didn't think this through. You got sloppy, did whatever you wanted to do, and didn't bother thinking about the people you leave in your wake. Not thinking about Naomi!"

Only whiplash would have shaken me more.

"What does Naomi have to do with any of this?" I asked. "Was it her who told you about this? Was it…"

And suddenly this all made sense. Mom finding out and Asa saying he wasn't the one who told her.

I lifted my finger. "Are you two plotting? Or working together on some messed up…" I pushed my hands into my hair, unable to believe this. "Dear God, Mom. It's not going to happen with Naomi. It wasn't in the cards for us, so stop trying to make that happen. Both of you need to stop."

She stood, closing the space between us. "It was Naomi who told me about all this, but it's me who's defending her. I know why you broke up, Alexander."

I stiffened and she nodded.

"So this just doesn't make sense. You wanted no baby with her. You made that clear. You made that known."

Because maybe, just maybe I didn't want her. Maybe she was too much, too similar to someone I already knew. So much I loved about Naomi, her beauty and drive for so many things, her goals. But I also disliked many things, enough to definitely count. How many times had her talk of children, being wedded *to me* with children, ended with her having nothing but a life at home, one in which she threw everything she built away, her life in medicine and what I knew to be dreams of a practice.

She'd said she would toss it away for me.

And even boasted about it. Like she actually believed that's what I wanted for us, for her.

I'd seen a woman first hand throw her life away. A beautiful woman who denied all her hopes and dreams, who played secondary to man.

My father.

So why would I want that? I didn't want any of it.

But even with all that, I just didn't want children when I was with her. I had no interest in it and it didn't matter how much Naomi fought me about the topic.

Or how much she ultimately lied.

I turned, as I had no way to explain any of this to my mom. I couldn't. It would hurt her too much, but she grabbed me, and once she had, that folder I noticed on the table was pressed to my chest.

Mom had placed it there.

"This is why she called," she said. "And if you answered her calls you'd know that too."

The folder fell to my hands when she let go and she stepped away, letting me open it.

Naomi had called a lot these past few weeks. She had, but I'd... I'd written her off.

"Your surrogate's blood work, as well as her family history," Mom said; she charged. "She pulled it when she analyzed your surrogate recently."

Johari's fall. Naomi had analyzed her.

I read the page, scanning down, and what I saw...

"Her brother has Down syndrome, Alexander," Mom said behind me.

I had walked off. I had stepped way, thinking only one thing. Johari had been so honest with me when I met her. At least, I thought she had. We had it all out on the table, everything I believed shared. But she didn't tell me this, about her brother.

This she left out.

# Twelve

**Johari** "You got some mail over here, darling," Ms. Sherry said, her call unexpected on this rainy late afternoon.

I adjusted myself in the CTA's bus seat, more than tired from the early morning shift. My feet hurt, cramped, and all I wanted was some time off them. The late shifts got me spent, but the early ones almost seemed worst, my body's internal clock so off these days.

I rubbed my hand over the reason why, my raincoat the only barrier. I barely showed at all, the small bump concealed by pretty much all clothing in my wardrobe at this point. But I knew what was there. I *knew* and every day that awareness grew more and more of that subtle life inside me. The presence let itself be known and I…

I felt it. I could this time.

Maybe not actually inside me. I mean, the baby was far too young, but I knew it was there. I could *feel* the evidence of the little bump below.

I smoothed my hand over it, cherishing the miracle of it. One day, soon, I should feel movement.

*That will make it really real.*

"Jo?"

Curbing my emotions, I faced out the window, the spattering

rain coating the city like teardrops.

I rubbed my face. "I'm here. Can you hold whatever it is for me?"

For years, the mail carrier had mixed up Ms. Sherry's and my mama's stuff. In fact, so much, Mama and Ms. Sherry decided to put each other's name on their separate boxes. Whenever the mix-ups happened, they would just walk the mail over to the other's place and my own mail was no exception. Since I moved, my packages would still occasionally sprinkle into their boxes despite being forwarded.

"Of course, love," Ms. Sherry said, a smile in her voice. She always had a smile there. "It's a pretty big one, too. Another one of these housing packets for places in California."

Laughing a little, I rested my head on the window. "You opened it, did you?"

"I didn't need to. It's stamped all over it and that's very exciting. This whole thing is wonderful. It looks like you have a lot of options on where to stay. You getting excited to move yet?"

"I will," I sighed, turning away. The bus stopped and I moved my legs, allowing another passenger to cut across my way. I was one of the last stops on this route, the final down the line. I crossed my legs. "Gotta get my match first. Won't know until I get that."

Ms. Sherry knew all about match day, the selection process that would determine what hospital my internship would be served at. I'd be a real doctor there, moving and shaking with other MDs. The selections happened once a year, so I wouldn't even be going into the match until I got closer to the move.

Hand on my stomach, I was definitely happy now I decided to take time off after I graduated. Originally, I made that decision so I could take some time to work, get my affairs in order before such a big move, and with this pregnancy…

Well, I'd definitely need that time to recoup now. Come time, I'd be fully refreshed and energized to go in. I'd be ready, all affairs and everything settled. I'd be putting in for hospitals in California, but also some here as a backup. Basically, things were up in the air, Chicago or California the future.

"But you will. You'll get what you put in for. You're a great doctor."

"Not technically a doctor *yet*, Ms. Sherry."

"But you will be. You will be."

I appreciated her kind words so much she didn't even know. I have been so far removed from kind words these days, really any words. My co-workers seemed to be the only people I conversed with anymore and then of course my peers at school. But with them, it was all professional, all friendly glances and small talk with nothing more and nothing less. It was only Roya who offered a more than welcomed conversation, checking up on me and seeing how I was doing. Like she always had, but then at the end of the day, she went home. I went home.

Just me.

I tilted my head back.

"Will you come by the house, Jo? To get the mail?"

"Um, yeah. I'm stopping by Thursday. Javan will be at your place, right?"

Silence on her end and I knew why.

She sighed. "There ain't no reason to be scared of your mama, baby. She don't mean no harm. She can be different, but that's how she is. You know she loves you."

*Loves me…*

That I knew, and I loved her as well. I loved her so much and respected her so much. I admired who she was and all her struggles, her fight to bring up two children, one of whom had special needs in a neighborhood that didn't always make that easy for a young mom. And she did that on her own with no help from anyone else. She beat the odds and I could only dream of being half of the strong black woman who raised me. She was all those things, yes, but she was also something else. And that something made me feel inferior, inferior to her to want to be something different. Because to my mama, for some reason being something different meant something bad. I was bizarre. I was unusual and being that wasn't okay to her.

I wasn't okay to her.

"I know she does," I said closing my eyes a little. I turned my head. "I do."

"So stop by more. And not just for Javan and me. You're

gonna leave soon, baby, and you'll regret leaving things this way between you and your mama. Y'all have both been so tense over the years and it doesn't need to be that way. It doesn't. Life is just too short for it, child."

I swallowed.

"And bring that man you're seeing. He was so handsome."

I could hear that one in my head now: "Jo bringing the white boy home to dinner, the *rich* white man who takes care of her, makes her think she's better than the rest of us.

*"She always thinks she's so much better."*

My heart charged, actually hearing my mama's voice behind the words and then the nausea surfaced, hot bile chasing steadfast up my throat.

The words really did make me feel sick. That they'd connected so negatively to someone so... so...

Alexander.

I couldn't think about him as it hurt too much. I didn't want to get this wrapped up. I had a plan.

And that plan wasn't him.

I ended things with Ms. Sherry after promising I would come home soon but remained shy of any type of commitment to anything more. Home could be her house. It didn't have to be Mama's.

The bus came to a stop and I raised my bag off the floor. I got it on my arm, and then lifted my hoodie over my head.

Getting my footing, I squinted out the window and a vehicle took my attention between raindrops. I only noticed it because the car looked so out of place out there, the rain sliding off shiny black paint so effortlessly.

The dark sedan with a silver emblem on the hood remained parked outside my duplex and I tilted my head, trying to make someone out, anything through the tinted windows.

*What's up with that?*

No one who lived around here drove anything like that.

My curiosity piqued, I got off the bus, the soft patter of falling drops covering my head.

The bus took off moments later, slow and through the passing windows, a man could be witnessed on the other side of that bus.

He'd gotten out of the driver's side, Hispanic and dressed in all black.

I'd seen him before, what seemed like so long ago outside of a busy café.

And I saw the man who he opened a door for, too. Ms. Sherry would call him a handsome man.

Alexander's patent leather shoes could shine in even the rainiest day. *He* shined like a polished copper penny. His long trench coat protected a fine suit, the large body beneath masculine in all a man's strength wherever the material touched. His driver had a second umbrella and Alexander took it, thanking him before escaping his own protection. He didn't use the umbrella given to him, though. He simply sprinted with it.

He sprinted to me.

He crossed the street with long strides, the rain sprinkling water droplets on the gray of his trench. He got to me and that same rain had broken up his dark hair, the water giving it a layer of sheen and clumping his thick eyelashes. He opened the umbrella over my head, his cheeks filled with color.

"Hey," he said, his voice rough a little with his labored breathing. I couldn't tell if it was from the brisk sprint or something else.

I pulled my hood down, my head protected.

"Hi," I returned as if this was normal, as if he should be here. And perhaps he realized that, too.

How unusual this was.

He severed eye contact, panning up and down the street before facing me.

"Can we talk?" he asked. "Can we talk out of the rain?"

My duplex ended up being the place I chose, allowing him to come in with me. I never signed any paperwork that said the pair of us couldn't consort and made no requests to have that condition added. He simply had been abiding by an unspoken request until this moment, a request to stay away and leave me to my privacy.

At least he had until now.

Alexander stripped off his coat once he cleared the threshold to my duplex, his umbrella closed and already shaken out from moments before.

I took them both from him. This place didn't have much, but I did acquire a coat closest in the renter's agreement. I went to put the personal items away.

"Thank you," he said, relaxing his long body when he took a seat on the arm of my couch. In his pressed suit, he could make anything fancy. Even sitting in such a casual way.

"No problem." I left him, going out of the room and to that hallway closet.

Down the hall, I stored my own raincoat, then my damp boots when I took them off. Any other day my stuff would have hung out by the door, but today an exception had to be made with Alexander's eyes on me. They'd been that way since we were outside, never left, and I felt them ever strong, his awareness of me and me of him.

I couldn't hide forever and did eventually come back to him in the living room.

All gazes were out in the open now.

That beam of his eyes hit me like a ray gun, a flare of brown on me in such an intimate way.

He found every angle—watching, searching. He hadn't seen me in so long, my choice being the reason.

I made no attempts to cover my stomach, but his gaze did leave me feeling self-conscious.

What else was new?

I pushed a thumb behind me. "I'm going to go change out of these scrubs. It's been a long day."

He blinked up, almost lost. "Of course. And I won't keep you. I know you've been working."

I nodded escaping again. My scrubs didn't show anything at all as I was barely showing, but I wanted to remove the temptation.

I didn't want to hurt him more than I already had.

I covered my stomach with a loose t-shirt, and then wrapped a sweater shrug over it all. Usually, I wore it on chilly days around the house.

Today the air chilled just perfectly for it, the storm and so many other things.

Lights flickered when I made my way back to the living room and both of our attention turned toward the flickering light fixtures.

"The storm," I told him, grabbing a candle I used for such things. "And shoddy lighting. Hopefully, we'll be okay, but just in case..."

I lit the candle between us and he watched me, no waver in that gaze.

He sat so properly in my living room, perfect and what I wouldn't do to give him a shove, shake him and make him laugh, make him fall with me.

I had fallen and the way he looked at me told me exactly why. I had a consciousness with him, a presence that was completely unobstructed when we were together. He was quite forward about it and unashamed by it. He didn't care who noticed. He didn't care at all.

"How are you, Jo?" he asked.

I could feel it, every ounce of his gaze like a prick to the skin.

He tilted his head at me. "How have you been?"

The candle lit, I placed my lighter on my coffee table, and then eased into my armchair, sitting across from him.

I moved my arms over my body. "Did you get my message? I gave an update of my latest exam to your assistant."

His hands came together, folding over his crossed legs.

His head bobbed twice in acknowledgement.

"I know how you are, how the reports say you are. But how are you? How have you been doing? Feeling? How. Are. *You*?"

He couldn't even let me read between the lines. He put it out there, all on the table.

Sighing, I followed the flicker of the flame in front of me, attempting to chase and maybe run away with it.

"Why are you here, Alexander?"

His intelligence couldn't be questioned and I bet reigned supreme even above the great minds I surrounded myself with daily. Knowing that, I refused to believe he was stupid, foolish. He knew I didn't want him here. He knew, but he came anyway.

It was he who sighed now, his large body moving up and down.

Standing, he crossed the short distance and came to sit on my ottoman, the closest he could be without taking me to him, taking me away.

His fingers reached to his beard, a restless action I'd come to notice he did when he was lost in thought, tense.

His brow furrowed. "I have a habit of not coming to you in the best way. I've done that before and because I have, I won't do it again. I need to ask you something and I'm going to give you the benefit of the doubt. I want to be open with you."

I sat back in my chair, not really understanding. "All right. Well, what do you want to be open with?"

Leaning forward, his hands came together. "Is it true your brother…"

He stopped for a minute, his eyes to the floor like he was thinking, pondering.

He lifted his head. "Is it true your brother, Javan, has Down syndrome?"

My brother's name, my brother's existence coming out of Alexander's mouth, forced surprise to be riddled within me.

And the surprise was far from good, more than unnerving.

I eyed him. "Why are you asking about my brother? Hell, Alexander, how do you know about my brother?"

A rise in my voice wasn't desired. But this was my brother he was talking about, a person I never mentioned and he had no right speaking of.

Putting his hands together, he breathed on his fingertips, then stared up at me. "I'm asking about him because it's important. And I know about him because your family history was pulled when Naomi did your work-up the day you got hurt. Your brother was born at the same hospital so Naomi had access to it."

And what right did she have to pull my family, *my brother's* medical history? No one asked her to do that.

I gripped my sweater, pulling it tighter over myself. "Well, your ex-girlfriend was out of line doing that. And I don't recall giving her permission to do so. Alexander, I'm sorry but that's messed up. If the ethics committee—"

"I need to know, Johari."

His voice boomed in the air, rough, terse. He had the tone of an executive, a boardroom official and me his subordinate. It seemed his fight for control was still in full bloom. But he couldn't control me. He couldn't control everything.

I stood and he joined me.

"Where are you going?"

"To get your stuff," I said, turning around. "Because you have crossed the line so hard right now, it's not even funny."

"Why are you doing this?" he bit out and I could see him physically biting. He was biting back words, his frustration. "I came here because I don't want to jump to conclusions. Because I don't want to cross the line and do something rash, something stupid. But you keeping something like this from me? Something so big when it could affect the baby…"

He shook his head, his hands moving over his arms. "I don't even know what to think."

He was all over the place, going every which way and, though, he didn't want to jump to conclusions, he did.

I took a step back. "You think I kept this from you."

"Like I said, Johari. I don't know what to think. This is a pretty big deal and—"

"That's the thing, Alexander. It's not."

He blanched, blinking. "What are you talking about? Of course it's a big deal. Your brother—"

"Isn't diseased," I said standing up to him. "He doesn't have something you can catch or spread. Did you ever stop to think and wonder *why* I wouldn't tell you something like this? Me 'with all my medical,' as you once called it. Me, Ms. Thorough and going to be a damn doctor soon, Alexander? Having a child with Down syndrome can happen to anyone. It isn't hereditary or passed down, at least not the type my brother has."

"Even if that's true, Jo, and I do believe you because I know *you know* your stuff, isn't that something you think I would want to know? Something important? Something worth mentioning? You're right to assume my ignorance in this, so why would you let me create my own theories and formulations? You could have just told me. You could have just talked to me. I would have listened. I would have understood, but you closed me off from it."

I said nothing and he grabbed my arm. He didn't pull me, just held me, and God, did I want to hold him back.

"I'm sorry if you misunderstood. If you thought *I* would misunderstand or... not want this. Not want this with you. I could see that being a fear."

He was right. It was. My brother was perfect. No, he was extraordinary and the simple fact of ignorance I had to deal with time and time again when people found out about him...

I didn't want to deal with it. I had no desire to fight the uneducated when Javan really did have nothing to do with the children I would reproduce. Even if he did, would that have been so bad? So terrible?

I guess to the majority of the world it was.

I said nothing and Alexander turned me, gentle fingers pressing into my arms, and moving, they came to rest on the sides of my face.

He shouldn't do this. Touch me...

"And any ignorance only comes from my own flaws. My own fears and has nothing to do with your brother," he said, swallowing. His face and eyes were so red. "I know what it's like to be in and out of hospitals. To be sick all the time, surgeries..."

He dampened his mouth. "I did fear that. I won't lie, Jo. That did scare me for the baby. But if it came down to it, if that had been the outcome, I promise you my love would be no less. I'd love our baby just the same."

He said our baby, not his, or even mine, but ours and...

My chest hurt, my breathing shallow. This was all too much. It was all too raw, too... loaded and I couldn't deal. My mind couldn't handle it, my heart. This wasn't my child. This wasn't *mine* and he couldn't say that. He couldn't because I couldn't go through that. No, I couldn't...

Not again.

A sharpness hit my chest, an intense fire that had my lungs squeezing from the inside out. I couldn't take in air. I couldn't think and I held myself, dropping out of Alexander's hands and to my knees. The world was at a full tilt and the panic had me holding my stomach, my baby.

I rocked, panting, trying so hard to find air, breath.

I wanted to feel it. I had to feel it this time. Before, my

pregnancy had been so short lived. I didn't even get this far. My body hadn't allowed me. It betrayed me. It did that despite how healthy I kept it, despite how much care I took to make sure I was fit to carry. It hurt me anyway. It wouldn't let me have something I didn't seek out for, but always wanted.

"No, no, no!" I cried, cradling myself, the little bump. "Please not again. No!"

Alexander caught me on my roll to the floor, his hands keeping me from hitting the carpet completely, and all the while I called out, the words not even making sense in my own mind. When one couldn't think, couldn't pass breath all logic soon swept away. I just knew taking air into my lungs wasn't possible right now and if I couldn't manage to do it, get things right, get my body right…

I'd lose everything. I'd lose my baby… just like before.

*Alexander* She wasn't breathing, nor was she responding to me.

And she held her stomach.

A million terrible things surfaced in my mind and all of them surrounded this woman in my arms, this woman who couldn't breathe and a child…

Our child.

My phone in hand, I attempted to let Johari know I was here, talking to her while juggling my phone. I had no idea if I could dial emergency with sweating fingers and her in my arms but I'd try.

I'd damn well try.

But a name crossed my screen before I could dial, a familiar one.

*Naomi Radcliff.*

*Could I be that lucky? That fortunate?*
Frantic words escaped my lips upon hearing Naomi's voice and no way could they be recalled. I was too out of my head.

Too scared beyond belief.

Johari curled beneath me gasping for air and I felt helpless. I felt worthless that despite all I had, my resources, all my money the woman I cared about was suffering in my arms. I refused to believe there was any finality to her condition. I wouldn't let myself.

Naomi, though thrown into this, quickly got what was happening on the other end of the line. She may have called for something else, but she got this, she got me and her background allowed her to help me. I had never been so thankful for my armchair doctor.

"All right, Alexander, listen to me," she said, calming, soothing. "I believe Johari is having a panic attack, okay? So what you're going to need to do is calm her down."

*Panic attack?*

Panic attack.

Johari choked, gasping and the position of her hands finally fastened onto me. She did have a hand on her stomach, but she had one on her chest as well.

*She's having a panic attack.*

"Alexander, can you hear me?" Naomi asked. "Do you understand? Just get her to calm down."

"I heard you," but that's the last I heard from her, the last she heard from me.

I put the phone down and reined all attention, all my focus, on her.

Johari.

I held her, my limbs readily aware of the want of that, the desire for so long.

I leaned in, touching the shell of her ear with my lips, embracing her.

"Johari," I breathed, holding her hands, holding her. "You can get through this, okay? Stay with me. Listen to my voice."

She trembled, tears shining her eyes and if that didn't cut me, sever me in two.

I swallowed. "You're having a panic attack, sweetheart. I need you to hear me, be with me. Tell me what you need. I'll do anything for you. Anything you need, I'm here."

And I would.

I knew that now.

Tears clumped around her lashes and a gasp of something familiar fell from her lips.

She kept saying, "I want to feel it." And when that statement passed, "I can't lose it."

She's scared she's losing the baby.

I rocked her. "You won't," I told her. "Johari, you won't. We won't. We're in this together. The baby and I are here. Both of us are with you. We're not leaving."

And I think that's what she needed to hear.

A hand stayed around her stomach, but the other came to me, gripping my hand.

I held her close in the flickering light of her home, rain softly pattering her window and her tears silencing between us.

# Thirteen

**Alexander** A wave of relief settled over me that I never decided to take up smoking, because times such as these, situations such as these would cause me to go through pack after pack. I actually felt much like an expectant father, my hand in my pocket as I waited, anxious for information I couldn't affect, nor help with. It was the worst spot to be, the unknown far more torturous than anything that could possibly be shared with me.

I rolled up my sleeves, my jacket gone and tie loosened long ago. I think it had been right around the time I helped Johari upstairs to her room. In fact, directly after that and before I called Naomi. Yes, that had been it. I believe Naomi hung up thinking the call had been lost and I didn't blame her. I sat with Johari a long time on that floor, her breaths evening beneath my hands while I held her.

I threaded my fingers through my hair, wondering what was going on. That really was the worst, the wondering.

Stair steps creaked behind me, and I whipped around from where I stood in the middle of Johari's living room. I was quite surprised I hadn't created a path with my pacing. I had done it enough.

Naomi descended those stairs, medical bag in hand, and how surprised I'd been when she had offered to come over. She said her shift just ended and she would feel better knowing her diagnosis on Johari had been correct.

I didn't fight her.

She'd been upstairs with Jo for so long and I debated nearly going in, only stopping because I knew Johari was in good hands medically. How many babies had Naomi delivered? Expectant mothers she cared for? The number got me lost she spoke of her patients so much.

Touching the bottom of the stairs, Naomi pushed her bag over her shoulder and I came to her, my hand returning to my pocket in more than a restless state.

"How—"

"She's fine," she said, and air touching my dry mouth made me aware of how much I hadn't been getting in. How long had it been since I took a deep breath? A good breath into my lungs?

Naomi pushed a blonde curl out of her eyes. "I do recommend she sees her own doctor as soon as she can. They need to perform all the formal tests and I already advised her of that. She understood. Of course she did. She knows how this all works."

"Then it will be done then," I told her, nodding. I knew Johari was on the task, but I would be there as well. Before I had taken a step back, let her allow me to believe I should, but I wouldn't anymore. This arrangement didn't work for me. It felt so empty of her, the baby, and that didn't sit well.

All time for later, though.

After acknowledging that she was understood that *I* understood what she told me with a head bob, Naomi made her way to the door, getting her raincoat back on.

"I really appreciate you coming over," I said. "Helping with this. You didn't have to and that means a lot."

She turned, adjusting the collar of her coat.

A small smile touched her lips. "It wasn't a problem, Alexander. As I told you, I wouldn't feel okay not knowing she was for sure all right."

And I believed her. Naomi did want to help people. That's why she had become a doctor, but this was a special situation. And what sent her calling me in the first place did linger on my mind. Her number had been on my phone before I dialed, which meant she'd been calling me about something and after my meeting with my mom, I think I knew what that something was. Up until this point, I was just trying to figure out how to broach the subject with her.

And being downstairs for so long gave me a lot of time to figure it out.

Naomi cracked the door open, the light shower misting in with the day, but I held the door above her, making her look up at me.

I slid my hand down the door. "I had a talk with my mom."

That seemed to be all I had to say.

Shifting, her bag slid down her arm and she braced it, tilting her head.

"I figured she would eventually. That had been why I phoned her I supposed," she said. She placed her bag down, allowing it to touch the floor. "It was needed information, Alexander. Johari could have already told you about her brother, but I felt it was important to make sure. You have a lot riding on this."

But what place had it been of hers? To step in?

My hand came to rest on the door knob as I looked up at her. "What ever happened to doctor-patient confidentiality? And how is pulling her family's individual medical history a requirement of doing a full work-up on her?"

She stared at me, stone-faced in her expression. "This was a special situation."

Which meant, she wasn't supposed to do something like that.

If I didn't already know.

"I knew you personally," she said, explaining. "I didn't want to see you taken advantage of."

"Yeah? How so? Johari already explained to me her brother's condition isn't hereditary. It could happen to absolutely any parent in the spectrum."

"Yes, that's true."

Of course, it was and never once did I question it.

"So what was the point of all this then, Naomi? Bringing my mom into this? She didn't even know about the baby. I told you I was waiting until Johari had hit her first trimester."

"I know and I apologize for that. But did you ever stop to

wonder the reason why someone would keep something like that from you? Someone who's doing something so important *for* you? You've got to think about what else she's willing to not tell the truth about, the potential of it."

From where I stood, the only person who had me wondering was her, her motives, her intentions.

And as far as I knew, we were done here. Her job was done.

"Thank you for your insight," I said, then widened the door. "And again, for coming here. I truly do appreciate that."

Her blanched look told me everything I needed to know about her dismissal, but she didn't fight me on the decision.

Nodding, she picked up her bag, taking a moment to pull her hood up before going out into the rain.

She turned around. "Don't get hurt, Alexander. You don't want to know what that feels like, how hard it feels."

But she hurt me, as well.

Betrayed me, as well so long ago.

I was never one to compare apples to oranges when it came to wrongs, deceit, but my ex was definitely playing the victim here. I did know hurt and I learned it from her first.

Rain surrounded her as she went toward her car parked in the street, but I didn't wait for her to get into it. I closed the door, and then took only moments to collect my thoughts. I wanted to check on Johari, at least once before I left her to her peace. I knew Naomi gave her a clear diagnosis, but I needed to see. I needed to be there.

I wouldn't wait in the wings again, not anymore.

I came across Johari's door on the upstairs level. I took her up here earlier after, well, her panic attack.

Standing there, I took a second before knocking. Last I had seen her, she'd been so out of it, spent in my arms.

I knocked twice, stepping back.

"Johari?" I added. "Jo, it's Alexander."

A soft, but sure, "Come in," sounded through the hall.

I turned the knob and let myself into her room.

A blanket covered her shoulders, her sitting there alone in front of the mists outside her window.

Turning on her bed, that blanket dropped from her shoulders

and how that subtle smile on her lips had my heart beating.

*She's all right.*

"I just wanted to check up on you," I said, and she nodded, allowing me to come in.

A shyness had her head lowering. "I'm kinda embarrassed. About what happened?"

"Don't be," I said, coming over.

A panic attack could happen to the best of us. Even someone in her position, her field of work.

I pushed my hands into my pockets. "And Naomi says you're okay. You and the baby are okay."

"She told me and can you thank her again for me? I mean, if you see her?"

I would if I saw her and had no problem with that.

Rocking back once on my heels, I watched her, then panned out the window. We had so many drizzly days like this lately and I was ready to be more than rid of them. I spent enough time behind dark clouds. I wanted the light. I wanted the sun.

"I understood what was happening. Eventually."

Her words had me turning toward her, a sadness in her eyes.

She shook her head. "But when you're in the rough of it, actually panicking it's hard to talk your way out of your head."

I felt a connection with her there. I too had lost my sense of reality before. I had never been one to buckle, even in the harshest and most volatile business dealings. But when it came to my sickness, my illness...

Yes, I definitely understood where she was coming from.

Movement on the bed had me eyeing an empty space. Johari created one for me, right next to her. She gestured to it with her blanketed arm and I didn't argue, wanting so much to be close to her. I think I wanted that from day one. But only until recently had I been bold enough to take it.

Smoothing my hands down my legs, I took that space, getting into *her* space.

And how she'd gotten into mine.

I watched how the rain streaking her window made designs across her brown skin, her cheeks I wanted to touch and stroke with my fingertips. Hers touched her stomach, her blanket the barrier.

I wanted to see. I wanted to hold her, both of them. She'd given me such a small peek before downstairs. In fact, I saw nothing at all.

"Johari?"

Her head lifted up, brown eyes on me.

I had no more words on my lips and I knew she searched for them, watching my mouth. Soon enough, though, she panned, in the very direction of my want and need. But how could I ask her to see, to be open with me.

To let me in.

Seemed I didn't have to.

"The last time had been so quick," she said, opening her blanket and there rested a small bump, a slight curve under her thin tank top.

I stared in wonderment, awe.

Getting closer, I drew in, humming over her and the tiny bundle between us.

She closed her eyes, me upon her.

"I lost it so quick last time, Alexander," she said, her voice stretched, hands curled on her belly. She looked up at me. "It's like I wasn't even pregnant. It's like I didn't even have one."

What she was saying settled itself upon me, the words and emotion behind them. She told me she'd never had a child that day in the café.

But that didn't mean she never conceived one.

Suddenly, events of before made sense, her in my arms downstairs, crying and pleading to feel something, someone.

She'd been through this before.

## Johari

"It was Jared's," I confessed, and rough fingers went to my cheek, making me look up.

He had these eyes like warmth in the night and sunshine in the day.

His hand cupped my cheek and a brush of butterfly wings could only be more gentle.

He guided my chin up, a finger curled under my jaw.

"You lost it?" he questioned and I nodded, feeling ashamed when I turned my head.

This was something else I should have told him. But something I didn't feel relevant. It had all been in the past.

I wished the hurt had.

"I wasn't more than sixteen and I was so afraid," I said, my eyes itching, hurting. "I was afraid for myself, afraid of what my mama would say."

His hand played with my hair, each stroke traveling deeply and fully.

"Was that your mom a couple months ago?" he questioned. "One of those women who saw us?"

I nodded, unable to forget. It was that event, which pushed me away even more from a woman I already had such a hard time connecting with.

As well as severed any hope with the man who'd been there with me.

"And she wasn't there for you?" he asked, and so gently. He treaded lightly.

He was there.

The thing about what he said, about my mama, was quite the contrary.

My mama *was* there. She was there for me and it had been the baby, the existence that brought us together in ways we'd never been. She'd been there for me. She really had, so when I ultimately lost the child… The baby gone…

"She was, actually. She had me young, as well," I told him, lifting my head. He remained cloudy through my eyes. "We shared that I think. We had a connection."

That made it so much worse in the end. We'd found something; we *had* something together. I needed her and she was there for me, willing and wanting to be.

I once overhead her say something to Ms. Sherry, something hidden in the night when she believed my brother and I were sleeping. She said I was probably grateful. She actually *believed* in her heart I was grateful to lose my child in the end. She said it freed me up and allowed me to get out, get out of here, and away from her.

It didn't matter how much Ms. Sherry chastised her for that, scolded her for the very thought and words. My mama had made her mind up. She believed something.

And I had no retribution.

"It crushed her when I lost the baby, Alexander," I cried, and I knew it had. I had seen that all over her face and felt it long after the baby left me.

I shook my head. "And it shattered me."

How much time had I spent at home, questioning any and everything about myself. I did have a plan, but that changed once I had gotten pregnant so young. That change hadn't been a bad thing, though. That was going to be my life and I...

I did want it.

My head dipped by Alexander's hand and when he kissed my head, I felt it all over, the heat coursing thickly inside me.

"You won't lose ours," he whispered, smoothing his lips over my crown. "We won't. He or she is ours."

I believed him he said it so strongly, forcefully like there was no other alternative. This child was destined to be, in the stars for us.

And *ours*.

His kiss felt like heaven on my lips and his hands to my skin, divinity. He used them to bring the blanket off my shoulders, then the straps of my top down my arms.

Firm lips pressed to the top of them, heating my already charged skin.

He gripped my shoulders. "I won't stop, Jo," he said, nearly pleading as he lifted his mouth and moved to the other shoulder. He brushed his lips again.

"I won't be able to. If I don't stop now... Step back..."

He was asking me for an out. In fact, begging me to.

But he wouldn't get that from me.

I let him pull me into his arms, pressing my body flush against his chest. Only pure rock could be firmer, *harder* and the force was a perfect give against my tender flesh.

Every nerve ending was heightened these days, slight touches like a stoke to a flame, and in his arms, I felt that, the fury of those intense sensations.

He stripped me of my top quickly, somehow needing that, me exposed.

But his fascination only lay with my stomach.

The swell of my belly remained tiny, but present, tightening slightly at Alexander's touch.

I trembled, his lips finding the start of a dark pregnancy line when he lowered his head.

Below me, he said things, but so far in my head, they were hard to make out. I got little more than an, "Amazing," from his lips, as well as "Beautiful."

Laying me down, he stripped off his shirt, his pecs jumping and dusted in dark hair.

I saw the man then, the vulnerable one beneath the suits and the money.

I saw the human.

Evidence of his cancer remained in the form of a scar above his left pectoral muscle and reaching out, I put my hand on it.

They connected his port there, the spot where he received chemotherapy. So much came with that scar, the reality of an intense battle before me. One never would know by just seeing him, the vast man before me with all his strength.

He descended that strength upon me, smelling of heat and tasting of flesh.

Over his scar was where I decided to place my lips and he breathed in, a harsh breath that sucked in what little air was left in the room.

His eyes pulled to the back of his head, a hum pulling from his throat in a sharp jump. Gripping my scalp, he drew me back to take my mouth.

His flavor couldn't be concocted, beard brushing roughly against my skin, tickling my lips. His hand pushed down the front of my shorts and when he gripped my pussy, I thought I reached ecstasy right there before him.

"Alexander…"

He guided me onto his lap that way, a hard and present erection firm underneath me. He unbuckled his pants and a mushroom head peeked above his belt buckle.

Reaching in, I gripped his cock, my thumb moving over the

dewy bead on top.

He bit my lip. "I need inside you, Jo. I can't wait."

The harsh tug of my hand was only replaced when he put on a condom, my arms coming to settle over broad shoulders while I waited. He pushed up on his knees, then took me with him when he lay to the bed, his weight settled on me like a thick blanket.

He kissed me, softly at first, before taking nips down my front, my collarbone, and then my breasts.

Already sensitive peaks extended, Alexander suckling on me.

My chest pushed up to meet him, my hips going up when he pulled down my shorts. My legs lifted with the release and I had never seen a man so ready, my spread thighs summoning him to lick his lips.

He kicked off his pants, hard and heavy. Muscled thighs speckled in raven-colored hairs and how the mass of him felt against my skin when he covered me.

Using his hand to guide him, he slid into my heat easily and filled me oh so tight.

His scent came with my breath, his mouth. He fit so well, but then again, didn't fit at all. His width forced accommodation, took it until acceptance.

Emotional, I closed my eyes, trying not to think. I just wanted to feel him, this moment. This moment that shouldn't be happening considering what we were to each other.

I just didn't care anymore.

"Take me."

And he did, harsh breaths moving over my lips, hands gripping my bottom as I bucked.

Hips smacked and fluttered against me and how quickly I knew he was ready.

Because I was too.

He waited for me, my high peak before falling with me into ecstasy. I spilled around him, pooling, then a sudden pressure enlarged an area already tight.

His release crashed into me with fervor and I found myself wanting his warmth. I wanted it badly, but the condom kept it from me.

A steady current of heat moved over my shoulder with his

kiss, words close behind while he remained inside me.

"I want…" he started, but then he stopped, his forehead pushing into my neck with his mouth.

I waited, listening but he didn't finish.

Then suddenly he was no longer inside me.

He pulled out, rolling to his back, and I watched him, a hand behind his head.

*What was he going to say?*

He seemed to let himself forget, using a hand to pull me to him. I settled my forehead against his rough skin, his hands coming up to cage my head.

He breathed across my cheek.

"I want you both," he admitted, finally, and his arms came to drop around me. They came securely, my throat fighting at the feel.

The love.

He looked up at me and I saw it there, deep in his beautiful eyes.

"I want you both, Jo," he said, swallowing. "I want both you and the baby and I know I'm not supposed to. It kills me I'm not supposed to."

The pain that was in his voice…

The struggle.

He shouldn't be saying this to me, any of this. This went against our agreement, our terms, but he said them anyway. He showed his heart anyway.

I turned in the direction of his kiss, letting his lips fall along my cheek.

"I want you both too," I said.

Because he shouldn't be the only one revealing his heart. He shouldn't be the only one willing to take a chance.

He watched me, awed when I took his hand and placed it to my stomach. I wanted us both to feel it.

We both *would* feel it.

# Fourteen

**Alexander**     This wasn't supposed to be my life and I thought that as I pushed through every day, allowed myself to move in the direction of promise and not a means to an end. Mere months ago, I had been heavy in treatment and not so distant before that, surgeries that left me more than cut open physically. Early journeys under the knife gave me hope, but enough of them had me spent, had me empty. By the time other forms of treatment started, I no longer anticipated a life. I couldn't, as I wouldn't allow myself the agony of wishing for one.

*Why do I have this? How do I have her?*

And I thought that with every doctor's visit, every sonogram in which I got the opportunity to be closer and closer to my child.

*My child...*

Mine and Johari's.

The cards weren't supposed to fair in my direction. I had been lucky all my life until I got sick and I figured that had been karma. I was being forced to pay for a lifetime of privilege, things of which had been bestowed upon me that I took for granted and I did. I never focused on what life would be like without the things I'd been given. I never cared enough. My thoughts only ached for their absence when having it all had been in the balance, but even those feelings alleviated eventually.

But those doctor's visits, those exams where I was honored enough to be a part of, I couldn't imagine the feelings they elicited ever alleviating. They had dug too deep, raw and fastened to my very being. My soul was wrapped up with every movement able to be made out by a sonogram screen and my life force continued on each time I got to hear the steady beat of the tiniest heart. It flowed, a small miracle of life and wonder and each time I heard it felt like the first. They never told you that.

They never did.

A thick, "I love you," fell from my lips at the latest, a mumbled, *emotional* sound and Johari turned toward me, her eyes warm as she lay on the examination table.

Her hand slid over mine and that's the first indictor my hand had come to rest on her cheek. I said the words toward the monitor, but my hand had been on no one but her.

She smiled then, the expression crooked on her lips.

"You love?" she questioned, her voice almost scared with the words. Her hand fell from my fingers. "You love…"

I kissed her, the doctor and his role in all this far from my mind. My only thoughts rested on the warmth I pressed my lips to and the soft beats, distant in the room but ever present in my heart.

"I love you," I told her. I told them both, needing them both to know, and it was only after she said it, too, said, "I love you" through tear-filled eyes I realized their knowledge wasn't the only something I yearned for.

*This is my life. This is mine.*

The days moved slowly after that, wonderfully slow with each passing day. I checked in with Johari in the mornings, and then picked her up after work depending on her own schedule. Today, I had a long day of meetings and rigmarole, but was able to work out picking her up on a day she escorted her brother home from school. She had the day off and when she did, she often made a trip of meeting him at school, then taking him to the park across the street before going home together. The two usually took the bus home, but today, I would be taking them. She wanted me to meet him, her brother, Javan.

*My life, my wonderful life.*

"My God. Is that Alexander Ricci I see there?"

My thoughts lost on my afternoon ahead, I almost missed the acknowledgement, turning my head in the direction of the elevators. A familiar face got off them, an old friend from my IT classes at Northwestern.

Yoshi Watanabe had been an exchange student from Japan, but ended up staying in Illinois long after graduation. I had actually been part of the reason for his stay. I helped him get a job at my dad's company alongside me.

"Yoshi," I greeted, shaking the man's hand firmly between my palms. He had been right. It had been a while since we'd seen each other despite working in the same building.

Stepping back, he took me in as well, scanning all over as I had been. He placed his hands on his hips, his trousers and button-ups a far cry from what I had to wear daily. People on the IT floor got to have many perks, dressing more casual one of them.

He shook his head with a wide smile. "It is you. What are you doing here on this floor with the common people?"

My old friend cut me to the quick. I pushed a hand behind my neck. "Stairwell is closed off on the west side of the building. I try to take the stairs when I can."

"Good man. A much better one than I."

"You're too kind. How have you been?"

"Busy, as you can imagine. But I'm sure nothing compared to you. Still a young CEO in training?"

His words had me chuckling. The job did literally have my name on it, when I was ready. Asa had already expressed no interest in it, and then, well, I had gotten sick.

But I wasn't now.

Grinning, I slid a hand in my pocket. "Easing my way back in."

Knowing exactly what I was getting at, he nodded. My illness was of course well known, especially around these parts.

He touched my shoulder. "Come. Say hi to all the fellas with me. They'll be happy to see you."

The "fellas" were the other members of the motley crew I used to hang with, some from college and others I had met while working here.

See, Yoshi and the rest of the gang may have worked in IT, but their duties went far beyond that of helping my colleagues restore their Internet passwords. *Ricci Financial* was up and coming with its dabble in technology, myself at the forefront of that project once my father had expressed interest in that market. I didn't get down here as much as I liked to and the other guys definitely let me have it.

"You know Earl." Yoshi pointed out to a stocky man in the corner, and then grinned at the man to his right. "And Gunther—"

"Alexander Ricci." The squirrelly redhead came over to me, nearly clipping Kit when he reached over her head to shake my hand. She jabbed him in the gut, him definitely giving her the right to do so.

"Hey, Gunther," I said to him, and then tilted my head to see Kit, the manager of this floor. She'd been here as long as my dad. "And sorry, Kit."

"Make no apologies for him," she said, and then smiled. "Good to see you, Alexander."

"Yes, very good." Gunther would be the one to jerk my chain. He was good about that. He chuckled. "What are you doing down here? We haven't seen you since…"

With all his eccentricities, my friend Gunther had gotten a little ahead of himself and said what probably everyone was thinking down here upon seeing me. They hadn't seen me in a while. Not since my dad passed.

"I'm sorry…" he started, but I waved him off.

"It's fine. It has been a while."

"Alexander was just passing through," Yoshi cut in, good about making the tone light in the room. The man had always been a joy to be around.

He patted Gunther's back. "I just wanted to show him what we've been up to."

"And we've been plenty busy." Gunther waved his hand, gesturing both Yoshi and me to follow him.

I said goodbye to Kit, then followed a set of stained pants away, Gunther's.

As I said, IT got many perks.

I would take dressing down any day than my stuffy suits at the office, and I had when I was down here. I recalled many days coming in wearing suits only to strip down to dress shirts minus the tie. Occasionally, I'd even wear polos if I knew I didn't have any meetings that day. It had been a good time and I was reminded of that as we circulated the floor, Yoshi and Gunther pointing out the many projects they were working on. They dabbled anywhere from cellular phones to the technology it took to make them and I couldn't remove the smile from my face. I may have majored in finance, but I always had a soft spot for innovation, technology. I was a tech nerd at the heart, though, one would never know by my fancy suits and polished shoes. I actually developed quite a few applications down here and as I noted before, I had been at the forefront of launching this Chicago technology division.

I came across one particular piece of software when Gunther sat behind his computer and showed it to me. It seemed they were developing a pedometer that would make counting steps, measuring food intake, and workouts far easier. Minus a clunky device, all one had to do was snap the piece on an article of clothing, very discrete in how tiny it was.

"Marvelous," I said really getting into it. I did miss this, missed getting into all this.

"Sweet, right?" he said turning around his swivel chair. "Yoshi passed this off. Told me it would be a waste of time."

Yoshi shook his head, sitting back on the edge of Gunther's desk. "Way to throw me under the bus."

"I do what I can," Gunther said, tossing his hands back behind his neck. Yoshi kicked his chair, making him fall foreword and I couldn't help my amusement. These guys were both still the same. Even after all these years.

"What have you been up to, Alex?" Gunther turned toward me. "I mean, besides running the office."

"I far from run it, but yeah, doing my regular day-to-day."

"And you're good? Doing well? I have to admit not seeing you worried us all a little."

I smiled. "Life has been well. I'm actually expecting. Though, it's still early yet. We don't know the sex."

I probably wasn't supposed to mention such things, the baby or Johari but… that was before. It had been before things changed. We changed.

Once *we* decided to have this baby, once I told her I loved her, all rules had changed and I knew those weeks ago in her bedroom. She was a part of my life now, both she and the baby. The logistics still were to be hammered out moving forward, but I believed we had time. I couldn't wait for that time.

Their eyes bugged out like I knew they would. No one knew about all this, at least no one outside of my family. I had been keeping them at arm's length for obvious reasons. I believed they would come around with time. Well, they would have to.

I got *congratulations* on both sides from my old friends and after a few promises of drinks with cigars, I noticed a moving box in Yoshi's cube across the way.

He chuckled. "Yes, after nearly a decade here I'm moving on. But not from *Ricci*."

"He's going to the Silicon Valley firm," Gunther said, tossing a stress ball in the air. "They're building that new division out there and Yoshi's been asked to head."

I had heard about this development of course. This division of *Ricci* would focus strictly on the tech side of the business, an endeavor sure to nestle us into that market.

I shook Yoshi's hand. "Looks like I'm not the only one who deserves a cigar. Let me know before you leave. We'll set something up. All three of us."

"You can pencil us in?" Gunther joked, nudging Yoshi who pushed him.

"He's joking, Alexander, and don't mind him. And hey, maybe I'll see you in Silicon Valley. The division's looking for leadership, too, you know."

What an interesting idea that would be. Though, I knew he was obviously joking. A long time ago, before I nestled myself into the life of my dad, I might have considered it. In fact, I think I did once upon a time. Like they said, before my dad passed being down here with them had been my life. I stepped up eventually, though, grew up when my dad died.

I patted Yoshi's shoulder. "You'll definitely see me out there to check up. Someone has to keep you men in line."

"And it better be you." Gunther pointed at me, stress ball in his hand. "And hey, head's up."

He tossed the ball, not much behind the throw. I mean, I was right there no more than three feet away, but when I bent down, reached to catch it…

A sharp pain nearly knocked me off my feet it hit so randomly. Dull and extremely hot, the pressure made a beeline, stabbing directly into my pelvis.

The ball rolled to the floor when I missed it and I stood, the pain radiating in familiarity.

Yoshi reached forward, his hand on my shoulder. "Are you okay, Alexander?"

Gunther had got up as well, but I lifted my hands, pushing air past my lips.

"Yeah, I'm fine," I said.

A dimming throb, the pain seemed to alleviate as quickly as it began, but I had to admit, it definitely could have knocked me on my back had I not had something behind me. I'd been leaning against an empty cubicle.

Yoshi and Gunther beside me, Yoshi's hand left my arm. He took a step back. "That happen all the time?"

It didn't, but it had before. I shook it off. I couldn't even feel it now.

"No worries," I said recovering. "I'm sure it's fine. I've been tiptop shape lately. In fact, the best of my life."

He nodded. "Even still, you might want to check that out."

"Especially, since we need another guy for the company baseball team." Gunther tossed the ball and I caught it that time, chuckling.

He pointed at me. "Don't need you dropping fly balls."

I always skipped the company baseball game. I never had time, but after what happened with me, my dad…

I tossed the ball back at him. I would make time this year.

Life was just too short not to live it.

Johari held the hand of a young boy beside the monkey bars, the two coming over when they noticed me.

I got out of my car, taking a moment to put away my phone. What happened when I caught the stress ball in front of Yoshi and Gunther didn't really alarm me too much. I had been perfect, more than the best I felt and that had been even before taking ill. I figured some insurance wouldn't hurt, though, so I did take the initiative and call my doctor. She'd been surprised to hear from me. We just had a checkup not too long ago and nothing had been out of the ordinary. But like Yoshi said, it didn't hurt to get that checked out. She agreed it wouldn't hurt to come in and I planned to have blood drawn again just before for us to go over.

Those assurances done, I waved to a woman, my girl and her brother.

Her eyes lighting up, Johari lifted her hand, absolutely stunning as the familiar dark strands of her hair cut across her face with her strides. She had such a glow and it radiated every day that past. I had a feeling only some of that had to do with her pregnancy. She was just good, full of beauty in general and that energized the air around her. The kid with her had that same radiance, a huge smile on his face that dared anyone not to get swept up in. I found myself grinning as well and that just couldn't be helped. Johari said her brother had Down syndrome and though I could see that since I was made aware of it, that definitely wasn't the first thing I noticed. His features because of the disorder were subtle, slightly flattened eyes with a smaller nose, and I realized I had seen him before. He'd been with the two women that night I kissed Johari, but he'd been turned away a little by one of them.

Johari pointed me out and he danced beside my girl, the two in puffy jackets. We were definitely starting to settle into that chill of the Midwest, the snow coming in soon.

I waved again, my breath able to be seen in the wind. Securing a button on my trench, I met the two about halfway from the street where I parked and their spot at the monkey bars.

I brought Johari in, kissing her cool cheek. Flushed with color, she warmed my mouth, my insides just as much.

"Hey."

"Hi," she said.

Her nose red, she looked so happy when she pulled away. More of that glow. Her pregnancy was in full bloom and I enjoyed the moments I got to endure in her pregnant bliss, holding her and the baby nightly, whether it be at her duplex or my home in the burbs. We'd been quite frequent visitors of each other's dwellings lately and we did spend a lot of time just being with one another and the baby. Her bump was still quite subtle and today, her jacket hid it in its entirety.

We were right around fourteen weeks, and like myself, Johari had been keeping the pregnancy under wraps. Her signing of the NDA had nothing to do with that. From what I could tell, Johari didn't want to complicate things until she had to in regards to the people of her life, her family in particular and I respected that. I had been more so doing the same thing for the most part. This was all so new to us, neither one of us having children before. And well, we recently decided to co-parent. We'd be raising the baby together. As far as in what capacity, we hadn't hammered out the details yet. We were focusing on us first. Us and this new experience.

I pressed fingers into her back, smiling at the young boy. "So are you going to introduce me to this guy?"

She laughed, rubbing her brother's back. "Javan, this is Alexander. Say hi."

He lifted his hand, kind of shy about it when he said, "Hey."

I greeted in a nod, sliding him a, "Hi there," which made his beam even brighter. I tell you, this kid could break down the strongest man's walls with his glee. It couldn't be helped.

Bending, Johari threw an arm around him, but stared up at me. "Alexander is my boyfriend."

*Boyfriend,* she'd said and this I didn't find myself minding. Not at all.

She moved on to squeeze Javan's shoulder, cupping his ear. "And he's here to get us ice cream!"

If this woman didn't unleash the magic words. Not only did I get an excited, "Yeah!" But also a fist pound, so I knew I had to deliver.

We ended up at what had become one of Johari's favorite spots. I seemed to have gotten her hooked on the ice cream at the Wrightwood Hotel, but seeing as how I found myself getting a scoop or two delivered to the car when she had me do the occasional runs I didn't mind.

We stopped there on the way to drop off her brother at home, the bowls of vanilla bean sweet cream devoured. Via Johari's directions, we pulled up in a neighborhood on the west side of town; it was lived in but not run down in the slightest. I actually frequented the area since I jogged just a block or so away from where those wonderful pieces of graffiti art resided.

I parked my Jag in front of a white house with gray shutters. "End of the line. Final stop for last minute passengers."

"Wait, wait! That's me. Don't forget to let me off."

Chuckling, I turned a little to my excited passenger in the back seat. "All right, bud. You can get off, but only if you promise we can do this again sometime."

I threw my hand behind me, getting a slap on the hand and an exuberant, "Yes!"

We bonded a bit, this kid and I. Johari ended up being out of the conversation most of the ride. He seemed to be a car guy as much as myself. We'd chatted about everything from hotrods to Porsches; this kid really knew his stuff and I admired that.

Through the rearview mirror, I watched Javan unbuckle his seatbelt, then go for the door.

Johari unstrapped as well. "Hold on, tiger. I gotta get your backpack out of the back seat."

"Oh, I can get it." I unfastened, pausing when I got a touch to my shoulder.

Johari waited until her brother got out of the car, but then her fingers came around the back of my neck. Our lips met briefly, but that did nothing to subside the feelings exchanged, the fire in my blood.

I held her side, making it all last for as long as I could before allowing her to pull away.

She said nothing, just smiled at me before getting out of the car and I took that for I did well today.

We did well together.

A click of my door, then I made my way to the back, retrieving a backpack for a more than excited little kid.

I handed it to Javan and he gave me another fist pound. He sprinted off like lightening after that, ascending the steps of that white house and Johari shook her head.

"Let me go make sure he gets in okay," she said. "I'll say goodbye to him and then—"

"Well, if it isn't the white boy who's dating my girl."

A casual stride in his step, the man clearly trying to get our attention walked down the street. He had his hand in his pocket, cautiousness apparent in his gaze.

I held the same hesitance, eyeing him. I pushed my hand around Johari's hip and a flick of his eyes made his awareness of that known. He stamped down the sidewalk toward us in the thickest boots, his puffy down coat giving the illusion of his size being about three times bigger than he actually was. When he got to us, he came about to my shoulders, but one would never be able to tell that with the way he stood up to me, sized me up.

Johari moved toward him from my hands before I could say anything and I had definitely been about to. This man disrespected me. I had no clue who he was and he only made my interest intensify at the way in which he regarded me.

Jo shook her head, pushing her arms over her coat. "Don't pay him any mind, Alexander. I haven't been his girl in almost ten years."

He panned her way, a gold chain shining around his neck despite the cloudy day. "But you admit you were, so I stand by what I said."

The summation had her chuckling, her eyes lifting to the heavens. "Right. Anyway, he's just messing with you."

Messing with me or not, I didn't really like how he approached me. But despite that, I could be the bigger person. Pulling my hand out of my pocket, I stuck my hand out to him. "I believe introductions are in order."

My hand stood in the wind at first, but eventually, he put his out, shaking strongly.

"Jared," he said, sounding disinterested as he tilted his head at me.

Johari kicked his boot. "Quit playing, fool. Alexander already knows about you. How we used to date."

The name hadn't clicked at first. He initially stated Johari was his girl, but the vague statement could have pinned him anywhere in the timeline of her past. But this was *the* guy, the one she told me about.

Squeezing his hand, I smiled before stepping back. "The drug dealer, correct?"

I hadn't meant much by it, stating fact, but I definitely got this man's attention. I got his as much as he'd gotten mine and imagine my surprise when his initial shock at what I said transformed into something else, a subtle smile on his lips when he stepped back and returned his hand to his pocket.

"Touché," he said, tipping his chin. "Me one, white boy one."

I hadn't been keeping tally, but if he wanted to all right.

The whole exchange had Johari grinning a little. She pushed a thumb behind herself. "I'm going to say goodbye to my brother. And Jared?"

His eyes flicked in her direction.

"Stop being foolish."

Surprise touched his eyes when he lifted his hands. He shook his head and Jo waved him off before popping up on her toes and kissing my cheek.

"I'll be back," she said. "And he's just messing with you. He means no harm."

I appreciated the warning, but something told me I got that on my own. He came at me one way, but ended in another. These two had a history, but whatever that had been seemed long in the past. She left us both, heading up the stairs and I leaned back against my car, waiting.

Jared shoved his other hand in his jeans. "Can you answer a question for me?"

I removed my gloves, warming my hands a little. "Depends on what it is."

A smirk touched his lips. "My girl in there," he said tipping his chin. "You serious about her?"

That one I could answer, returning my gloves to my hands before burying them deep in my trench coat's pockets. "Very much."

"And no funny business? She's isn't some side piece for you?"

I watched the house. "She's the only woman in my life." Though there could be the possibility of another.

We hadn't found out the baby's gender yet after all.

Jared bobbed his head twice at that and then, backing away, he sat on the stairwell of one of the neighboring houses Johari went into. He lit up something a bit more than a cigarette after he sat, watching me over the smoke.

"Where y'all meet?" he asked, offering me a hit.

Denying, I raised my hand. "A business arrangement. It eventually turned into something more."

"Hmm."

His cheeks hollowed on the drags, the cool air filled with the sharp current. I let him have his moment to himself, but a cracking door killed the silence.

I assumed Johari would be coming out that door. She just went in after all, but a woman came out, a black woman of slight age. Especially around her eyes. She wore a colorful wrap around her head, a hesitation in her eyes I took for only distrust. I assumed because she beamed the expression directly at me, a complete stranger to her only paces away from her position on the porch. I realized I had seen her before, as well as the soft features that made up her face.

My girlfriend had nearly every one.

I took a step away from my car, removing my hands from my pockets. "Good afternoon, ma'am."

My greeting, "Good afternoon," did come back to me, but not without hesitation, as well as a cool stare to tag alongside it. Her eye contact broke as quickly as politely allowed, and then she went about her business. She descended her porch steps in house slippers, crossing the sidewalk to get to her mailbox in front of the house.

I got no more acknowledgements after she got her packages, but Jared sure did.

She stared at him, but he made no motion to move.

Nor did he stop taking his hits.

He simply nodded once at her, taking a deep drag on his blunt and all that did was send the woman into the deepest of scowls.

I ended up getting a little of it too I was so close.

Grunting, she walked away, her house slippers scraping the walk. She paid us no attention after that. She went back into the house as quickly as she'd come and my curiosity of her only heightened. She'd been one of the women outside that night I kissed Johari and I had a sneaking suspicion of who she was, especially after Jo said one of the ladies had been her mom. She'd also held Javan's hand that night.

*That must be her.*

"A nice little piece of work that one, right," Jared said, pulling me out of my thoughts. He put out his blunt under his Timberland boot.

I leaned back to my car. "Johari's mom?"

"The one and only. A straight pill. She ain't never liked me much. And good luck with that yourself."

Not understanding, I shrugged and Jared chuckled.

He stood, pushing his hands into his puffy coat. "Let's just say you don't got as much pigment as she's used to. So that's already a check against you."

I guess I couldn't say that didn't make sense. I had run into the same obstacles myself with my own family. It seemed it didn't matter where we lived or how we'd been raised. Johari and I'd have the same judgment no matter our backgrounds. I supposed my mom was right, but that's where her correctness stopped. I wasn't ignorant to the world around me and though it was unfortunate, I'd be ready to deal. I didn't have to come home to those people and neither did Johari. Knowing that, them and all their judgment, meant they were non-factors. They were insignificant, at least when it came to this issue.

"Then there's just the fact that the woman has issues. She treats Jo like shit."

Jared got my attention again, my head tilted.

"How so?"

He shook his head. "Just straight cold on her. She cares, but she's like ice to Johari." He shrugged. "I always figure it was because her girl did better."

"Better?"

He faced me. "Better than her. Better than she ever did for herself. A lot of us want to get out of here and well, Jo actually did. She is getting out, doing her doctor thing."

I thought about that, watching as Jared passed me, and surprisingly, he put out his fist, waiting for me.

I pounded it.

"Look out for her," he said. "I don't trust you, but I trust my girl so that's enough for me."

I appreciated that and very much respected it, respected him. My snap judgments of before came to the forefront of my mind, me assuming something about him because of what my brother found out.

It seemed one couldn't judge people on paper, their character.

"I will," I told him and he smiled, just slightly at me.

"Don't get in her way," he said. "She's let too many people do that to her, me and her mama included."

I could imagine he was referencing the pregnancy, the pair of them getting pregnant so young.

I stared up at a white house, a home with a mother and her children inside it. I didn't know how her mom had gotten in her way, but with her chill, her cold…

I think I had an idea.

## Fifteen

**Johari**  His flavor explodes in my mouth at first taste, the smooth steel of his cock sliding along the bumps of my tongue. I loved doing this for Alexander, his rough pants and offers up of submission.

Under my lashes, he was beneath me, a hard chest gleaming in sweat and stomach tightening in six perfect sections of rock. Did I say six? I meant, eight. He could easily make me forget his strength when he was like this, hot and bothered. An iron bicep reached up, his fingers fisting his hair while his other hand came down on the back of my head. He fought his strength then—that powerful drive he could jolt into his hips in a single sharp thrust. His tongue curled and ran over sweat beading above his upper lip.

"Come to me," he said, twisting his fingers in my hair. He tugged, trying to force me off him but I wasn't ready. I enjoyed his taste too much.

I sucked, the salty twang of his pre-cum setting me off and sending an intense heat deep into my tingling pussy. The pregnancy made me so wild these days, unable to be sated unless I had him at least once a day, unless I had this.

The mushroom head touched my throat and I gagged, making him call out.

"Johari, come."

*No.*

Bobbing above him, I played with his fleshy sac, gathering the loose flesh with a ready palm, and he groaned, my hair pulled at the root striking a shockwave through me. I could do this all day, listen to him all night while he said my name and let me please him. Alexander tended to like to do all the pleasing. He didn't like submitting and I found such a challenge in breaking him of that. It turned me on to no end.

When his calls became too much, I thought about turning back, giving in and letting him turn this whole thing around, but I stayed for the long hall.

His hand gripped my naked bottom with the first few jets of his release and pain struck me deep in my core, my own release building.

I held it back, slurping and swallowing him down and he allowed me, his dark hair mussing on the silky sheets of his California king. I rather enjoyed making love in his bed. It allowed him to stretch out, his vast frame covering nearly both ends with his length.

His teeth coming over his bottom lip, his hand released my scalp a little. His eyes opened and I watched awareness come back with a blink of his warmly colored eyes. Eventually, he saw me. He braced my shoulder and pulled me up to him.

He kissed me sweetly then, his mouth swollen from the number he did on my own mouth earlier tonight.

I had never been kissed more softly or intimately than exchanges with this man. It was like he wanted me to feel it, really let me know how he felt and how he wanted me to feel.

Parting, he brushed my ear when he moved his lips. He stated nothing but a, "Your turn," before pushing me on my knees. Sex could still be done missionary at this point in my pregnancy, but there were few men who didn't enjoy doggie-style.

I guess he and I had that both in common.

Hands spreading my cheeks wide, Alexander sent a sharp current of air directly into my sex and soon, he tongued my folds and sent shocks across my vision.

An intense ache left my throat, my thighs quivering as he widened me and pulled me apart for him. His tongue tunneled, burying deep within and I submitted, pushing my bottom up and offering my heat to him. He enjoyed that, gripping my ass and I cried, his name a rough ballad from my lips.

He rose up, his harsh weight on my back. He slid in easily after that, perfect entry into my core and how much I loved the feeling of him. We stopped using condoms after appropriate testing, the chance of pregnancy obviously not a fear, and how that made the experience so different. I felt so close to him, no separation and the feeling tugged at my heart every time.

Water coated my eyes at that first slap to the back of my thighs, Alexander balls-deep within me. He grabbed my breast, nipping my shoulder and I put my hand over his.

He played with my pussy from the front, tender strokes to my clit and I couldn't breathe. I could only feel. I could feel Alexander, his hand between my thighs and his massive body caging me in, caring for me and loving me.

His hand escaped my tender flesh and rested on my stomach. My little bump wasn't so little anymore, though still modest at fourteen weeks. Each day the baby's presence was there and these intimate moments with Alexander made the whole thing so emotional. I was feeling my child more and more every day and…

It was wonderful.

Alexander kissed my shoulder, grinding his hips with vigor, making me sore, and making me feel wonderful. Suddenly, his fingers were in between my thighs again. But they weren't there long. He stroked me once, his finger gathering my juices.

His hand maneuvered behind and I felt the smallest finger between my cheeks, him already filling the opening below it. He knew what that did to me and his pinky invading my ass caused jolts to power through my entire body. I was done. He made me done.

His pinky probed, his hips doing the rest and he whispered, "Come for me. Come with me."

He shot off again, warmth so deep within. Nothing should feel this good. Nothing should be this powerful.

His release was long, intense along with mine and we fell together.

We rested as one.

Something woke me up and it wasn't my phone. I had set an alarm for tonight, an appointment I couldn't miss when the hour got a little later. Alexander and I turned in early, but I intended on getting up before the day. I had made arrangements to call a couple of good friends, but the alert on my phone didn't wake me for the appointment. Something else did.

Something under my hand.

A faint but present sensation moved within me, a timid vibration soft as if a flutter of wings.

I focused on it, my hand on my belly and when those wings flapped again, I froze.

*No way.*

Closing my eyes, I couldn't feel the movement with my hands, but I knew it was present. The awareness rose deep within.

I covered my mouth, the water burning my eyes from the influx of forming tears.

*I can... I can feel...*

"Alexander?"

I called for him, feeling for him behind me. My touch ran cold and I turned, his place on the bed empty.

I ripped away the sheets quickly. I knew he wouldn't be able to feel the presence. But I wanted him to know.

*I can feel the baby. I can feel.*

Leaving the room, I poked my way into every entry, Alexander's high-rise condominium intricate, but there weren't a whole lot of spaces he could hide. My feet slapping the polished floor, I quickened my steps, my hand on my stomach.

"Alexander—"

A light down the hall took my attention, the bathroom right at the entryway of his handsome dwelling. We had a closer bathroom, the master connected directly to his bedroom, but maybe he got up to get a drink and headed there right after. The kitchen was close by.

I went there, cradling my belly and those flutters seemed to flap with my excitement.

*Almost there.*

My hand touched the door, moving to knock. There was absolute silence in there, then what sounded like a soft moan, a grunt. A sigh followed and I stepped back.

"Alex—"

The door opened and he was there, the epitome of male perfection with tousled hair and sweatpants hanging low on his hips. He was barefoot, wide chest before me, but how he presented himself stopped me from touching him or sharing words about the baby.

Shallow but definitely present breaths left his lips, his face flush and lids pink above.

Opening my mouth, I went to ask if he was okay, but his soft smile cancelled the words.

He brought me in, trim beard tickling my forehead with this kiss.

"What's up? You okay?" he asked, pulling away. A hand came to rest on my back and his breathing had leveled out. He seemed fine now.

*Maybe it had just been in my head.*

My excitement couldn't linger and I fused my fingers with his, bringing them over to my belly. I lifted my t-shirt and placed his hand right there, the very spot of the fluttering sensation.

"Jo?" he questioned.

"I felt it," was all I told him. "I can feel."

His brow jumping, he let his hand settle then, moving closer to me. Like I said, he couldn't possibly feel it. But it seemed him knowing about the movement had been enough. Dampening his mouth, he kissed me again on the forehead, the smile on his lips moving to my neck.

He pulled me in against that doorframe down the hall, the two of us just holding each other. Just holding the baby.

Emotional, I didn't fight him when his finger moved up to remove a tear from my eyes. This was all just so wonderful, something so new and amazing.

He kissed my lips, strong hands caging my face.

"Our little soccer player woke you up, huh?" he asked, his words warming my mouth.

I nodded, laughing through my tears. I was going to get up anyway, but this was an excellent alarm.

His flavor potent, I enjoyed the taste of it, trying so hard to drench us both with the emotion clouding my eyes. Eventually, I got myself together enough to pull back, asking him something.

I placed my hands on his chest. "Everything okay? You weren't in bed."

Blinking, it was like he just seemed to notice that. "Yeah, fine. I'm about to head back there. Just finishing up."

Not wanting to impose, I gave him his space, but he caught my bed shorts between two pinched fingers. He tugged me back.

"Thank you for telling me," he said. "About the baby."

"Thank you for this."

A light touched his eyes when I said that, and though he smiled it didn't quite reach his eyes. He gave me a chaste kiss, then backed into the bathroom. He waited, closing the door until I cleared and I headed back the way I came, shaking my head with my hand on my stomach. Today was already such a special day. And now to have this…

My grin wouldn't stop as I made my way into Alexander's living room. Cushy, his home had the layout of a skilled designer's hand and I was awed by the handsome furnishings and ornate sconces softly illuminating the walls in their late night setting. Alexander had a view of the entire city of Chicago up here, *Ricci Financial* in sight before Lake Michigan went wide ahead.

I got my workbag, imaging a life in which I woke up to it every morning. I could imagine that. How so much had changed. Only months ago I had been heading into my final year of med school and now, I was imagining a life of yes, more complications, but very much more fulfillment. Talk of the immediate future hadn't been exchanged too much between Alexander and me. We were going by days, not wanting to rush.

Booting up my computer, I was about to find out where my friends were going to be headed to next, the people I met along the way on this medical school journey. I had made friends all over the globe in forums and other chat rooms who were going through medical school such as myself, and most of them had recently gone into the match. They'd be finding out where they'd be placed for their residencies in a matter of months, and all so busy, tonight was the night we chose to talk about where we were going. I was excited to hear what fields they decided to focus on. These people had gotten me through some of the most intense trials and tribulations of school. We were all the dearest of friends, each other's resources in this tough world of medicine.

*Wait until they hear about this.*

My hand on my belly, I smiled. Many of them knew I wasn't entering the match this year to work for a year, my intention to get caught up financially before moving away from everything and everyone I had ever known. But none knew of this new development, the baby. So many things had changed.

I guess I had a little, too.

I actually wanted to get their opinions on some things. I had been thinking about a lot of stuff since getting pregnant, finding Alexander.

*Come on. Just one more time.*

Like the baby heard me, those soft flutters started again and my heart squeezed. Hands came down my arms and I sat back with them.

"You're not going to bed?" Alexander asked, coming around. He took the chair next to me, putting a hand on my stomach.

I smiled at his automatic response to do that. He did that a lot, reaching for both the baby and me at the same time.

I couldn't stop my heart from bursting, watching him.

"Not immediately," I said, checking the status of my connection.

Alexander's brow furrowed and I tipped my chin at the monitor.

"I'm talking to some online friends about the match," I said. "Where they intend to go. They're all over the world so this is the best time for all of us."

Alexander knew all about the match process, as I talked about it from time to time in passing.

"I also want to mention the baby. Though, I won't go into

detail for the obvious."

This made him chuckle.

Moving in, he separated himself from the baby, grabbing my hands.

"I hope you're not referencing the NDA. You know, we're beyond that. You can tell anyone you like."

I figured that was unsaid. This was no longer a business relationship and hadn't been for a while. I got the funds, but had only used what was needed to pay back Jared. He used that to settle his debt with Hakeem, no more fears there. The man only wanted what was owed him and after he got it, he went about his way, my brother and Jared's brother Erick no longer on his radar.

The money settled after that, the initial money Alexander gave me. I didn't know why at the time. We weren't dating then. Maybe my heart just knew. We had no more transactions.

It was just us now—us and the baby.

"Yeah, but this situation is kind of complicated. I figured a regular, 'I'm pregnant' wouldn't suffice."

His dimple pushed up into his cheek before dark hairs started.

"I guess I get that," he said, kissing my hands before lowering them. "Your top picks are in California, right? When you go into the match next year?"

Again, something I had explained to him.

"Mmhmm. Family practice."

His smile always made him so handsome, his eyes lighting up. "You'll be good at that."

I knew I would. I had been working so hard for it. But life did throw you curveballs sometimes and when it did, sometimes adjustments needed to be considered. I didn't anticipate getting pregnant and definitely not meeting him, loving him. That's what I wanted to talk to my friends about, what was next for me, their advice.

Absentmindedly, Alexander's fingers came to rest against my belly again and I grabbed them, kissing the back of his hand. "We should talk about all that."

His eyes left the monitor. We'd both been watching it, the welcome screen coming up.

He tilted his head. "What exactly?"

"My match, the process. The baby. Us? I've been thinking about it and I wouldn't mind holding off."

"Holding off? What do you mean?"

What did I mean?

I chewed my lip a little.

"I guess holding off on California and going into the match at all. A life of medicine will always be there. It will always be there for me when I'm ready." The words felt weird to say, but not exactly bad. Medicine would always be there, but this… him…

Dark lashes shifted, his thoughts taking him away for some reason. I wanted to know his take on what I said, but I had to say, he wasn't giving me much.

His hand came down his beard, his lips tight with his silence, my belly jumped a little.

The baby wasn't the cause, though. Far from it.

A ping chimed on my monitor and that caused him to look up. He fell out of his thoughts then, taking my hand.

He kissed the back of it.

"We'll talk about it," he said, and then stood. Cradling my head, he moved in to brush a kiss on the crown.

The feeling I enjoyed, but the dismissiveness of the action not so much. He was being dismissive, rushing away.

Letting go, he smiled at me. "Don't stay up too late, okay?"

We weren't finished, but he was right. I did have a call. I watched him walk away, a slowness in his step, and thoughts of why faded at the sound of many voices. My friends had chimed in on the call.

*I guess we'll talk about everything later.*

My phone's alarm buzzed me awake before work, but the crick pulsating in my neck made me linger under the sheets a bit longer.

I rubbed at it, a sleep-fog keeping me out of it and gazing around an empty bed, I didn't even recall getting there. I stayed awake a pretty long time last night and the last thoughts I recalled were in front of my computer screen.

I groaned feeling for my phone. A message typed on the front kept me from the time and I waited for the blurriness to leave my eyes.

"You stayed up too late," the message said, then, "but don't worry. I think I got to you before you spent too long sleeping on your computer. I took you to bed around two o'clock. The aspirin is for your neck, by the way. Hopefully, it helps relieve any if at all soreness. I'll see you after work. I love you. - Alexander."

The aspirin was where he said it was, two small tablets on a china saucer and near that a tiny daisy.

I brought that daisy to my nose, the fresh scent humming through my senses. My friends assured me last night that any decision I made would be the best for me. They told me to take my time with it and that I had their support either way. They also granted me their well wishes, love for me, the baby, and Alexander.

I had been working toward something for a long time, which was why I *still* couldn't make any permanent decisions about rearranging the details of my career. Say I stayed and did work here, I would be saying goodbye to California and my goals of being there, working there.

I stared at Alexander's text and I knew *that's* what made this decision so hard.

Because I loved him, too.

*He said we'd talk about it. Everything will be okay.*

I wouldn't let myself linger on any decisions later on that day when I got to work. There would be no point in having anxiety surrounding all the thoughts which would have no solutions until talked about later anyway.

Upon closing my locker, I lingered in the break room for a bit after changing into my scrubs. I wouldn't have too many more shifts at the hospital, my education almost done. Very soon, I would have to make some decisions, big ones and not just for me.

I settled my hand on my stomach. Roya hadn't been too much help these past few weeks either. Truth was I didn't need support.

I needed someone to tell me what to do, what was right.

Someone coming into the backroom had me dropping my hand and looking over my shoulder.

Our gazes intermingled immediately, myself and Dr. Radcliff.

Blinking, she simply stared at me. I believed surprised, surprised to stumble upon someone. Maybe even surprised to see me. At such a busy hospital, we managed to be passing ships. I didn't even see her in the NICU whenever I visited Roya these days, too many passing bodies and shifts.

I nodded at her, which she returned before going over to her own locker, her white coat over her shoulder. It seemed I was coming in and she was leaving.

I rolled the dial on my lock once, securing it, before deciding to take care of some unfinished business.

The doctor had her back to me when I approached her and like before, my presence ran unexpected across eyes behind thick blonde curls.

"Is everything all right?" she asked, a curiosity in her gaze. I could only describe this event as unusual. Me approaching her wasn't common.

I smiled a little, wanting to put her at ease. Things were good partially because of her.

"I just wanted to send a thanks your way."

Her hand slid down the locker door a little. "A thanks, Johari?"

I nodded, shrugging. "I mean, you came to my rescue all those weeks back and I know I thanked you already that day, but…"

"It was no problem," she said, waving what I said off when she widened the locker. She put her white coat in there, exchanging it out for a jacket better suited for the weather. "Anyone would have acted."

"But that anyone happened to be you. Not only that, but you made a house call. That means a lot to me, a lot to us."

No longer distracted, her gaze panned over to me, my hands smoothing down and framing my belly over my scrubs. The pregnancy usually could only be seen that way, the bump still modest.

Her hand leaving her locker, she tilted her head in my

direction.

"Everything's all right then? I mean okay, with you and uh, the baby?"

Her asking, wanting to know meant something in ways she'd never know. The doctor had always been so dry. But perhaps, that's why she worked with babies and was so ready to help me considering my... interesting situation. She had a soft spot for babies.

I supposed we both shared that.

I ran my hands over my tummy.

"More than okay. I guess a simple panic attack couldn't get us. I'm super embarrassed about that. I definitely should have known what was happening, but when you're in it..."

"You forget," and she said it as if she knew, as if she understood and I was sure she had. She was a doctor.

Her fingers played with her jacket's hem. "I'm glad you're all right. You still have a long road ahead, from what I remember. Just consider this a small speed bump along the way."

So encouraging of her to say and she remembered where I was in my pregnancy. I had to commend her on that and a spark of respect grew for this woman but not because she was my superior. I admired her on the most basic level, a woman and a human being. This was an unusual situation I put her in considering she used to date Alexander and though their history was unknown to me, she definitely didn't have to step in and help me. She did, though, and beautifully.

I figured we were done here. I had bothered her enough, but I turned at another surprise, which fell from her lips.

"You recently put in for matches, right?" she questioned adjusting her coat's collar and when she did, she had a small smile on her lips. "Are you excited? It will be no time before you and your classmates will soon find out where you're placed."

And how this woman and her care surprised me again. I could only assume, as she knew how things were. She'd been through all this before, hadn't she? The craziness of the medical school and then near the end, the match.

"They will soon, yeah."

"'They,'" she said. This seemed to confuse her. "Won't *you* be one of them?"

"Not immediately no. I decided to take a little time off before going in. I plan to be matched out in California, which is a big move. I want to take time to prepare for it."

"So you'll be going in next year?"

The ultimate question and one I, myself, had no answer for at this moment.

"Maybe not," I started, and then didn't really know where to go with this conversation. It would get kind of awkward if I went any further, but I guess I had opened that door by being so forthcoming. But Dr. Radcliff seemed cool, though. She really did so maybe I didn't mind so much confiding.

"I decided to... to keep the baby."

This stopped her, her turning around as she'd reached for something in her locker.

Her eyes narrowed. "What does Alexander have to say about this?"

But as soon as she let the words go her eyes flashed. Like she realized she wasn't supposed to say them.

She waved her hand. "Never mind. It's... It's, uh, none of my business."

But I didn't want her thinking I was taking something from him. In fact, it was quite the opposite.

"We're seeing each other," came out of my mouth, and after it did, I had no thoughts of regret. We were seeing each other.

And I loved him.

Her lids slowly widened with that, her head lifting and lowering.

"I see," she said, turning back toward her locker. "And so you're staying here. Being placed *here*, and not uh, not California?"

"Maybe not at all," I told her. An inclining of judgment could be heard in her voice in her last statements.

Something I didn't like at all.

My hands fell from my belly. "I might be putting everything on hold. This was so unexpected. You know, the baby, and well, Alexander."

Something happened with every word I said, like I was

watching my body from outside myself and with each new bit of information I shared, I yearned to slow my pace, pull them back. I went on the defense, defense of *my* decisions and in doing so, I didn't take into account who I'd spoken with.

She was close to the issue, *too close* considering she dated the man I was currently with, and in all my attempts to let her know my decision was mine, I may have rubbed salt in the wound a bit that my life maybe, possibly could have been hers.

My stomach turned at the realization.

Feeling I did enough, I averted my eyes, rubbing my hands down my scrubs. "Anyway, thank you for everything again. I appreciate what you did for me, truly."

Her lips parted slowly, then she blinked away, too. "Of course. And good luck. Good luck with your decision."

Taking that for what it was, I decided to make my exit quick, the air in the room all but sucked out.

Mostly because of me.

"Johari."

My lids covered my eyes. Turning around, I faced her, surprised by the look she gave me. It was one of seriousness. In fact, I'd only witnessed doctors give it before sharing bad news with their patients. The expression was grave and because it was, it sobered.

She came forward. "I know this might be inappropriate, but I'm going to share something with you because I think you need to hear it. You're about to make a really big decision and I don't want you to make a mistake."

Slowly, I moved my arms over my chest. "What do you mean?"

Grabbing her bag out of her locker, she brought it up over her shoulder, her fingers playing along the strap a moment before she spoke.

She sighed. "I think you need to know something about Alexander and though, you might not want to hear it—"

"You're right. I don't," I said, cutting this off as I felt I knew where this was going. And she was right. This was inappropriate. "If you have something negative to say because you guys used to see each other…"

"It's not about being negative, Johari."

Her voice chilled in the air with its volume, striking me still and making me silent.

She pushed her golden curls out of her eyes, breathing a little. "It's not about me throwing him under the bus or whatever you're thinking. It's about you and the decision you are about to make based on your feelings for someone you clearly don't know because if you did…"

She dampened her lips, her fingers moving over them. "Alexander and I dated off and on through grad school, then later when he matured up enough to have just one woman on his arm. I ended up being that one woman and things did get serious. But I went into the relationship with a complete understanding. Settling down wasn't an option for him at that moment in his life, and children might not ever be. He expressed that, adamantly from the beginning. He didn't want them. I think that may have had something to do with his father. Though, he wouldn't admit that. It was just something I picked up over the years watching them together. Well, before his dad passed."

Lost, I had no words for what she was saying. He didn't want kids…? Ever? But that was so different now. He was so different.

I put my hand on my belly. His care, his current affection for our unborn child couldn't be more opposite.

Lowering toward the benches in front of the lockers, my thoughts were strewn, tossed about in a maze.

Dr. Radcliff closed her locker.

"I honestly thought he'd get over that," she said, taking the bench beside me. "And I guess with you he eventually did but…"

Her head shook, eyes gazing up. "He wasn't when he was with me. He absolutely did *not* want children, but that's the thing about life. Sometimes you don't get a choice."

I didn't understand, my eyes narrowing.

She went on.

"I got pregnant eventually. *We* got pregnant and Alexander…" Her teeth went over her mouth. "Well, he wasn't happy. We were going to have this child he didn't want and…"

Her words flustered her, this conversation got to her. Dr. Radcliff was always so put together, but this… this was shaking her.

It was rattling her.

She swallowed, staring up at me. "I lost the baby, Johari. Didn't even make it to my first trimester."

I had… absolutely nothing to say to that. We shared something there, something so tragic.

*He never said anything.*

I didn't understand, shaking my head.

Watching the woman who told me, I saw that loss there, deep in her blue eyes while she stared empty ahead.

My lips parted. "I'm sorry."

Her nose red, she sniffed a little, but no tears did this woman shed.

She all but pushed them away, facing me. "I'm sorry, too, Johari. I'm sorry I wasn't strong enough, strong enough to stand up to him."

*Him.*

The word chilled and I didn't get it. I wouldn't, I…

Her jaw moved. "Alexander made me get an abortion."

The world stopped mid rotation, my reality cancelled on a single tilt. She couldn't be telling the truth. No, she was lying.

"He…" The words dried over my mouth and I swallowed empty air. "He *made* you."

Her hands rubbed down her pants. "In so many words."

Her smile was crooked, sad when she looked up. "He didn't flat out tell me, but the insinuation was definitely there. The pressure."

"But he didn't say it. He didn't actually tell you to get one." I was grasping at straws, I knew. But this wasn't Alexander. This wasn't *my* Alexander, someone so warm and loving.

Dr. Radcliff crossed her legs. "He didn't want children, Johari. He didn't and he put the pressure on me to end the pregnancy. He didn't drive me to the clinic. He didn't physically remove the baby from me, but make no mistake that Alexander Ricci ended it. And I can only gather now that all this, with you…"

She stared at my stomach then and my hands went over myself, protecting.

She sighed. "Are the actions of someone who recently stared death in the face and is trying to make things right. You know he was sick, right?"

I nodded, dampening my mouth.

"So nothing he does can be taken at face value. He's just recently recovered, Johari. I'm sure he's all over the place, confused, and do you want to be on the other end of it when he gets it all back and changes his mind? Goes back to that bachelor life and leaves you stuck with a child… and no career?"

Words ticked at my throat, but grew lost at the many thoughts that circulated my brain. The thoughts rang heavy on me, hurting intensely, vigorously…

And did nothing to alleviate the current vise-like squeeze of my heart.

"Just think about it," she said, standing up. "Think about the choices you make now. Because after you do, you might not get a do-over. I most definitely didn't."

Her words had me aching, shuddering and I couldn't defend myself, defend him. How could I when I didn't know the whole story and how dare I when I knew exactly what she'd been through? I couldn't. My consciousness of her pain, the for sure *ache* she had to have for the loss of her child…

She stepped away after that, turning briefly to say only one more thing.

The "Sorry," that left her lips sat heavy.

Mostly because it sounded genuine.

# Sixteen

**Alexander** "What am I looking at?"
I stared out the window of the small downtown practice. I reached for the day. I sought for the light, but I couldn't find it among the passing cars.

In my peripheral, my doctor could be seen taking a seat on the edge of her desk, her hands gathered in her lap.

"We'll start with hormone therapy. Then if we need to…"

"Chemo?" I questioned, finally facing her. I had been lost for a moment, a long one while staring out her window.

Dark hair sprinkled with graying strands framed an aged face.
The distinguished black woman nodded. "Correct."

My fingers moved up to cover my mouth, falling over the short, coarse strands of my beard. She didn't even put surgery on the table, nor radiation.

*It's beyond my prostate.*

I sat there, stark-still, at words I heard before and terms I chillingly knew the meaning of. No one should know these things. It just wasn't right and with my clear understanding of them, it was almost worse this time. It was worse because I knew what I was in for and more horrifyingly tragic because…

My thoughts pushed out other factors because if I went there, if I let them in for only a moment, I'd break down completely. This consultation would be over. I would be worthless, gone.

*I can't think about the baby… Jo.*

Dr. Bradbury's voice went far away after that, her explanations of what she found and where we were going pushed off into a fog, which couldn't be busted out of no matter how strong the fists. It was like I was watching everything happening in her office from behind a veil, outside of myself. I only came back when she touched my shoulder and only finally took in speech again with her next words.

"You must tell your family," she said. "You waited too late last time. You shouldn't try to deal with it by yourself for so long. You need support. Beating this is just as much mental as physical."

How could I? How could I ask for support when I was about to be someone else's support, two people in particular?

My days, my time continued on after that and they went very similarly. I saw no need for a change in routine, alarm, and wouldn't let myself go that route. I went to work. I lived my life, but hiding the symptoms…

That was the real struggle. I often had to cancel meetings, fear of letting on and allowing people in my circle to know, my colleagues and clients. There wasn't a week that went on without at least some type of symptom, various aches and pains and my doctor's constant calls didn't help in regards to keeping me out of my head. She wanted us to get going, start this process again while we had an early diagnosis, but I couldn't help thinking to what end? Would I be dealing with this issue my whole life? Would I constantly be told I was fine until I wasn't? I just knew right now I was fine. In my current state, I could live my life, but once I went into treatment again that was it. I had cancer again. I was sick and feeble and weak and couldn't easily succumb to that. I could deal with a little pain, to feel normal for a while longer—to *be* normal.

The hardest part was hiding everything from Johari. She was the closest. She was the toughest and my condition most definitely pushed a distance between us.

We didn't talk as much as we used to, examinations for the baby all but silent and my bed more empty than not. She chose to stay at her house most of the time. In fact, shortly after my most recent diagnosis.

*"You must tell your family..."*

"What do you think of this one?"

I blinked up, a small baby outfit held out in front of me. It was pink. We recently found out we were having a girl, a tiny angel.

*Get a grip on this and be present here. Today.*

Forcing myself into my body, the present, I scanned the tiny outfit in the busy department store. These trips were rare as Jo tended to make them by herself.

*By herself...*

I was already abandoning her, the baby.

Refusing to let myself think that way, I smiled at the outfit, then the woman behind it. Johari never looked more beautiful, her pregnancy really showing behind a floral top, which framed her small bump, and with that flush on her cheeks... just wow.

"I like it," I told her, trying to ignore the look behind her brown eyes, the questions.

I was getting those more and more as well.

Dr. Bradbury's consultation had been nearly a month ago.

Not thinking about it, my reality remained here. In fact, *this* was my reality. Jo, our baby, and me.

I reached for the tiny outfit. I would see my child in this.

I was determined to.

"Let me hold this for you," I told her, then took the initiative and reached over, pointing out another outfit I believed she'd like. I had to be here for her. I couldn't give into my personal weaknesses.

*Johari*    What he just did there... That distractedness that bordered on disinterest and even worse, dismissiveness...

He'd been doing that more and more, a call of his name distant in the wind with his thoughts and anything else, more of the same whenever talking to him. He heard nothing half the time and spoke to me even less, not even wondering why I stepped away, stepped back…

I started the conversation with him about what his ex had told me dozens of times over the past few weeks, but lost my confidence on the subject due to my fear of the outcome.

But why didn't I have the right to know? To have my questions about who he was at the heart answered. I had so much to learn about Alexander, but at least *thought* I knew what seemed the most important.

I believed I knew the man's heart, but if all of what Dr. Radcliff said about him was true, I wasn't sure I knew anything about him at all. That scared me to no end and so was my reason for my retreat. Once I opened that door, Pandora's box couldn't be closed. I would have to make a choice then and it had to be the right one. Our baby was the only person who mattered in this situation, the only person, and nothing else could be taken into account.

Least of all a broken heart.

Alexander held that baby outfit, so tiny in his hands as he followed behind me as I stepped through the aisles. At one point, he stopped, almost lost in the tiny jumper as he stared at it.

His large fingers brushed across the collar, his gaze all but empty.

Like he was out of it.

Most days, he didn't even look happy anymore. In fact, he looked miserable. Deep bags rang under his eyes, as if missing sleep. He was still polished, still perfect in the way he carried himself, but something was missing.

And he even seemed to be losing weight.

Those pretty clothes he wore hung loosely on what used to be the broadest shoulders, pressed pants hanging baggy on his legs. Something was clearly eating him up inside and I couldn't help wondering if it was guilt… me.

I closed my eyes away from the thoughts, so tired of the pretending. I didn't want him to pretend. If he wasn't happy, if he truly didn't want this anymore…

That baby outfit lowered to his side when he looked up, his smile crooked at me. "Remember when we said we'd talk? About you and California?"

My feet stopped immediately where I stood and my heart did something similar. The twinge went deep like a sharp crack to a wall and I had no idea why. Perhaps, it'd been the way he said it. He sounded so sad, almost conflicted.

He tapped the outfit in the center of his palm. That was how small it was. "We never did talk about it and I've been thinking about it. I've been thinking a lot."

*He's been thinking a lot. A lot.*

I had been thinking, too, but no options could be created in my mind about my final decision regarding my career. I had no solutions because things had gotten so much more complicated. I had so many things to talk about with him first.

His jaw moved a little, his cheeks hollowed. He really had been losing weight. Maybe even sleep too over this, though, I couldn't attest to that as I'd stepped away. I hadn't slept over at his house in what seemed like so long.

He swallowed. "I think you should go. I don't think your plans should change."

Breathing, I attempted to settle the current in my lungs. I swallowed, too. "You do?"

He nodded, fingers feathering through his dark hair. How even that seemed to lose its blackened color, his brown eyes faded as well.

"Medicine is what makes you happy," he said. "Medicine is what you've worked hard for and that's what you should do. You shouldn't change that. You should never change what you want."

But he had, hadn't he?

*My God... she was right.*

Turning away, I pretended to stare at the little baby outfits, something that used to make me feel so happy.

I covered myself. "So what does that mean for the baby?"

"What do you mean?"

I closed my eyes. "I mean, you here and me there. What does that mean for the baby?"

Because she was all that mattered. She... not the ache, never the ache.

"It won't affect the baby, Johari."

"How so?" He seemed to condescend me now, play with me. "If her parents aren't together…"

"No." He came to me so quickly, instantly, and with his haste, I had seen more presence in him than I had in literally weeks.

His hands came to my arms, burning me when he pulled them away from covering my chest. His hand on my cheek did the same, stabbed my heart the same.

He rubbed his thumb along the sensitive skin of my jaw. "I want to be with you. That hasn't changed. It's just…" He stared away for a moment. He looked up. "This would be temporary."

"Really?" I said, stepping back. I left his hands midair. "Then what? You come out to meet me? Leave your legacy here?"

"Maybe."

The whole thing was laughable, but I didn't partake. I thought it might set off a chain reaction, make me cry or do something else stupid like that.

My nostrils flared. "This plan clearly wasn't thought out."

He cringed, twitching as if I slapped him. "I'm just proposing what I think should be done. We can talk about the specifics. That's why I brought it up."

"I think you brought it up because it all was starting to really bother you. You were feeling… I don't know. Messed up and maybe even trapped by it. You said the first thing that came to mind without even really thinking about it."

His head shook slowly. "Johari…"

"Do you even want this baby, Alexander?" I came right out with it. And frankly, it should have been said weeks ago. If he didn't want this baby I had a right to know. If he didn't, he owed me that.

So many emotions rushed his handsome face—shock, confusion—but even with his dramatic changes, this man could still take my breath away. He could still take my heart.

His hand came down his sculpted beard. "What is this?"

"What is this?" I repeated, nodding my head at the words. "This is an out. This is me giving you permission. Because if you don't want this baby anymore, just tell me—"

"I don't know where this is coming from." He was angry now, angry at me. His face painted red, charged with emotion. "I don't understand why you'd ever say something like that to me. Why you'd ever question I'd... I'd want to be with you."

"I don't know, Alexander. Because maybe you haven't been here? Because you *haven't* noticed the baby or me and it gets worse every day. You're absent. You've checked out and I noticed you still haven't answered the question."

"I may have been busy, 'absent,' as you say, but I've never once given you a reason to think that I didn't want you, or the baby. This whole thing is ridiculous. This conversation, everything."

"But is it? Have you? Never given me a reason that is."

He shook his head and I came forward, my heart breaking every step. Mostly because I knew what I had to say and after I did, everything would change.

"Did you make your ex-girlfriend have an abortion?"

The shock ripped through his face, wrecking and tearing apart a man who already seemed so out of himself. I expected this to shake him, but not to break him down, shattered him.

The words started slow. "Who told you that?"

I noticed immediately he didn't deny it and I blinked away, a burning hot in my throat. "So it's true."

"No. I..." He started several sentences with his lips, but never once did he finish the statement. Never once did he defend himself.

His hand severed the air. "Who told you that? Was it Naomi? Did she confront you?"

"And what if she had? God forbid she tell me the truth. The truth about you and the shitty person you clearly are."

I fought to move around him, but he caught me, still so much stronger than me despite his clearly weakened state.

His hands came down on my shoulders. "Well, did she tell you that she stopped taking her pills? That she didn't care about how *I* felt or what we discussed as a couple about our future, one in which she completely agreed with. It wasn't until she got pregnant that I knew the truth, that she was telling me what I wanted to hear so she could—"

"Trap you?" I shook my head. "You arrogant son of a bitch. No woman would ever do that to her child, would put them in such a horrible position with their father for such selfish reasons."

"But she did," he said and though the words came out strong, not wavered, the expression on his face told how this was all affecting him, the conversation and the words I said.

He let go of me, his hands to his sides. "What is it you want to hear, Johari? You said you wanted to give me an out, but is this one for you?"

I twitched. "What are you talking about?"

His fingers came through his beard, his hand falling away. "Do you really want to know the truth or what you *think* the truth is? You must think I'm stupid. That I don't know how you made up your mind about who I was only nanoseconds after you knew my name. Do you want me to admit I didn't want children? Because I didn't. I grew up in a family with a father, though despite his love for his wife and children, was completely absent. And when he was there, it was all my brother and I could do to make him proud enough so he'd break away from work, making money, to pay us the briefest amount of attention. He did all that only to have the world not give a damn about him when he died despite all the time he sacrificed, time away from his kids and family, for them."

His words struck me silent and I only quieted when he got closer.

He pushed his hands into his pockets. "My dad, God rest his soul, was the only model I had for a father-figure. And wouldn't you know it? When it came to me, the apple didn't fall far from the tree. I knew my faults. I knew who I was as a person, so pardon me if I didn't want a life where my kids felt they needed to prove something to seem worthy of my time. I didn't want kids when I was with Naomi and I was very honest about that with her. Too bad she wasn't the same with me, because maybe, just maybe if she was truthful, there could have been a future there for us. There wasn't though because she lied and I was made out to be a selfish asshole who didn't want kids."

My throat closed up, no hope for any speech now.

But Alexander seemed to have enough for both of us.

"Is that what you wanted to hear?" he asked. "That I'm that guy? That asshole who made a woman do something she didn't want to do?"

"No. Of course I wouldn't."

"No?" He shook his head. "Well, I'm not. And you should go to California. You should live your dream and not let anyone stop you. Stop using this pregnancy or me, as an excuse to hold yourself back. My God, you'd think you would learn after almost being trapped here before. The baby you had with Jared and then the thing with your mom—"

"What thing?"

The words weren't meant to be said and I understood that the moment his lids covered his eyes. But by then, it had been too late.

He opened his eyes, pushing his hands into his pockets. "Jared talked with me the day we got Javan ice cream. That she has issues with you, holding you back, holding you here."

Leave it to him, huh? To intercede when he had no right. And now, he made me look weak in front of this man.

I could tell by the way he stared at me, actual sympathy in his eyes.

Pushing the cart, I attempted to move on, away from this, all this bullshit.

His hand stopped me, coming down on my shoulder.

"Jo—"

"Don't," I said, turning around. "And don't ever."

I had no idea what I meant by that. But when I pushed the cart down the aisle this time…

He chose not to follow me anymore.

# Seventeen

**Alexander** The phone rang the same time the knocks of an expected visitor drummed through my apartment and as the name struck no urgency within me to answer, I let the call fall to voicemail. Only one person calling got my attention these days and that hadn't happened.

Johari didn't ever call.

The word "Mom" stayed on the phone screen and I let that be the end of my focus on the device, choosing instead to go let the visitor into my home. Like I said, they were expected. The familiar coveralls and rounded figures of the movers filled the hallways leading into my high-rise. They tipped their hats to me, knowing what to do. This was the second day they'd been here, the last day, and they got right into finishing up. They pretty much packed away the small stuff, the big stuff such as my baby grand piano (more for looks than actually play) covered in white sheets. My kitchen counters and shelving all covered in the same material, the purpose to keep away the dust. No one would be here for a while. No one would be here to tend to it. The movers left the last room alone until today, the baby's room. I wanted a chance to pack up the baby's things myself, as they would go to a separate storage area. Only she would have access to that. Only Johari.

My chest vacuumed at the sight of an empty nursery, but not

because I spent so long on it. Truth was, I hadn't stepped foot in it until the last day Johari stayed here. It just didn't feel right, too many memories.

The day she first saw it came to mind, the first night she stayed in my home. Hand on her belly, the glistening chandelier had caught every bit of amber-coloring in her dark eyes, an awe on her face that got me every time I saw it. She took in the walls of colorful paper and the collages of art that moved with the intricacies of street design. I hadn't been able to get an actual artist in here. I hadn't had the time, but I got pretty close, she said that.

"You did all right," she'd said, a modest smile on her lips that told me I more than did just "all right." She told me we could perfect it as time went on. She said we had time. But we didn't have time and tragically, neither one of us knew it. That day had been perfection. That day had been the paradise of the unknown.

"Want us to get this?" one of the movers said, pointing at the silver crib still intact. It was the only thing that remained in the baby's room outside of packed moving boxes, those colorful walls of art bare now.

Moving my hands down my mouth, I shook my head. I could take care of breaking down the crib.

The man gave me a shrug that told him of how insignificant any of this was to him. He had a job to do and it wasn't to argue with me. He grabbed a box, and then his female colleague behind him grabbed another, the two of them leaving me in an empty room.

Needing a moment, I got a drink of water, the movers passing me by as they went in and out of rooms. My little items would go away to another storage unit, out of the way so when people came to clean occasionally they wouldn't have much to do. I wouldn't be here to move things around and keep them busy. I would be going into treatment soon and very much by myself.

I had people to tell about my illness, my condition, but also, like before, too many people to worry about me. It was that sole reason which kept me silent and alone in this new journey to get better again, get healthy.

I saw no point in telling others as my doctor advised. The

hormone therapy could work and I just wanted to do things this time around on my own terms. That meant going away for a while, my mind defaulting to familiar ways. My family's property in the country provided me with vast environment and the absence of the stresses of the big city. That's exactly what I needed. I needed the quiet, time to get myself together and give myself a chance of the therapy working. The doctor had been right about one thing, though. This disease was just as much mental as it was physical and my family there, stressing there, would just be a burden for my recovery. If I was forced to take more extreme measures of treatment, that's when I would call. This was the plan and I already wrapped my mind around the specifics of it. I needed to give myself a chance to lick this and then…

I could go back to the way things were, when they were perfect or at least, starting to get there. The only person I owed anything to in regards to an explanation was the woman I loved and I did love her.

I loved her enough to let her go.

My calls went unanswered since our fight at the department store, but I hadn't given up. I had a messenger set up with all the details regarding what was going on with me and where I would be. All the information was at the ready for her when she wanted to hear it. I'd left many messages letting her know that. If not ready, she'd find out anyway. She would when my legal representatives came to find her. I set up a plan for her and the baby. They'd always be cared for even if…

Swallowing, the water went down my throat thickly, but I made myself keep it in.

"We got the last of it," a mover said to me, a big box in his hands. "Just need the crib."

*The crib, yes. I should do that.*

I nodded to him, and then headed back in the direction of the nursery. I grabbed my phone on the way, figuring I would do all this like ripping a bandage off from a cut. I could break down the crib and listen to my mom's voicemail at the same time, getting them both over with.

The toolbox sat in the corner of the baby's room, already

there from previous use. The changing table had been broken down with it, as well as other items, which used to be in here.

I retrieved a screwdriver out, and then brought it over, laying my phone on the top of the box. After starting the voicemail, I squatted, going into loosening those tight bolts. My mom's accented voice traveled through the room and I took a moment. It had been a while since I talked to her.

"Hi, darling," she said, warm always, no matter the time that passed, nor the circumstances. Even when she was angry at me as a child, a softness always lingered in her European voice. "I know it's been a while, but I wanted to give you time considering how things were left between us before."

I fought myself from smirking, shaking my head while I loosened another bolt. How she downplayed how she disrespected me before, me, my baby's mother, and my future.

I ran my hand over the bars of the crib, then jingled, removing a bar quickly. I had to go quickly. I couldn't do this thinking.

"That day's sat heavy with me. You probably don't think so, but it has and I…" Her voice faded off for a minute, a pregnant silence in the air before she continued. "I want to talk to you about something I've found out. I went to our lawyers recently about some contractual tweaks I wanted made, our estate planners."

I closed my eyes slowly, my heart stopping as I anticipated her next words. Those were *my* lawyers, but they were hers, too. Like she said, they were our family's.

"You changed your will?" she questioned, and I blinked.

*How did she know? Did they tell…*

"Don't worry. No one told me," she started. "I snooped. Your file was on Ira's desk."

Ira… Our estate planner was old. He did tend to leave things around.

I sighed, pinching the bridge of my nose.

"You left it all to her?" she said, nearly whispering the words were so soft. "You left everything you have to her and… the baby?"

My weight settling to the floor told me I'd stopped breaking down the crib and my hand coming to my mouth let me in on why. Hearing it out in the open like that, the ache in my mom's voice, the anguish as if… she lost me for a second time.

"Are you okay, sweetheart? I mean…" Her voice stopped again and she took a moment. "Of course you are. You promised me. You promised you wouldn't keep anything like this from me again and if that's the case, that means you did this for other reasons. Reasons I probably should have listened to the first time."

I looked up, the phone so far yet only feet away. I reached, my fingers moving in the air. She wasn't there really, was she? Just her soft voice.

"You love her, don't you?" A shakiness touched her voice, an emotion that bled into the call. "You love her and I stomped all over that, didn't I? I stopped all over you and your decisions."

I moved my arms resting them over my raised knees. I had never heard her this way before. The soft hum of her voice rang heavy, almost dripping with something…

I took it for remorse.

"You know, I never told you but my parents disagreed with my marriage to your father. They thought he was too serious, too cold and stifled me in all my conquests. But these were my own father's, his goals for my life. I desired more of a simple one. I desired your father and what they saw as cold I read between. We shared something, your dad and I, something only the two of us got, and back then, what I would have given for someone else on our team."

Asa and I rarely did see my grandparents. In fact, we were only sent over to France to see them, my mom never along for the ride.

I gripped the screwdriver in my hand.

"I want to meet her, sweetheart. And I'm so sorry for how I've been, how I didn't understand. I just want to see you and the baby and your love. How is she coming along? Healthy I hope?"

She had been. Though, I had no recent updates.

How I missed her.

"We all need each other," Mom went on. "But anyway, please check in with me. I need to see you and your family. But if you aren't ready, if you need time, I do understand. I've hurt you and

I'm so sorry about that. I'm sorry for not understanding and not being on your team. I promise you I won't do that again."

One thing she had never done, never in my whole life was break a promise to me.

I supposed I had been the only one doing that.

A weight so heavy upon me before lifted and I hadn't even realized it had been there until the force alleviated. She delivered me something I didn't realize I needed. That was her support, her love.

I needed a member on my team.

That would make all this so much easier to deal with... endure again.

"And if you're not ready to speak to me at least contact your brother. You know how he worries."

I smiled a little, my nostrils flaring with emotion. One would never know I was the oldest, my brother always looking out for me, worrying.

*I had pushed him away too, hadn't I?*

I pushed everyone away, but it's the only way I knew how to deal with all this. It's all... It was all I knew.

I really was my father's son. He did the same thing. None of us knew he was sick until well...

He was pretty much gone.

My phone in hand, I dialed someone. I *did something* I shouldn't have been so scared to ask for before. And I was scared. In fact, terrified.

But I didn't have to go through it alone.

"Alexander, thank goodness you called."

That relief steadied an accented voice, as well as put hope in my heart. I was so much like my father.

But I didn't have to be him.

"Mom," I said swallowing. "I need to tell you something. And after I do, I... I need your help with something else."

# Eighteen

**Johari** I stared at the papers in wonder, baffled by the content they contained.

*This can't be right. He didn't...*

"Mr. Ricci is ready for you, Ms. Russell."

The young girl stood ahead of me, so familiar with her pleasant expression and professional demeanor. We'd done this before, she and I.

I wasn't a stranger to the *Ricci Financial* building.

Getting myself together, I grabbed the documents I had been too busy to look at. I all but brushed off the lawyer who approached me on my way out the door today. He said he had something important for me, a folder chock full of information, and once I realized who it had come from I wanted nothing to do with it. He'd said it was from Alexander and...

What if he was serving me with the same information I had been about to serve him.

Unreasonably hurt, I blew past the man in the smart suit and twisty white beard. He told me he was required by law to leave the paperwork for me and if I didn't take it, he would leave it by my door. That had been the only reason I took it, not wanting my neighbors or anyone else to get their hands on unidentified documents. They could have had my personal information on it or something and I couldn't take the risk.

I grabbed it in a hurry then, rushing past the man so I didn't miss my bus. I had been so rattled I just let the big folder sit there next to me. I couldn't deal with it then. I had my own worries that I had to brace myself for, my own burdens.

How I wished I looked at the papers, read them before coming.

I followed the young woman down a hall, her silky black hair flowing in a posh, high ponytail behind her. We'd gone behind familiar glass, but that's where all the familiarities stopped. Even still, I held my breath in the direction of Alexander's office. It had been right there. I could see it.

*Did he really...*

I fought myself from going in that direction to find him. I wasn't a lawyer and maybe I didn't understand all the documentation he had delivered to me. It had been in a bunch of legal mumbo jumbo that even this medical student couldn't take in. I just knew my name had been there, myself and references to our baby.

My hand rested on her, her form deep within but totally present. She made her presence known constantly now, no mistake that she existed. I came here for her. I did so because I didn't know what else to do. She'd be here in no time and then me leaving shortly after that. The year would go quickly and I needed a plan. I needed something in writing. I was scared. I couldn't take the risk I would lose her. I couldn't.

*The Estate of Alexander Carlo Ricci,* the document had said.

*Why would he leave it all to me?*

"Hello, Johari."

A Ricci had said my name, but it hadn't been Alexander.

His brother, dashing in every way a man could be, only remained subpar in my eyes. Not many men could hold a candle to Alexander Ricci's sweeping dark hair and captivating amber eyes. In fact, I wasn't sure many at all.

How ironic that he finally called me by my first name today, reaching out to shake my hand without any type of resentment in his eyes. He almost seemed jubilant about my presence. Perhaps, because he was happy, ecstatic by what brought me here and how this all turned out in the end. I was here to relieve his brother of a burden he never felt Alexander should have in the first place.

"You came to see me about a potential custody arrangement," he said, guiding me along. The administrative assistant left us and he led me to the door on the far side of his office. His office was grand, but not of the same standard as Alexander's. Where Asa's windows were large, Alexander's were larger, his vantage point bigger of the distant Lake Michigan.

I could say nothing in return as he led the way because I had been so frazzled in so many ways. Especially by the most recent, the room he took me into.

The boardroom I had been in before had my heart jumping into my throat by the familiar area, the history there. Alexander and I first connected here and for me, something even deeper blossomed even that early on. I was sure of that fact now.

Patent leather shoes stopped on hardwood as Asa Ricci turned around in a navy suit, which displayed the vast length of him.

"Don't worry," he said. "Alexander isn't in the building today and doesn't know you're here. He hasn't made an appearance around the office in weeks so him accidentally walking in won't be a problem."

*Weeks?*

And I didn't miss what sparked behind Asa's green eyes after he'd said the words or how his gaze drifted off into the room, his mouth a firm line.

He gestured to the table and I followed him, taking a seat on the other side. My documentation went on the top, but Asa was very much without anything in front of himself. He didn't even have a pen.

Upon stroking his beard, short, blond whiskers pulled through his fingers.

"So a custody arrangement," he said, placing his hand to the table. "You've decided you'd like something in writing in regards to co-parenting with my brother."

As I said, I had been scared. What if, when it came time after the baby had been born, Alexander decided to be vigilant and serve me with papers himself? And worse, what if he tried to take the baby away for some reason? He may not want her, but his family might decide they did. She had his last name and would have blood rights to anything he had.

That complicated things.

All this had been going through my head since the time of our fight and even before considering the unknown answers to his secrets of a life long before me.

I stared at the binder his lawyer presented me with, all that information so heavy on my mind. It seemed Alexander had been vigilant in the end, hadn't he?

"This is your right as the mother of the child," Asa went on. "But what I don't understand is why you sought me out for such a thing. My brother's funds could have provided you with any attorney you liked. I know because I drew up the figures for him."

Truth was, I hadn't touched that money since I paid off Jared. It didn't feel right. In regards to why I chose Asa, the decision was because I thought he'd help me. He never wanted Alexander to have this baby. Least of all with me and I thought I would have his support, his help.

He was also the only lawyer I knew.

My gaze still on that folder, that weight in front of me, I still said nothing.

"Johari—"

I pushed the folder toward him, all words coming in my direction ceased. Swallowing, I put my hand on it. "Read the document. Please."

Because I had been confused and ignorant to all the legal verbiage and he would understand it. There's no way his brother had left everything to the baby and me. He wouldn't do that if…

If he didn't want us.

Asa turned his head, eyeing me a little. But when I didn't make any words of backing down, he did as I asked. He opened that folder, *read* those documents and as the width of his eyes increased while he read, my throat squeezed, my heart as well.

"Where did you get this?" he asked, turning pages quickly. "Who gave it to you?"

"A man approached me at my home. Bombarded me with it

almost. He said he was required by law to—"

"Feeble looking? White twisted up mustache?"

I blinked.

His eyes lifted above the paper. "Our family estate planner."

I supposed that made sense and estate planner? Why had Alexander done this? I supposed that made sense with his riches, being prepared in all that, but why do this now? And why do it at all?

"This is legit," Asa said, hand going down his mouth when he turned another page. "Was a note left with this or anything? From Alexander?"

"I don't think so." Though I hadn't gone through it with a fine-toothed comb. I had been too shocked by the contents.

"Our estate planner probably misplaced it," Asa said. "He's terribly old."

He was and I remembered that clearly since the encounter was only this morning. He also had a lot to give to me and I had been resistant.

"He left you everything," Asa went on, but with the soft tone of his voice and the faraway look in his eyes, I wondered if those words had been even to me. He didn't even read the pages now, sitting back. "He left you both everything."

He confirmed exactly what I thought, that Alexander did do all this—he did leave me and the baby everything. The baby would be taken care of for the rest of her life and that was something I couldn't change. Even if I refused, then it all went to her. He took care of her, forever.

"He loves you."

As he said it, he wasn't angry by the words or even confused by them. His voice held that of an announcement and his expression…

That of awareness.

That moved over his awestruck eyes. "Have you talked to him?"

"I haven't. It's been a little bit. That had been on me, though. He's tried to call but we had a fight."

He nodded. "So you've had no contact?"

I hadn't, but I wished I did. I wished I understood. He said some out of line things to me, but that... that probably had been because he cared.

*God, I've been such a fool.*

He didn't want to stand in my way. He wanted me to succeed. Even if that meant losing me.

Asa pushed the documents toward me. "You need to talk to him and once you do, can you call me? He's shut me and our mom out and like I said, hasn't been around here in weeks."

Which didn't seem like him at all. Alexander wasn't a lazy man. He ran his business and with nothing but the upmost professionalism.

"I just want to make sure everything is all right with him," Asa went on. "We've been very distant since he decided to do the surrogacy and I don't think he'll respond to me."

A phone ringing through the air, intercepted me saying I would. Asa checked his phone. I think going to end the call, but once he saw the name, he answered.

"Hey, Mom," he said and I definitely understood that. I would have answered, too, even with all my history with mine.

He told her one moment, then looked at me. "I'm sorry, Johari. I have to end this meeting."

"Completely fine." This meeting shouldn't even have happened. I should have contacted Alexander from the jump. I knew that now.

I got my stuff together and Asa stood with me, his hand over his phone.

"Just please have my brother contact me if you get a hold of him. Last time he went AWOL like this he'd been sick—"

Upon biting the words, he shook his head like he was trying to remove the concept of them. He shook my hand and I promised him I would try to get a hold of Alexander. After that, he took his call in the boardroom and I left to make my own as well.

"He really left everything to you? You and the baby?"

My hands dropped between my legs, my feet rocking me back and forth in one of the NICU's rocking chairs. I was silent like I had been so much of this conversation with Roya. Hell, like I had been so much of the day.

She came around a crib containing a sleeping little miracle, Roya's fine silk wrap brushing against her cheeks. "Because he loves you."

Her words struck no question, no ounce of one in her voice whatsoever. I said nothing once more and she sat in the rocking chair across from me. The pair of the chairs were for the parents who swung through here.

She leaned in. "What did he say when you called him?"

The question, so innocent had me looking up and staring so far away. I rubbed at my eyes feeling so emotional for some reason. It could have been the baby. It had been before, but this felt a little deeper. It felt loads.

"I tried a few times, Roya. But nothing."

I attempted more than a few, in the bank lobby before I even left the building, then again on the bus ride over to work, and even a couple more times during my shift today. Each time, I got no dice, his deep voice sending me to voicemail every time. I made one final attempt just before coming up here, my shift over for the day.

And still the same—nothing.

"I don't think he's ignoring me or anything. I just..." I swallowed. "I'm kind of worried. Why did he leave everything to me? I mean, why now? And then there's this thing his brother said. He said the last time he'd done sporadic things like this he'd been sick."

*Sick...*

Could he have been?

My brain reached for signs, tells that I believed at the time, had been his dismissiveness, guilt even from being in a situation he once wanted but now had second thoughts about. But had I been mistaken? Had he been sick the whole time and I just missed it? I looked beyond it because I'd been consumed in my own thoughts about him.

That's the thing, though. With the way he presented himself

the last few weeks I saw him, illness could have been the conclusion just as easily as my own theories about him.

Roya's hand down my arm soothed, helping but not relieving. "Don't jump to that just yet. And I mean, give the man at least twenty-four hours. How many of his calls had you ignored before finally returning to him today?"

I doubt she meant that in any negative away, but it sat hard, heavy on my chest.

I covered my body, rocking. Why hadn't he at least left a note? Something that told of his reasons for delivering me such a huge thing, the baby such a gift? I combed through that binder and found nothing. The contents held nothing but a man sharing his life, giving it over as if it were nothing.

Checking my watch, I at least might get to answer some of my questions. I planned to go to his place, but a feeling chilled me to the very core that my arrival would also go without any answers to my questions. I tried his house phone more than once too, but that?

That had been shut off.

A body passed from behind clear glass on the door and Dr. Radcliff's blonde tendrils could be witnessed just before the window ended.

I got up, telling Roya just a second before rushing out of the NICU with nothing but a feeling and some hope in my chest.

"Dr. Radcliff?"

I caught more than her attention, my voice a little louder than I hoped.

Startled, she stopped, her head tilting. "Johari? Everything all right?"

No, everything was not all right, but I didn't know how to come across sounding more concerned and less crazy.

I took a breather, my pregnancy more than catching up with me even with the short distance. "I wanted to ask you if you've had any contact with, Alexander? Anything at all recently?"

The question clearly threw her, her head twitching a little. "I... no. I haven't. What's going on? I mean..." Her hands rose. "None of my business."

She probably had something there, but I made it her business the minute I approached her. Knowing that, I bit back my pride and brought my courage to the forefront. This was now the fourth person not counting Alexander's many co-workers who hadn't seen him lately, so this wasn't about me.

Listening, she stood there for every word I spilled about the situation. Though, I left out the part about Alexander giving the baby and me his estate. That didn't seem relevant. I simply kept the details on Alexander and his current scarcity, ending with something I did feel she needed to know, my fear he might be keeping something as large as his health to himself.

That rested across this woman's features like I knew it would. She clearly cared about him, maybe even more than she let on.

Her hand came to her mouth. "And you stopped by the apartment?"

"I was headed there now. But the line, it's been disconnected."

A large breath lifted her chest. "Okay. All right."

"Do you know anywhere else he might be? Anywhere he might go?"

"There is a place. His family has property out in the countryside. He spent the majority of his treatment there. He didn't want the world to see him that way. He barely let his mom and brother out there, keeping himself away."

That sounded so much like him. And I did know him, didn't I? Even with all that happened, I felt I did know him at the heart. I did know his heart.

Bringing out my phone, I brought up a map application. "Is it easy to get to?" I could try there after his house. I wonder if Roya would let me borrow her car. I could get it back to her before her shift wrapped. She was working second shift tonight.

"Well, it's…"

Dr. Radcliff's voice fading had me looking up, her eyes on my phone, me.

Shaking her head, she pushed her hands in her pockets, biting her lip before facing me.

"It's uh, no problem at all," she said. "I'll give you directions. You'll get there in no time."

# Nineteen

**Alexander** "Dr. Dubois has agreed to relocate to the States. She's the best oncologist on that side of the world and will be able to offer you around-the-clock care," my mom said, rushing back into the library. She'd been gone for a moment, her best negotiating done while she was on her feet. I supposed I got something from her there. She put her phone down. "And I don't want you to have to worry about any of that. Financially, it's all been set up."

I sat back on the lounge in my family's study, shaking my head, in awe at my mom. We'd both been on the phone all day and most of the day before, me on my own calls. I was making arrangements to move, but not even where I believed only twenty-hours ago. I would be going to California, heading on a new adventure and, though, unexpected where that would lead me considering I'd be in for the most recent battle of my life, that was okay. I was ready for it. I *would be* ready for it. I was doing things differently this time and with my family in my corner, I knew I had this. I called my mom mostly for support and she gave that and so much more.

"You didn't need to do that, Mom." She didn't have to do any of this, arrange for the best doctor from France to come to me, just *for me.* I supposed on the books my mom got the woman a job on the West Coast, but really she'd be there for me.

Her smile went warm, my mom so beautiful. She came over to me, putting her hands on my cheeks. She kissed my forehead. I guess the fact not mattering that I was pushing thirty-two.

I had hopes I'd see quite a few more of those, birthdays.

She placed her hand on my neck. "Now, you let a woman do what she needs to do for her boy," she simply said, picking up her phone again. "And if you decide to go somewhere else, whether that be California or wherever, the doctor is extremely flexible. You should be able to start treatment anywhere and she'll go with you. But you have to understand, Alexander, you might be too sick to travel at some point..."

"Mom." My hand went over hers. "Please, I don't want you to worry about that."

"But I do and you should. Promise me you'll slow down if..."

She couldn't say the words and I wouldn't let her. I stood, threading my fingers in hers. "I will and you'll be the first person I call if I start to see things headed that way."

And I wouldn't break that promise to her. I was done breaking promises.

This seemed to sit well with her, moving across the aged lines at her eyes. She patted my hand, and then came around the lounge, taking a seat.

She looked up at me. "Are you sure you want to be working during all this? I mean, you can work here, right? Be close."

We had this talk before. She didn't understand my reasons for wanting to go away and it seemed, though, she still didn't, at least she accepted them.

I took her side, picking up her hand again. "I won't be working, Mom. I'll be living."

Something I knew to be completely true and my certainty of this decision told me that. Not once had the prospect of something excited me so much, but *this* excited me and after making so many calls, I realized work on the West Coast would be possible. My old friend Yoshi had been right. They did need someone out there, someone to run things yes, but someone who also had something to contribute to the new technology division. They'd been more than happy to have me when I called, wanting to establish myself there.

It was all ready for me when I was ready to take it. The doctors would be set up and everything.

I smiled at my mom. "For too long, I'd been working not for myself but for Dad. I love investment banking. I love business, but I think that's him. I want to try me for a bit."

"Even while you're sick, sweetheart?" Her hand went down my face.

I squeezed it. "Especially. I'm not going to hide from my disease anymore. I'll treat it as an old friend. Kill it with drive and motivation."

"Damn right, you will," she said, the words bringing tears to her eyes. "I'm so proud of you. Your dad would be proud, too."

She had no idea how much those words affected me. All I ever wanted was to please my father and if doing something for myself would actually do that? That'd be the ultimate dream.

Out back a man made his own calls, my brother. He paced, a phone to his ear while he made logistical/ financial plans for me. Again, something else I didn't ask to be done for me. My family went to the mat for me and couldn't be convinced otherwise. Asa had already gotten housing set up and notified the appropriate parties here of my transfer. Again, all these things were in place for when I was ready to have it. Whether it be next week or a year from now.

I didn't have to worry about much thanks to my brother and it seemed his latest job was done. With a breath, he put his phone down on the patio table, taking a seat in one of my mom's gardens.

Mom kissed my cheek. "Talk to him. I know he's not handling this well. You know how he pretends."

I did know, my brother the worst actor in the world. I told him I was sick just yesterday, my mom calling him to come home from work.

His gaze had averted at the words and after I told him of my plans, he buried himself in them, making them his own. He didn't want me to know, how much this all was overwhelming him and maybe, even hurting him. I knew his process so I let him go, fully intending on coming to speak with him later.

My mom lifted her phone. "I have a few more calls to make. I want to set up a delivery service for your food. You shouldn't have to set foot into a grocery store."

215 | B a b y ,   B a b y

Also, something I didn't ask her to do, but I supposed both she and my brother had a process.

She put her phone to her ear. "I also have an event to set up. Tell Johari to keep the twenty-third open, all right?"

A smile split my lips. "Why?"

"Because Grandma is throwing a baby shower. In fact, the first of a few. My grandchild will want for nothing by the time I'm through. I've already contacted the major news outlets."

How awful to have Jo sucked into this crazy world I came from.

How terribly, awfully wonderful.

My mom's party chatter took her away and I left her to it, taking my phone with me. I had plans to call Jo after all this was settled. I wanted her to know I had a plan. California was for her, yes, but also for us. She'd be able to live her dream, work on the West Coast for her passions, but I could have mine as well too. The drive to move had been influenced by her, but the desire to live? That had all been me.

Green eyes flashed to the glass patio door when I cracked it open, my brother watching me take steps down the stairs.

He dampened his mouth. "Seems we own many properties on the... on the coast," he said, clearing his throat. He pushed a hand through the short blond whiskers on his face. "You have your pick of the litter, so whatever city you both settle on you'll be good to go."

"All right. Thank you."

He nodded when I arrived in front of him, his gaze following as I took a seat on the cement bench next to him.

He cleared his throat again. "And everyone knows you're coming. You'll have no interruptions with your bank cards or anything. Fraud shouldn't be cutting you off for unexpected activity."

"Well, that's good." I leaned forward, putting my hands together. "And everyone knows I'm leaving? Well, eventually when I do."

I planned to head off as soon as Johari was placed.

"Yeah." He lifted his phone. "Everyone at the firm."

"Thank you, Asa. I really appreciate that."

And if my brother's throat didn't clear for the third time. He chewed the inside of his cheek, his gaze averting. All this was overwhelming him. Face filled with color, he seemed as if he might explode from all that swirled around inside him, all his thoughts, all his worries.

The two of us sat silent in my mom's garden and being around him, a simple act of being outside with nothing but the air around us, the weight of how much I missed my brother settled upon me. There used to be only hours between when we'd see each other, but more recently, I had made that weeks. And even when we did have interactions they had been business related, nothing personal. He didn't care to hear about where I took my life because he didn't accept it. He'd been adamant about that so that only left neutral topics.

His gaze hit the cobblestone walk below. "You go MIA for weeks and come back with this."

A smile touched his lips, a weak one.

Probably because he'd said this to me before.

He faced me. "If you die, you jerk… if you put me through that again…"

I put my hand on his shoulder, rubbing. "You forgot already? I'm not allowed to die. You already told me that. *Yelled* at me that."

Laughter broke tension that was so serious, and Asa sat back with it, pushing his arms over his chest.

"That's right," he said, shaking his head. "So I'm holding you to that."

I nodded. "I know."

My hand falling from his shoulder, I sat back against the ivy-covered wall behind us

"But are you really going to leave all this?" he asked. The Chicago skyline rang clear in the distance, *Ricci Financial* amongst it. "I know you're still working for the company, but who will run things? That was supposed to be you. You were working toward it. A Ricci should be behind it."

I eyed him, finding what he said funny. "You're forgetting there's two of us."

The very notion had his eyes widening. "Could you imagine

me? We may have both been the Princes of Chicago, but you're definitely William in this situation. I'm just the spare."

But he didn't have to be. He was just as brilliant as I was in the boardroom and maybe even more so. Dad had always stacked his cards with me and I never understood that. I supposed my brother's love for fun had distracted my father. It was hard to see past all that when it came to Asa, the serious man that lie underneath the lifestyle handed to us.

"Anyway, can you see me here? Being all serious?"

"Can't you?"

His only response to that was a quick turn of his head and a blink of his eyes. My brother could do anything he wanted, but just had to believe he could first.

He sat with those words for a moment before turning my way. "You going to call Johari now?"

When Asa told me Johari came to him about custody arrangements I… hadn't been surprised. With our fight, things had been left very open-ended between us and she was preparing. She *should be* preparing. I told her she should leave, go for her dreams and did so without any plans prepared for the two of us as a couple whatsoever. She had been right that day. I came to her with nothing but words and no actual plan to back them up. If anything, I no doubt came across as releasing myself from my obligations to our baby and us. Precisely, why I had been so vigilant in getting these arrangements made for us now. I wouldn't go to her again unprepared. After she had our girl, she'd be applying for matches in California and I'd be ready for the move, sick or otherwise.

I pulled out my phone. I felt ready to call her now, tell her everything. She'd probably disagree with me going with her, but I didn't care. I needed to be with her.

I needed to live life.

"I'm surprised she hasn't contacted you herself."

I looked up at Asa, shaking my head. "Why?"

He seemed confused, blond eyebrows drawing in. "Well, I told her to. After you had your will changed and left her and the baby everything. It really freaked me out. I told her to call you and—"

"Wait. Ira contacted her already? About the will?" I made plans for him to do that, but not so soon, not until I had left for treatment.

Now, he really looked perplexed. "Was he not supposed to?"

"No. I mean, he was but…" I pushed my hand into my hair. The old man always had been terrible about dates. I dropped my hand into my lap. "He was, but he was supposed to do that after I had left for treatment. I mean, my original plans were to go out to our family's property to do it."

He blinked. "You were going to do that? Again, and not tell us?"

So many things I did wrong, but attempted to right them now. "Yeah, but I knew that wasn't the right call to make. I wanted to prepare and get everything together before telling everyone. That included my estate, but Ira wasn't supposed to deliver all that to her until I had gotten settled. He was supposed to do that and tell her where I was."

Asa rose up slowly. "I, uh, read the paperwork, Alex, and nowhere did it say where you'd be. Johari brought it with her and showed it to me during our meeting. It was just your plans for the estate. Nothing more."

Absolute dread filled me at the words. I left a note, a detailed one explaining everything.

Ira must have lost it in the transfer, our family lawyer elderly and known for such things from time to time.

*What must she think… A document telling her she got everything with no explanation.*

"Honey?"

Mom's voice caught me midway off my chair. I needed to go fix this, call Johari right away.

Mom came down the cement steps, her phone in hand. "I think I have your phone, hon. I just now checked the messages from yesterday on this one and there are a bunch from Johari. I think I picked yours up by mistake."

*What?*

Her phone held out to me, I exchanged it with what I believed to be my own. Her picking mine up by accident at some point would make sense. We did have the same phones, all of us did.

"I'm sorry I didn't notice sooner," she said, watching me scroll through it. "I got a bunch of calls from a number I didn't recognize yesterday and my default is to ignore them. And with all the calls I was making for you…"

"It's fine, Mom," I told her, pushing the phone to my ear. There had been a few calls. In fact, many. Listening, they all started with the same. She wanted to talk to me.

But then she *needed* to talk to me.

They got more urgent with every message I clicked over to, and varied throughout the day. They varied until the final one late last night.

"Alexander," she started.

And everything went blank for a moment, her voice just having that way. How much I missed her.

"I'm trying to come out to see you, but I think I'm los—"

And that's how it ended. That's how she left me. I assumed the call got lost, so dialing, I attempted to get to her.

An automatic voice stopped me at the first attempt, sending me straight to voicemail.

I tried again.

"… please leave a message at the tone."

"Johari, it's Alexander. I know you tried to call and I'm sorry there was a mix up with my phone. Please call me back. I need to speak to you, sweetheart."

I ended it there, but my phone in hand I found I couldn't sit with that.

I needed to go to her.

"I'll park the car," my brother said, dropping me off at the entrance to Chicago Community Med. He opted to see me to the hospital despite me letting him know I had no problem going myself. I let him because I felt *he* needed to do so.

I rubbed his shoulder, thanking him before heading inside. I figured it was a safe bet Jo would be in. She usually had a clinical at this time on this particular day. I normally wouldn't have bothered her but her calls sounded so urgent, her voice.

*"I'm trying to come out and see you…"*

Had she stopped by my apartment? I hadn't been there, staying at my family's last night with all the chaos.

The automatic doors separating for me, I headed towards admitting. The nurse there raised her head.

"I'm looking for one of your doctors. Well, she's a medical student."

"The name?"

"Johari Russell."

Awareness flashed in the woman's eyes, but she shook her head. "I'm sorry. She's not in today."

What she said kind of threw me off a bit. I didn't have Johari's schedule tattooed permanently to my brain, but I didn't think my memory flailed when it came to times she was here. She was pretty consistent with the time she spent here over the last few months.

Thanking the nurse, I tapped the counter and stepped out of the line for the others waiting to go around me. My phone returned to my hand and I attempted to make another call. I tried a couple more times on the way here, but the same thing. Voicemail.

"This mailbox is full."

My last one to her voicemail box had been lengthy and I bet my worry could have challenged hers in that final message. I guess I couldn't help it. She just sounded so uneasy when she called me, and now, her not being in…

*Maybe she took a sick day. She is pregnant.*

Banking on that, I rerouted, heading back the way I'd come. I would stop by her house. She was probably there and all this worrying was ridiculous, unnecessary on my part. I almost hit the doors when I spotted a familiar face.

Johari's friend Roya looked knee-deep in paperwork, her cheeks flushed. She seemed busy, stressed, but I did go over to her, calling her name.

She gazed up, her recollection of me settling over her face. "Hey—"

"Hi. I hate to bother you, but have you seen Jo? I thought this was her normal time to be here, but the nurse at admitting said she wasn't in."

What was weird was how the mention of her friend changed her expression. She frowned, adjusted her hijab. That's when the bags under her eyes really made themselves known. I finally took a moment to take them in as well as her well-wrinkled clothes. I had only seen Roya a handful of times, but she was usually more put together than this.

"No," she said, moving the clipboard in her hands underneath her arm. "And if you see her, tell her it was real fun getting to work today."

She started to leave, but I gestured her to stop.

I shook my head. "What do you mean?"

"I mean, she borrowed my car. She borrowed it to go to *you* but she never brought it back. I had to take a cab home last night and the bus today. So when you see her—"

"Wait." She said so much and I needed a moment. I rubbed the back of my head. "You said she went to find me."

She nodded, a curiosity in her gaze when she tilted her head. "Yeah. Didn't you know? She called you like crazy yesterday, but you weren't answering. Eventually, she decided she was going to go to you after her shift. I thought she was going to take the bus to your house, but then she came to me asking to borrow the car. She said she needed it to go outside the city. Dr. Radcliff told her about a place you might be at so—"

I apologized to Roya for leaving, but I had to go. I had to...

Naomi was in her office, a place I had been to a few times and how her eyes enlarged at seeing me, seeing me tense, seeing me pissed to hell. And once that door closed...

"Where did you send her?"

My hands went down to her desk, the sound cracking the air. *She's not answering fast enough.*

"Naomi—"

"Who? What?"

She was condescending me, playing me for a fool and she wouldn't do that again. She played games with me for the last time.

I came around her desk, my jaw working. "Roya said you sent

Jo somewhere. You sent her after me and she never came back."

Her face paled. "What?"

"Exactly. So where did you send her? I swear to God, Naomi."

"I just told her about the cabin. Your family's property? She wanted to know a place you would go. She thought you might be sick again and—"

I had no more time. In fact, I felt I had zero. Because if Johari went where Naomi said she did. If she tried...

But my steps were ceased at a hand on my arm and if I didn't have the control I had, the strength, the fury erupting inside me would have sent it flying off.

"Alexander."

"You're going to take a step back," I told her, slow as I turned around. "You're going to go back to your chair and you're going to continue what you were doing."

Her hand left me gradually, carefully. Her arms returned to her side and her face flushed bright like the hot anger inside me.

I lifted a finger at her, my shoulders, my *body* shaking. "And when I get back, after I go get her, you better hope to God I don't press charges."

My family had chosen our property in the country for a reason. It was beautiful, but the location had been its true value. Deep and remote, it couldn't be found without detailed instructions.

And absolutely *no one* could find it without a guide.

Naomi knew that. She had to as she'd been out there before, which meant she knew exactly what she was doing. In fact, chillingly so.

Her hands coming together, that read all over her face. She sent Johari out on purpose. She sent her to get lost.

Considering how she'd helped me before, helped *Johari* before, I highly doubt what she did was planned. Naomi was a good doctor. In fact, a great one and she did go into medicine to help people. *That* alone would force her to help someone even if she didn't want to. This situation, though, Jo needing help to get out to me...

Gave her an opportunity. She got one in which tempted her,

allowed her to do the wrong thing.

Disgusted, I turned, but her voice stopped me.

"I was just trying to help."

"And I hope that's the story you keep telling yourself," I said, not facing her. "Because if this all goes south, you're going to need something to help you go to sleep at night in your prison cell."

I never did get her reaction to that last statement.

I was too busy calling my brother to bring the car back around.

## Twenty

**Johari** A light shone through the window of the back of Roya's Chevy Malibu. Bright, it burned, a white-hot poker shooting itself straight through my vision.

Moving, my breath gathered in thick puffs before me. The first night I kept the heat low, knowing I wouldn't have it forever. I had to conserve it. I didn't know when someone would find me.

I didn't know *if* someone would find me.

Falling, I lost the light, my limbs I... I couldn't even feel anymore.

My fingertips blue...

I closed my eyes, the light too bright, too much.

"She's here. Alex!"

*Alex...*

*Alexander.*

Squirming, I tried to move, shaking life into my numb arms. I need to. I had to find the strength.

Holding my stomach, I reached for her, the baby.

*He's here. He's come.*

But I felt no internal flutter this time, no signs of life. She didn't do it all the time, but I always felt her presence. She was always there. Especially, when I was overwhelmed, or, or happy.

*Where is she? Where is she!*

I couldn't find her. I couldn't reach for her and the panic rushed me like a crashing wave. The bile climbed an already dry throat, my tears burning my tired eyes.

My feet fell suddenly, the door forced open and heat brought me in, beautiful eyes staring down at me.

Alexander brushed a hand over my brow, calling to me, saying something, but I couldn't hear him.

*I can't feel her.*

His jacket pulled down his arms, a light behind him guiding his way. He unbuttoned his shirt then, but I had no idea what he was doing until he hugged me to him and gave me the most charged heat I ever felt. His body radiated a wonderful sauna and how close he drew me into him even more. His button-up shirt he closed over me, then his coat around us both. All the while, he kept saying, "It's okay. You're going be okay, sweetheart."

He rocked me, the tears falling down my face. But it wouldn't be okay. How could it if...

If I didn't feel her?

# Twenty One

**Johari** The nightmares came like shadows, vast and rolling in dark clouds behind my lids. Sheer terror kept me in my sleep, the wonders of the unknown locking me into my own head. I had no idea what would become of opening my eyes, so dark dreams kept me in.

The alternative terrified me, the reality of what would become upon opening my eyes.

The dark labyrinth eventually loosened, forcing me out no matter how hard I thought. I found the light then, the day.

It found me through my own bedroom window.

Disorientation took on new meaning, my own bedroom surrounding me, my body aching and hooked up to beeping monitors around me. This should mean something to me, or at least make me calm since I'm in a familiar place.

It flooded back like a damn breaking underneath powerful waves. The car… The car with no heat… The countryside…

The baby.

*My* baby.

Our baby.

Panicked, my hands shook, heading toward my stomach.

That's when I discovered I wasn't alone.

Alexander had beaten me to it, his arm covering my waist as he lay beside me. On top of the blankets, he had me curled against him, fully clothed and holding me to him.

He held us both.

His large fingers covered my stomach as if reaching, pulling for her. Would he do that if... if...

The tears stung my eyes, his name upon my lips in gentle pants.

His head popped up to the sound of them, his eyes searching the room upon coming out of the same slumber I had.

He found me immediately, though, reaching up, touching my cheek.

"Jo."

My name a whisper on his lips, he sat up, caging my face with gentle hands.

"God, Jo."

He brought my face toward him, doing nothing but settling his forehead on mine, his breaths rushed and tight from his lips. His arms fell around me, his strong frame, and I fell into them, feeling so much loss and taking comfort in what he gave.

I shook, my hands patting his chest, but too scared to go lower, to feel.

"The baby," I breathed against him. My body no longer chilled from the cold of the car. It was something deeper.

Something far worse.

His arms strengthened around me and I buried myself into his embrace.

"I couldn't feel her, Alexander. Not in the car. I stopped feeling her—"

But then he did something, something that brought me life and returned my meaning. He moved my hand to where his had been and our baby made herself known, so deep inside.

"She's okay," he said embedding tendrils of heat softly onto my cheek, my lips next.

His lips went firm, hard against mine.

"You're both okay," he breathed. "Both my girls."

I laughed. We were his, weren't we? It hadn't mattered if anything had happened to try to disrupt that. We were his. We'd always been.

"What happened?" I asked, breaking away slightly. I found

his beautiful eyes. "Why am I here? How did we get here?"

The time had been such a blur, the only thing I remembered, the *last* thing was Alexander, him and his strong body, in his attempts to bring me out of an environment so cold.

He smoothed a hand down my face. "I had you transferred here from the hospital. After you got out of the worst."

The worst…

I didn't even remember the hospital, everything so lost in my mind.

The night had been so fuzzy, the night terribly cold and with not a lot of heat. I had to conserve it. I got lost so quickly, the backwoods a maze with no way out. Rather than burry myself deeper, I decided to wait it out, using blankets Roya had in her car. She didn't have many, but what she did, I used to cocoon myself in, rationing the heat of the car to take me through most of the night.

"That had been so smart," Alexander said upon hearing it. He held me, his hand on my head.

He said even still with my thoughts to conserve heat I had suffered hypothermia, something I had been well aware of while it was happening and that had nothing to do with my medical background. But everything felt so good now, so warm and wonderful in his arms.

*Is this real?*

I closed my eyes, letting him rock me. He'd been the only person I had been able to get a call out to in the roaming area. I got too far into the woods before I realized no other calls could be made, but he found me.

He got to me in time.

How stupid I had been to try to go out and find him, but it seemed, at least according to him, I had no chance from the jump.

"Naomi knew," he said, explaining so much to me that suddenly made sense. He smoothed a hand down my cheek. "She knew what she was doing. She told you to go out there knowing you'd get lost."

Why didn't I see the signs? I had been blinded, led on by her care, which I clearly had mistaken as just professionalism. At the heart, had been a woman, one crushed and broken. In the end, I had everything she wanted. But even still, I dismissed that away. I took her help time and time again not knowing that I was breaking her with every word of acceptance.

I listened intently, Alexander's words so bitter about her. Had she been wrong? Yes, but at some point, I should have stepped back and put distance between her and me. She was too close to all this and her snapping would have been I was sure only a matter of time.

"That doesn't make it right," he said, shaking his head. "What she did."

I hadn't said that, but I did know where she was coming from.

Naturally, Alexander's next thoughts were to press charges, but I had two minds about that. Perhaps because I understood where she was coming from.

I took Alexander's hands, putting them on our girl. Curling into him, I let him focus on us.

And what a relief when his body settled against mine too.

We sat there together. In fact for what felt like so long, and in the end, we relished that, what *this* was and what we had. This moment, our family, was what was most important and I think in so many moments of that...

He let his heart be at peace.

Together, we decided no more drama. I couldn't stand it anymore.

Especially when he confirmed my greatest fear.

"Why didn't you tell me?" I asked him, nearly in tears again. So many tears today, too many. He couldn't be sick. He couldn't be after I found my way back to him, after *we* found each other, but to that, he only smiled at me, placing his hands on my cheeks. He kissed me then, his eyes closed and when we came up for air his forehead rested on mine.

"I'm going to make you a promise. Are you listening?"

I nodded, my eyes so puffy. "Yes."

"I promise these are the last tears you're going to shed over me being sick," he said, brushing a tear from under my eye. He then kissed under each one, his warmth and love so close. "And that my illness will never again keep me from you."

And I'd hold him to that promise. I'd hold it to either one of our dying days…

I planned for those to be far in the future.

It turned out the pair of us didn't have much longer together than those meaningful moments we'd spent alone in my bedroom room. It seemed I'd been called for.

My brother rushed into the room, bypassing Alexander completely. It was like he didn't see him there, or maybe he did but I had been priority.

Javan tackle-hugged me, closing his eyes, and though, weak, I found the strength for my guy.

"Hey, dude. It's okay." I was unsure of how much they told him, but he at least knew I'd been hurt. He at least knew that.

I held him for what seemed like an eternity and in that hold, sometime Ms. Sherry had come in.

Along with Mama.

The whole room silenced, a change of tone I had no idea what to do with nor had I been prepared to handle it. I didn't know if it was a bad tone, tough. I just was put in a spot of the unknown, my family here, Mama, and Alexander.

He stood immediately of course, Alexander. He nodded to them both and not surprised, Ms. Sherry smiled at him. They shared a warm exchange when their gazes collided that I couldn't identify and I wondered how many conversations had been commenced in my absence.

By this time, Javan had pretty much crawled onto my bed, under my arm.

"Are you okay?" he asked, rubbing his face against my side.

Leave this kid to break the weird tone.

Alexander touched his shoulder. "She's doing fine, bud. I told you not to worry."

"I know but…"

I hugged him, kissing the close-cropped hair on his head. "Alexander told you right. He just caught me in here sleeping, being lazy."

Javan laughed and I loved that. It meant he was okay. These stresses were beyond anything he could help and I seemed to be out of the dark. Alexander told me that and I trusted him.

I trusted him with everything and more.

In the eyes of a child, my few words seemed to make things okay for my brother and I was grateful for that. But the adults in the room told another story with their gazes. I had never seen my mama this way.

A darkness brimmed under an aged woman's eyes, one that told of stress and no anger. Had she been stressed?

Had I made her so?

Her hands twisted together, she looked unsure of the situation, what to do or when to do it. That's when Ms. Sherry put her hand under my mama's elbow.

Almost as if Mama needed it there for support.

She rubbed my mama's arm before approaching my bed and bringing me into a hug, that left me unconfused on her thoughts of the room. She didn't care. She just needed to know I was safe, okay.

"You got a good man," she said, whispering the words in a tight squeeze. "He only left the room when your mama needed time with you. They traded off."

They had?

They had and I saw that on my mama's face, those bags under her eyes. I wanted to talk to her and maybe Ms. Sherry and Alexander sensed that. It had been she who suggested she and Javan come back and Alexander who gave the call on where to go.

"How about ice cream?" he asked, making my brother perk up. He laughed, tugging at his shirtsleeve. "I got some at the store last night for your sister."

"We can bring it up to her!" Javan bounced and that sent Ms. Sherry smiling.

She put a hand on his head. "I like that idea, but no rush. We'll eat ours first before coming back up."

A wink to me said she was keeping him at bay to give me more time, more time alone... with my mama.

Javan smiled, too, but he looked unsure of when Ms. Sherry pulled his hand to leave.

Alexander tugged on his shirt. "She'll be okay. She's got your mom."

My mama.

*"They traded off."*

I did have her and I always had. In my trying times, she had always been there for me and that's something I never had to question—ever.

Javan's vise grip did leave me and together, all three of them left the room. But not before Alexander placed a kiss on my forehead, giving my arm a squeeze before passing my mama. He nodded at her, greeting her with a, "Ma'am" before letting the two of us alone.

And if my mama didn't nod kindly to him back, her tough exterior broken if not the littlest bit.

The door closed behind Alexander when he tugged it, then it was only me and the woman who raised me. To my side she came and when her hand went down on mine, the one covering my stomach...

Our cupped hands framed a belly only hidden by my sheets. There was no hiding my daughter, she was there and her existence was in the open now. I thought long and hard about telling Mama about the pregnancy, but each time, I came at full stop with the decision. I had no idea how she'd take it, or *if* she'd accept her considering the circumstances in which she'd been conceived.

A warmth spreading across my mama's lips told me I should have held faith and the tears in her eyes started mine.

She smoothed a hand over my belly, going behind mine.

"His?" she asked, squeezing, and I nodded, telling her, "Yes."

This baby was Alexander's and nothing about that I would keep. I couldn't keep it in and wouldn't ever again.

I wondered about this conversation so many times with my mama. I figured it was one I would have to have eventually, as I started to show, but never had been in a rush. I mean, what could I have said? I decided to be a surrogate? For money? I feared this woman's judgment so much, then when this baby actually did come into existence, my anxiety rang even worse at what would happen as silly as that may seem.

Mama would wonder about me, me and Alexander and why someone like himself would chose to be with me. I saw nothing but negativity when it came to a response to this whole situation from her. I knew that because I knew my mama.

At least, I thought I had.

A soft, but present, "I'm glad," fell from her lips, genuine words that reflected not only in her voice but her eyes. She always had so much tension, but today, she had none.

She sat down with me, her hand in mine as I explained everything that happened. I was sure she knew all this. She had been here, but coherent unlike myself. But I had to go there, tell her everything that happened with Naomi and the trip out to the country. I had to start at the beginning. She needed to know how Alexander and I met and our original relationship. This I knew could open the floodgates, but as she sat there, listening intently, I found the tension relieving. It didn't go away completely of course and it probably never would, but it was a start.

"You kept this from me," she said at one point, but it wasn't a question. Her words rang of statement, as well as the tension they caused to return to her eyes.

"I'm sor—" I started, and I hated myself for it. I promised Alexander I wouldn't do that anymore.

And now was a good time to start.

But her sorry came before I could retract the statement, as well as her hand coming up to my face. She touched me, so warm and I couldn't remember the last time I felt this close to her.

Nor if she ever apologized to me.

I felt in there we had a start. We had something.

And God, if I hadn't hoped for that my whole life.

# Epilogue

## 40 Weeks Pregnant...
### ...and then some.

**Alexander** She fell upon me like a whisper, a hint of the softest wind.

Arms pushed around my chest, Johari failing in all attempts to surprise me. Her belly gave her away every time.

I unfolded her fingers, lifting her hand to my mouth. A ring resided there on her third finger, ready and waiting for its mate. We decided to wait on that, marriage.

We both wanted the baby to be a part of the wedding.

She breathed me in, her warm breath sliding like the brush of a blanket on my back.

"How do you feel?" she asked, her clear smile forming its upward curve into my skin.

Her belly pressed and I lowered my glass to the sink. I had gotten up for a minute, getting a drink.

Holding the sink, I let my head fall forward, pressing my lips to that diamond solitaire on her finger. Her joy when I gave this to her over dinner I'd never forget. It had matched mine that night.

I let her form into me, then slumped, gripping the sink.

Her stilling behind me didn't go unnoticed.

"A little tired," I said, exaggerating my breathing a little. It was cruel I knew. I was tired, but had energy for this, her.

She froze, her hand falling down my chest.

"Oh?" she whispered, worry behind her voice. She started to pull away, but I gripped her hand, pulling her back.

Looping my fingers in hers, I faced her, reaching out with her hand in mine.

My finger brushed sweetened brown skin, her chin lifting with the softest touch to her cheek. Her lips parted and dark lashes lowered. How she changed so much in this pregnancy, her glow radiating in the tiniest tint throughout her entire body.

I lifted her nightgown, revealing that to me when I took it over her head. Large, dark areolas stayed pert with the rise and fall of the fullest breasts, the skin tight and so rosy.

I touched her, making her breath intake when I covered her nipple, squeezing between two fingers.

"But you said you were tired—"

Her mouth had the sweetest taste, succulent and pure like fresh raspberries.

I brought her to me, my hands framing her belly, our child. I told her I was tired, but I let on, playing with her I guess. We'd been doing this a lot lately, having at each other, and I supposed I was giving her a hard time. Our attempts to induce her pregnancy had been an interesting one, sometimes mere minutes between rounds...

And I had been the last to complain.

I kissed her, drawing in her flavor, but her hands on my shoulders attempted to keep me away. As well as her soft words.

"Alex..."

My thumb brushed over her bottom lip, swollen and warm from my mouth. I smiled at her. "I'm never tired with you."

And I hadn't been, doing so well. I supposed my doctor had been right about my state of mind. Because my response to treatment had been more than a positive one. I was here now. I was here with her every day and every hour and...

I couldn't see that changing, not for a while.

Hormone therapy had gone more than well, over the rough of it and my strength returning. We took it day by day, my doctors watching my condition actively. I'd been working with my mom's doctor and my own, and Dr. Dubois would be following Johari and me when we moved to California early next year. So many changes were going to be made, my new job starting soon, and of course Jo's as well. She'd recently graduated and was ready to be matched with the hospital of her dreams on the West Coast.

The changes in our lives had all been positive. I wasn't free and clear of cancer, but had strong hopes I would be again one day. The pair of us counted our blessings every day because not only was I doing well, but we had a healthy baby, more than full term.

Now if we could just get her to have it.

I caged Johari's face with my hands, lifting it to have her mouth and her hands fell away from my shoulders.

A kiss to her mouth had her gasping and a taste of her tongue shaking. Her hands to my boxers, she slid me out, pumping me, and I let her. I let her get me ready.

"Couch?" I asked, biting her bottom lip and the dimple that pushed into her cheek, making her smile, let me know my answer.

My finger slipped into her heat the moment I brought her into the living room, pressing her bottom against the sofa.

Turning her, I needed to see those globes, her ass just as rosy as the rest of her skin.

I gripped, watching the brown flesh push through the spaces of my fingers.

I guided her to the arm of the couch, lifting her knee to it and her head fell forward, her breathing hiked and shallow. She reached, gripping along the back of the sofa and I pumped her, two fingers then three in her sweet heat.

"You okay?" I asked, kissing her back. I always checked on her, more and more due to the obvious. She could go into labor anytime.

Her only response was to push her ass out, that beautifully round bottom.

"Don't make me wait," was all she said. Her legs spread and that glistening heat called me to take a greedy taste.

I engorged, licking along her lips and fresh juices had me even more greedy. I pumped myself, a stroke to every sweet taste. I needed to be ready. She said she didn't want to wait.

"Alexander, please."

Her head turned, her eyes sought me out, and I stood tall, holding her underneath my arm. If she weakened I'd be there. I would never leave her.

I shoved myself to the hilt, quick and full and she called out, my body submitting to the pleasure. Her arms went shaky a bit, giving out, but like I said, she wouldn't be left to fall.

I held her, pumping my hips and she gripped the sofa, the material beneath her nails tearing sounds into air. Reaching back, she grabbed my hips, summoning me for more, needing me to do more and I obliged, kissing her back when I slammed my hips into her soft bottom.

The smack of my thighs rang through the air, Jo's body submitting, giving in to my labored task. A cloak of her hair covered her face and I pulled it back, reaching to grab her breasts.

"Alexander, Alexander…" she breathed quickly in succession, and I bent, twisting her nipples and driving my hips.

"Jo…"

I kissed a trail down her back, my feet taking a stance on the carpet as I felt the build. Her hand squeezed my thigh, sending a roar from my chest from the wonderful pain and when her fingers came between her legs to touch herself, stroke herself…

I slammed, hard and full. Letting myself flood her, I called her name, her walls pulsating and humming around me.

Heat flushed my cock and I rubbed her back, letting her take me, enjoy me. Moving my hips, I drew it out and didn't fall out of her when either one of us was done. I simply lowered my arm, letting her rest and that's when I hugged her.

"I love you," I said, breathy with no space between us. I made that space tighter when I gripped both her and our child, our little girl. We decided to name her Ruby and I couldn't wait to meet her.

"I love you, too," she said, moving her hand on mine and then a breath sucked in, her relieving it slowly as she rubbed her belly.

"Jo?"

My next question was to ask if she was all right. I did that instinctually, but it turned out I didn't have to this time.

She smiled at me, reaching behind to touch my cheek. She

said only two words then.

"It's time."

*Johari*  Twenty hours… Twenty hours of breathing, feeling. I brought my hands over my stomach, attempting to soothe myself in a state of serenity, but that proved to be difficult.

I felt *everything* and the warm water surrounding me only helped to a certain point. It was the hands that got me through, the body around me.

Alexander brought me in, bringing his hands down my arms underneath the tub's water. We opted for a natural birth, the setup in the bedroom, and with every sharp hit of pain, I questioned my sanity of that decision.

"You're doing great," Alexander whispered, his breath to my ear. He squeezed me. "You're perfect."

My coach, my best friend.

Falling back into my place of peace, I lay into him, him in his swim trunks behind me. Across from us both, we had a full team, a ton of people rushing over to Alexander's place. We moved out of the city, a temporary situation until we moved to the coast. It seemed neither one of our places had been baby friendly, and I wanted to nest a little before heading onto the next chapter of my life. I'd be matching up with hospitals soon and Alexander would be joining me, corporate head of *Ricci Technology Incorporated.*

He was living a dream such as myself, something he shared with me.

I was so proud of him and proud of us, us for how far we'd come and the little blessing we were about to bring in together.

Roya couldn't keep the grin off her face, staring at us. She was helping the midwife with the birth, as well as coaching me.

Her vantage point full, she stared up at me. "Almost there, babe."

She'd know. She and the midwife had an excellent view. At least everyone else was out in the living room, my family and

Alexander's both.

And *that* had been interesting, our families meeting, but surprisingly they found some common ground.

They cared about us after all.

They'd all rushed over the minute we called about the birth and once here, it was all we could do to keep them out of the bedroom. Especially Alexander's mom, a feisty European ball of fire.

A soft, "Sweetheart?" came from behind me, along with a brush to my sweaty brow. Alexander was there smiling at me.

He kissed my cheek. "Ready to push?"

*Push?*

*Push.*

A ball of panic hit my chest. My mama… she hadn't come back yet.

I sat up, the water sloshing. "Mama—"

"I'm here. I'm here," she said, and then she was, an entire bag of ice in her hands as well as a Styrofoam cup. I assumed she got them both at the local gas station and how she gave me the craziest side-eye when I told her about how today would go. She didn't understand it, a natural birth confusing her like many things I did.

But she was there every step of the way.

She put the cup down, kissing my forehead before taking her place by my side. She was there and I had my other support behind me, my man whispering everything perfect into my ear. He said everything he needed to, everything to get me through.

Sharp, several sensations clouded the water beneath me. The world went hazy but I fought through it, a tiny bundle floating into the midwife's hands. My midwife's name was Susan.

A few passing moments of the unknown went over me after the tiniest little body slid into my midwife's hands. It was unknown how the baby would be, if she was healthy and happy. Alexander and I already had me tested. The baby wouldn't be like my brother—she didn't have Down syndrome—but even if she had, she would have been perfect. Our Ruby was perfect no matter what.

Cries hit the air and there she was, placed on my chest, my

bathing suit top. I had felt her for so many months, kicking inside me but nothing was like this. Nothing was like meeting her for the first time.

My tears hit my chest and her cheek, a little wrinkly baby like my own pictures as an infant, the faintest brown to her skin of her father and mother.

I kissed her cheek, staying there and Alexander's hand covered her head. That's how small she was, but she was healthy. I could hear Roya say that somewhere in the distance.

"Perfect," my mama said and it was she who got the first picture, saying she needed to show Ms. Sherry and Javan who were out in the living room, resting and waiting for news. She said this, that she would leave, but she just kept taking pictures, tears welling in her eyes.

I rocked Ruby, unable to believe I just created this tiny miracle. And not only that, but that Alexander and I had created this little miracle through chance, through circumstance.

He hugged us both from behind, Ruby and me.

"Sweetheart, you have the same birthday," he whispered to me, and I laughed, completely forgetting that today was my birthday.

What an excellent gift.

# About the Author

VICTORIA H. SMITH
->>>- Romance Author -<<<-

Victoria H. Smith has a Bachelor's Degree in Political Science. She puts it to good use writing romance all day. She resides in the Midwest with her Macbook on her lap and a cornfield to her right. She often draws inspiration for her stories from her own life experiences and the characters she writes give her an earful about it.

In her free time, she enjoys extreme couponing, reading, watching Scandal, and general geekery in the form of Sherlock and DC Comics. She's a bestselling author and the 2014 Swirl Award winner for Best New Adult Romance, as well as the recipient of the 2015 AMB Ovation Award for her new adult romance FOUND BY YOU. She writes both new adult and adult fiction in many genres, but mainly focuses in contemporary interracial and multicultural romances.

# OTHER BOOKS BY THE AUTHOR

## FOUND BY YOU SERIES

Found by You **FREE ON KINDLE UNLIMITED**

Loved by You **FREE ON KINDLE UNLIMITED**

Brody **FREE ON KINDLE UNLIMITED**

Enthrall **FREE ON KINDLE UNLIMITED**

## THE SPACE BETWEEN SERIES

The Space Between **FREE ON KINDLE UNLIMITED**

The Dividing Line **FREE ON KINDLE UNLIMITED**

Drake's Destiny **FREE ON KINDLE UNLIMITED**

## MORE TITLES

Sugar Love **FREE ON KINDLE UNLIMITED**

Only Love **FREE ON KINDLE UNLIMITED**

Holiday Fling **FREE ON KINDLE UNLIMITED**

## AUDIOBOOKS

Found by You

Loved by You

**Drop me a line! I love hearing from my readers! <3**
Email: victoria.smith775@gmail.com

**Other Links:**

**Blog**: http://www.authorvictoriahsmith.com/
**Facebook:** http://www.facebook.com/AuthorVictoriaHSmith
**Twitter**: VictoriaSmith76

**Sign-Up for My Newsletter for the Latest Release News!**

http://eepurl.com/2F-Q9

~

CPSIA information can be obtained
at www.ICGtesting.com
Printed in the USA
LVOW04s1734111116
512626LV00008B/666/P